# TEARS (
# an Easy(

by

**Brian Parker**

MUDDY BOOTS PRESS

This is a work of fiction. Names, characters, places and incidents are the product of the author's imagination and are used fictitiously. Any resemblance to actual events, locales, or persons, living or dead, is purely coincidental.

Notice: The views expressed herein are NOT endorsed by the United States Government, Department of Defense or Department of the Army.

# Tears of a Clone
## an Easytown Novel

Copyright © 2016 by Brian Parker
All rights reserved. Published by Muddy Boots Press.
www.MuddyBootsPress.com
Edited by Aurora Dewater
Cover art designed by Luke Spooner

# Works available by Brian Parker

### Easytown Novels
*The Immorality Clause*
*Tears of a Clone*

### The Path of Ashes
*A Path of Ashes*
*Fireside*
*Dark Embers*

### Washington, Dead City
*GNASH*
*REND*
*SEVER*

### Stand Alone Works
*Enduring Armageddon*
*Origins of the Outbreak*
*The Collective Protocol*
*Battle Damage Assessment*
*Zombie in the Basement*
*Self-Publishing the Hard Way*

### Anthology Contributions
*Bite-Sized Offerings: Tales and Legends of the Zombie Apocalypse*
*Only the Light We Make: Tales From the World of Adrian's Undead Diary*

# ONE: FRIDAY

"*Stop! New Orleans PD*," I shouted. "Drop your weapon and put your hands up."

The man I'd chased for six blocks stopped and raised his hands slowly, but he didn't have a visible weapon. My partner, Sergeant Drake, and I were following a lead on the Paladin, a vigilante who'd taken it upon himself to clean the streets of Easytown, when our suspect attacked another victim not far from where we were.

I had my service pistol at arm's length, aimed directly at the center of the perpetrator's back. He wore some type of black composite armor that shown dully beneath the full moon, and a helmet with a face shield. I'd seen video of that armor diverting knife blades and it had even taken at least one bullet without slowing him down. In a practiced motion I pulled the Aegis, my personalized laser pistol, from the paddle holster on my hip and placed the .45 caliber SIG Sauer pistol back in place under my arm.

I wished Drake wasn't two blocks behind us, huffing along as fast as he could go. I could use his size to help me manhandle the suspect when I had to cuff him.

I was eight feet from the vigilante that our local media had dubbed "the Paladin" since he allegedly attacked—and murdered—two-bit thugs and rapists, rescuing the population from the criminals that the police department couldn't stop. He was like a modern day knight of justice; a real, live superhero.

And the public loved him.

"Put your hands behind your back," I ordered.

He didn't comply. "We want the same thing, officer," a heavily synthesized voice drifted out from behind the mask.

"What? Put your goddamned hands behind your back or I'll fucking shoot you," I hissed. "Do you hear me?"

"No need to be rude," he replied. "I want the same thing that you do. I want every tweaker, ganger and murderer to pay for the things they've done."

"You don't know shit," I countered. "Put your hands behind your back!"

He slowly lowered his hands, but they didn't go behind him. "I'm cleaning up the streets. Something you don't appear capable of doing."

"And we allow everyone to have their day in court. The same right you'll be granted once I take you in."

"So you're the guy, huh?" he asked.

"What?"

"You're the detective assigned to the case against me. Good to know."

I advanced two steps. "Is that a threat?"

He shrugged and I twitched the end of my laser pistol in response. "Ah, ah. Keep your hands up where I can see 'em."

"I like to know who's keeping an eye on me," the Paladin replied. "So I can keep an eye on them."

"You son of a bitch," I spat. "If you go near anyone I know, I'll kick your teeth so far down your throat that you'll be shitting enamel. You understand me, nutcase?"

"You're fighting the wrong war, Detective. There's something *much* bigger happening in this city."

"The only war is the one you started against everyone else down here. Before that, it was only mildly dangerous."

His chin jutted upward, indicating a point behind me. "Your partner made it."

I didn't need to turn. I'd heard Drake's grunts of exertion from a block away. He may have been massive and an intimidating physical specimen, but his cardiovascular system was definitely lacking. "On your knees, Paladin."

"I didn't pick that name, you know," the perp stated as he began sinking to his knees. "It's a stupid nickname."

"I'll be sure to put it in my report," I retorted. The Paladin was in a position of weakness, so I risked a glance over my shoulder to see where Drake was—which was all the perp needed.

The world around me exploded in green smoke and a fist came out of the cloud to my right, sending me flying backward.

"Oh, damn!" Sergeant Deshutes laughed. "Rewind that, play it again."

The street light's video feed rewound and I relived the humiliation of letting a perp get the drop on me before escaping into the darkness.

"*Bam!*" she shouted at the monitor.

"Shut up, Sandra," I muttered, staring at her darkly through my swollen eye. "Don't you have a desk you need to ride or something?"

"That paperwork can wait," she said. "This is a once in a lifetime opportunity. It's not every day that I see a Kung Fu master get his ass dropped with one damn punch."

"You've got a short memory, then," I replied, referring to the incident at The Puss 'n Boots a few months ago.

"Oh no, I remember your pummeling by penises at The P&B."

I blinked slowly, unimpressed. "Have you been waiting all this time to use that one-liner?"

"You don't like it?"

"It *was* pretty dumb," Drake said.

She thrust her chin out. "Nobody asked you, Muscles. Alliteration is clever and shows a high level of intelligence— something you two obviously don't have."

"Alright, Deshutes," Chief Brubaker interrupted, walking in from the hallway. "Get back to the desk. The lobby's starting to fill up. I want it cleared before lunch."

"On it, Chief," she replied, stepping away from the monitor. "These low class cops are boring me anyways."

I watched her leave in annoyance. Sandra and I were good friends, but I hated being the butt of any joke.

"Okay. Tell me what we've got," the chief ordered.

"We had intel that the Paladin would be on Jubilee Lane on Thursday evening. Drake and I went over there to investigate evidence of another attack by the vigilante—"

"What kind of evidence?"

"A dead drug dealer in an alley, two massive knife wounds originating in the upper abdomen and terminating just below the scapula on his back," Drake cut in. "Stabbed completely through. His product was dumped around his body and ruined by the rain."

"Same M.O. as usual," Brubaker stated. "You're sure it was the same guy and not a copycat? I don't want the media giving this guy credit for murders he didn't commit."

"The dealer's head was separated from his body," I clarified.

"Well, damn."

We'd managed to keep the decapitation details out of the vid feeds, so the likelihood of a copycat was slim. The Paladin had garnered the media's attention by using a sword or long knife to murder his victims. The blade was either super-heated or used lasers because the severed veins and arteries cauterized instantly; there was almost no blood at all.

The media focused on the idea that the vigilante was cleaning up the streets, rescuing the citizens of New Orleans from the filth that seemed to be everywhere, not the illegal aspect of his actions. *They made him seem like a goddamned hero.*

He may have been murdering bad guys, but that didn't make it right.

"So, yeah. We went over to conduct the investigation on the dead drug dealer," Drake continued, "and we hear a scream down the alley. There weren't any drone units or uniformed cops available to assist, so we went to check it out."

"That's when we saw the Paladin and gave chase," I finished.

The chief eyed my purple eye dubiously. "I guess you didn't learn your lesson about waiting for backup, did you, Forrest?"

"I had him, Chief. It was only one guy, there wasn't a need for backup."

"The evidence would say otherwise," he retorted, pointing at my face.

I couldn't argue with him. I'd let the Paladin get the drop on me. It wouldn't happen again.

Chief Brubaker straightened up and yelled down the hallway. "From now on, no officer from my precinct will attempt to apprehend the Paladin until drone support has arrived. Is that clear?"

Mumbled responses answered him and he nodded to himself. "Deshutes!"

"Yes, Chief?" Sandra's voice echoed off the cinder block walls.

"Put that in a memo and send it to every officer in Easytown."

"Got it!" she replied happily. She loved doing paperwork, which was one of the many areas where my opinion of police work differed from hers. She was happy as a clam being the desk sergeant and never leaving the precinct. I wanted to get out amongst the population every opportunity I got. That's where the real police work was—not filing damn reports.

I loathed the paperwork aspect of my job.

Brubaker stepped back into the homicide office. "Forrest, I want to hear you say it."

"Oh, come on, Chief. I'm not some rookie who's gonna—"

"Say it."

I bobbled my head side to side sarcastically as I said, "I won't attempt to apprehend the Paladin without the proper drone support."

"Good. Now, find me that vigilante and put him behind bars."

Chief Brubaker stepped backward into the hallway and disappeared. "Does he think I'm some sort of goddamned rebel or something?"

"You *did* get yourself into a lot of trouble a few months ago by refusing to wait for backup."

"But, I took you with me for the bust," I reminded him.

"And I ended up buried under the statue of a horse."

I waved dismissively. "Details."

"Okay," Drake said in the serious tone that I'd learned meant he was ready to work. "Unlike you, Detective, I have a family to go home to. So let's work on some of those 'details' today so I can get out of here."

"Hey, that hurts me right here," I replied, pointing to my chest. "I have things to look forward to in my personal life. I just upgraded Andi's AI to a faster processor."

The big man stared at me through lowered eyelids. "Damn, we need to get you a dog or something, sir."

Drake was right. I didn't have anything to go home to. My days consisted of hanging out at my friend's restaurant for lunch, and working. My nights were usually filled with more work and fiddling with Andi's components to improve her interface as much as I could afford to do, although recently, I'd been seeing a state cop named Avery when our schedules synched up.

"Fine," I relented. "The Paladin's latest kill was here," I tapped a map of his previous kills on the vid screen and a dot appeared. I typed a few notes in the details box and closed it down.

Looking at the map, the guy had no discernable pattern except staying off The Lane itself. Everything else was fair game. "I wonder why he's avoiding Jubilee. That's where a lot of his targets hang out."

"Cameras," Drake replied. "The Lane is saturated with cameras and drones watching over the customers. He's avoiding the cameras…even the hidden ones."

⚜ ○ ⚜ ○ ⚜

I wiped angrily at the brown spots of coffee the machine had applied liberally to the front of my white shirt out in the hallway. One minute I was thinking about what to say to Dr. Jones to get me out of our session and the next, my shirt was ruined by the goddamned coffee maker.

Technology and I didn't get along.

"What the hell happened to you?" Dr. Jasmin Jones, the NOPD staff psychologist, asked when she opened the door.

"I read an article that said coffee was good for your skin. Trying it out."

She grunted. "Everyone knows that you don't read, Zach. Come in, you're late."

I followed behind the doctor and she gently closed the door behind us. I'd been in her office easily a hundred times over the years. I had an aggressive personality and a rough demeanor with suspects. It had gotten me forced into the department's anger management courses and eventually landed me in the shrink's office. Now they didn't even bother sending me to anger management, they just shipped me off to her.

Old-school print books lined the shelves in her office, making her an oddity among the staffers at the NOPD headquarters. I'd only seen her open one of those books in all the years I'd been coming here. It was a giant tome called *Diagnostic and Statistical Manual of Mental Disorders — 39th Edition* and she'd plopped it on the desk when I came to get her opinion about a possible profile on a serial killer who'd been stalking Easytown's robotic pleasure clubs.

I'd followed the false trail that the killer laid for me and her unofficial opinion had helped put me on the right track. She'd also been there for me when Paxton Himura committed suicide across the table from me.

"Have a seat," Dr. Jones said, indicating the couch.

I lay back and closed my eyes. "Man, this is the life, right? Getting paid by the city to take a nap."

She sighed. "You're in one of *those* kinds of moods today, huh?"

One eye popped open so I could see her. "One of *what* kind of moods, Doc?"

"The one where you feel compelled to be a dick for no reason."

"I— Sorry," I amended and sat up. "I don't want to be here. What do I need to do to leave as soon as possible?"

Dr. Jones crossed a leg over her knee, exposing a shapely brown calf. "You know the drill, Zach. Talk me through what happened this time."

"I, uh… Heh," I chuckled, remembering the way the suspect had cried like a baby when I snapped his wrist. "I defended myself against a knife attack."

She shuffled through some papers. "Says here, you broke his wrist and stabbed him with his own knife."

I cleared my throat. "Well, that…ah, did happen, but it was unintentional. I didn't *stab* him. When I broke the wrist, his hand flopped over onto the back of his forearm and the blade went with it. His own momentum carried him into the knife and it went into his ribs."

The folder closed. "How long are we going to do this, Zach?"

"What? Have meetings where you determine that I'm totally sane and an asset to the police force? Probably for the next ten years or so."

"Yeah, that's not going to work for me. You've always got an excuse for why something isn't your fault. You have serious accusations of police brutality against you this time."

I shrugged. "It's Easytown. Either I'm brutal or I'm dead. The judge always sees it my way."

"Judge Carlson is getting ready to retire, Zach. You know who's next in line until the governor makes an official appointment? Hennessey. You know who Judge Hennessey's golf partner and bass fishing companion is? Todd Jefferson. Is this starting to make sense to you now? It's not a game."

*Fuck.* I'd stiffed Councilman Jefferson during a murder investigation at a sex club a few months ago and wouldn't let him leave until everyone else was released. Rumor had it— Teagan's rumor mill—that when his wife found out that he'd been visiting hookers in Easytown, they split up. She took the kids and left him with nothing. I'd thought it strange that he showed up at my award ceremony for the fight at the cathedral, but maybe it was his way of keeping an eye on me.

I couldn't afford to have the city's highest-ranking judge against me—or against the precinct for that matter. Carlson always overruled anyone who tried to censor the iron fist we used in Easytown. What worked in the French Quarter or Village de L'Est, where I lived, wouldn't work in Easytown. Those thugs would eat up the cops from other parts of the city. The district was simply too wild.

"If Hennessey overturns Carlson's rulings, then the city will lose revenue," I countered. "The only thing keeping that district afloat are police drones, uniformed patrols and plainclothes officers working the crowds without fear of reprisal for doing whatever needs to be done to keep the tourists and customers safe."

"I understand, Zach. Heck, your stories were enough to make me get two Dobermans, reinforced steel entry doors and shatter resistant glass on all my first floor windows. Judge Hennessey is an idealist. He's spoken out publicly many times that he feels that law enforcement has been allowed to have a heavy hand in the city for too long."

"And since the other precincts don't actually use that same heavy hand—" I left it hanging in the air.

She nodded. "Exactly. So, back to my original question, Zach. How long are we going to do this?"

"I didn't mean to let him stab himself," I replied, holding my ground. "When faced with a life or death situation, I made the call to eliminate the threat. It's not like I killed the guy."

"*This time*. You were lucky, Zach. A few more inches toward the victim's back and you could have gotten him in the kidney."

I sat up off the couch and held my hands up. "Whoa. Don't call that criminal a *victim*. He was wanted for murder and tried to kill me. He's not a goddamned victim, he's a murderer."

"Bad choice of words on my part. Sorry."

I forced the anger to simmer down and lay back against the pillow.

"I'm not questioning whether the *murderer* needed to be stopped," Dr. Jones continued. "What I'm *asking* you to do is to think of the political climate that's brewing downtown. Let that temper your responses, Zach. Councilman Jefferson would love to have Judge Hennessey make an example out of you."

I set my jaw and thought about my problem for a moment. "I can try to be easier with them."

"That's a start. I'm not asking you to allow yourself, or anyone else, to get hurt. Could you have controlled James Cochran with a wristlock instead of breaking his wrist?"

"Probably."

The room became quiet and I turned my head toward the shrink. She had a grin on her face that stretched from ear-to-ear. "What is it, Doc?"

"After all these sessions—all these *years*, I finally got you to admit that there may be an alternate solution to a problem than the one you chose."

"Do you want a mark on the scoreboard or something?"

"No," she answered. "You wanted to know what you needed to do to get out of here early today...well that's it. We talk about the difference between black and white, my way or the highway, and the futility of an office worker like me questioning the actions of someone out in the street. Well, today, you actually opened up to some advice and I'm very happy that you're at least willing to see the other side of an argument."

I sat up once again and pushed myself off the couch. "If I'd have known all it would take was a compromise, then I'd have done that years ago," I said as I walked across the room to the coat rack where I'd placed my coat and hat.

"Maybe you should apply your newfound insight to the opposite sex more often, Zach. You'd be surprised how far meeting in the middle will take you."

I grunted in acknowledgement. "See you next week, Doc."

# TWO: FRIDAY

"Hey, baby. You look cold and wet. I… I can make you *hot* and wet," an inexperienced voice called from the mouth of a darkened alley

I glanced at the hooker who beckoned to me. She wore an expensive-looking white, water repellant jacket that hadn't been dug out of the trash, a black mini skirt with cliché fishnet stockings, and earmuffs poking out over light pink, shoulder-length hair. Honestly, she couldn't have stuck out more in Easytown than if she'd been wearing a sign that said, **"Fresh Meat."**

If she survived her first week on the job, she'd know better than to ask me for sex.

"I'm a cop, sweetheart," I warned her.

"Oh, I *love* cops," she replied, stepping out of the alley and closing the distance quickly.

She wore a prosthetic on her right leg below the knee. It was high-end tech, not the junk amputees in Easytown usually wore. Up close, I could tell that her clothing didn't just look expensive, it *was* expensive.

The diamond studs in her ears confirmed my initial thoughts. "What sorority?"

"Huh? I'm trying to make some money and have fun at the same time, you know?" *Lie.*

We saw it all the time. Sororities and fraternities had their pledges do all sorts of crazy things down in Easytown to show their dedication to the organization. We'd had males pick fights with district toughs and attempt to ride the police drones like a bull, girls stripping in front of uniformed cops and performing sex acts on each other in front of live news feeds. This wasn't the first time I'd seen one of them force a girl into prostitution to prove her loyalty to the sorority.

"Don't bullshit me, kid. What sorority?"

"I won't charge you. It'd be a freebie since you're a cop. You look like you'd be a blast to fuck."

"Do you see the news vids? People die *every day* down here. Street prostitutes usually don't last more than a few days. Is that sorority important enough to you that you'd risk getting murdered for it?"

"I—"

"Shut up." I pulled out my phone and said, "Andi, video from my last prostitute job."

I held the phone flat and holograms of the crime scene photos from two days ago projected in the space between me and the girl. The images flipped rapidly through the mundane location photos and then slowed down when the close-ups of the body began. Sick fucker had pulled the prostitute's intestines through her anus while she was still alive.

*Where was the Paladin that night?*

The girl retched and looked away. "That was three blocks from here, just a little bit further up The Lane," I said. "Casey Bond; she was pledging a sorority too. That was done to her while she was alive, screaming for her mother at first and then for a merciful end to her pain. We have witnesses."

I reached out and grabbed the girl's chin, forcing her to look me in the eyes. "What sorority?"

"Sigma Tau Epsilon."

"Which school?"

"Tulane."

I released the girl's chin. "Andi, stop the playback. Thanks." As I slipped my phone back inside my coat, I whistled for a cab.

"What are you doing?"

"Saving your life."

An orange and blue taxi halted at the curb and the door slid open. I grabbed the girl by the elbow and tried to steer her toward the car. She wouldn't budge.

"I won't get into STE unless I get a guy to pay for sex with me." She slid down to her knees and pawed at my crotch. "You don't know how hard it is for a girl with a prosthetic to get accepted into a sorority. Please. Let me suck your dick, right here."

I looked around the area, but didn't see anyone watching or any cameras set up. "Where are they?"

She found a spot on the ground that seemed extremely interesting.

"Where are they?" I repeated.

"One of the sisters is a computer science major. She hacked into the camera up there to watch."

I followed the direction she'd nudged her chin. *Son of a bitch*. The sorority had hacked into the city's security camera network. These goddamned hackers were getting out of control.

Her head fell forward into my leg and she began to cry softly. For a moment, I considered getting into the cab with her and riding a few blocks to make the watching sorority girls think she'd successfully landed a john, but pushed the thought aside. It wouldn't teach the girl a lesson and it sure as hell wouldn't affect the sorority.

I tilted my fedora back and stared directly at the camera. Then I pulled off my glove and stuck up my middle finger, mouthing the words, "Fuck you."

More department sensitivity training was coming my way, I'm sure.

"Hey, let go of me," the girl squeaked when I grabbed her upper arm in a vice and pulled her to her feet. Then I physically dragged her toward the cab.

"It's for your own good, kid."

"Ow! You're hurting me."

I laughed at her naivety. "This is nothing compared to what you'd experience if a real john came along or if one of the district's killers got to you."

I shoved her hard into the open doorway and she fell across the seat before sliding down to the floorboard. Somewhere along the way, her leg had detached, so I picked it up and tossed it inside as well.

"*You're an asshole!*" she screeched, clutching her leg.

"You're welcome," I answered and slammed the door.

"They saw it come off," she sobbed. "They saw it come off… I'm done."

I ignored her and reached through the open front window to tap on the navigation screen. A woman's face appeared. "Where would you like us to take you?"

"This is Detective Forrest, NOPD. This passenger is to be returned to the Sigma Tau Epsilon house at Tulane. No deviation in the route is authorized."

The girl screamed obscenities from the back seat.

"Are you paying the fare?" the taxi dispatcher asked, glancing from me to the girl cursing loudly in the back.

I sighed and swiped my credit chip over the green scanner. "How's that?"

"Everything appears in order. This passenger will be returned to Tulane. The estimated travel time is thirty-seven minutes. Do you require a confirmation of drop off?"

"Yeah, why not?"

I leaned inside. "If I ever see you down here again, I'll arrest you and send you out to Sabatier Island for a few days."

"Fuck you! You ruined my life!" she squealed.

I pulled my head out and patted the top of the taxi. The car pulled slowly into traffic and I genuinely hoped that I'd never see the girl again.

In one last defiant gesture, she spit out the window at me. "I *hate* cops!"

"Heart of gold, buddy," I congratulated myself and walked toward the coffee shop where I was going to meet Drake.

"Andi, add Sigma Tau Epsilon to the list of sororities actively trying to get their pledges murdered."

"I didn't know we had a list," Andi replied.

"Start one then. And add the sorority that Casey Bond pledged."

"It's already been shut down by Xavier."

"Thank God. Put it on there anyways."

"You got it, boss."

"Thanks."

I pulled the duster close to my body to ward off the chill of the steady drizzle. It was in the low 30's and would probably snow—or more likely ice—overnight, creating a nightmare for commuters, even with automated vehicles.

Snow in New Orleans. Ninety years ago it would have been unheard of, but after the Russo-Chinese-Indian war everything was out of whack. It wasn't uncommon to have a few storms every now and then down in the Big Easy.

Easytown, the district where I worked, was a slum in the eastern part of New Orleans. Six square miles of reclaimed land that used to be the bottom of Lake Borgne. The land was built up by squatters at first, the derelicts of society. Then the city added it to their neighborhood map, paved a few roads and opened it up for settlement, full of promise.

Poorly-built houses, run-down apartment complexes, warehouses and the clubs along Jubilee Lane were the only thing Easytown boasted these days. The district's clubs offered every vice imaginable, for a price. If it couldn't be found on The Lane, then it wasn't a lucrative pastime for the business owners. Pay 'em enough, though, and they'd get you anything.

As I continued walking down Jubilee Lane, awash in the glow of neon lights from the various clubs, I was wary of the sights and sounds coming from the clubs. For the most part, the business owners did a good job disguising the horrors that awaited the unprepared, which is why we had so many murders down here. To a seasoned Easytown veteran like me, everything was a threat—which may explain why I was constantly in trouble for allowing situations to escalate.

"Hey, cop!" a patron yelled from the line in front of Club Megasonic, one of Tommy Voodoo's thumper joints. "Go fuck yourself!"

I stopped and turned slowly toward the kid. He had to be sixteen, maybe eighteen if I was lucky, wearing a synth-leather jacket and sporting a ridiculous spiked hairstyle that I'd seen a few of the kids with recently. Noticing that their hair looked like a porcupine made me feel old.

Again, I couldn't let a little thing go. Call it a chip on my shoulder. Call it a need to be in control. Didn't matter how you labeled it, I wasn't willing to let some punk get over on me.

"What did you say to me, kid?"

"I asked how much money you earned sucking dick in the alley," he replied, grinning like an idiot.

His buddies laughed and slapped him on the back. From my peripheral, I saw the doorman edge toward the entryway and reach inside.

"Taunting an NOPD officer is grounds for immediate arrest, jackass," I stated.

The doorman reappeared holding a pulse blaster. He was within his legal authority to keep the crowd under control, so this could get ugly if I didn't end it quickly.

"What are you gonna do about it, old man? We got the numbers on you." He flashed some shiny metal object. "And we got the tech. You ain't gonna do anything."

"You're right. I'm gonna ignore your comment and chalk it up to stupid youth. You kids have a good night."

I turned back toward the coffee shop and started to step off the sidewalk when the kid continued, "That's what I thought. Pussy. We woulda mopped the floor with you. Bloodhounds rule this joint!"

"*Bloodhounds?*" the others cheered.

That did it.

I whirled back around and took two rapid steps toward the line. "Did you say 'Bloodhounds'?"

"Yeah! We rule this shithole!"

"Never heard of you," I answered.

The ganger who'd been talking slid a silver weapon of some kind from his sleeve and aimed it at me. "You ain't heard of us?"

I held up my hands and the old wounds in my back began to ache. A few years ago, several gangers found out where I lived and jumped me at my old apartment. They stabbed me twice in the back before I was able to disarm them.

I gestured for the doorman to put his gun down. "Whatchu doing, bacon?"

"That man over there has ten or fifteen terawatts of fuck you pointed at *the Bloodhounds*." I added as much sarcasm to the last two words as I could manage. "You should probably put down the weapon."

As one, all four of them turned toward the doorman and I pitched forward, pushing the muzzle of the weapon toward the other gangers. The kid squeezed the trigger and the small gun erupted with sound as shotgun pellets tore into two of his fellow Bloodhounds. I kept one hand on the weapon to control it and knife-handed his larynx. He released the weapon and slapped at his throat, uselessly trying to uncrush his windpipe.

The fourth ganger started to pull another weapon out of his belt and I shot him in the face with my .45 service pistol.

It was over in less than six seconds. That's how fast and brutal Easytown was: people who didn't keep their wits about them ended up dead.

I watched as the Bloodhound with the crushed larynx began to turn blue. He was really hamming it up. "If you relax, you can get a breath. All you're doing now is killing yourself."

His legs began convulsing. "I can't assist you with committing a suicide. That would be unethical. Ah, shit..."

I straddled the kid's chest to keep him from moving around too much and pulled out my pen.

"Goddammit!" I shouted. "This is my favorite pen, asshole."

Once the push-button and ink cartridge were removed, I jabbed the metal cylinder into the soft flesh beneath his Adam's apple and pushed through the rubbery flesh of his trachea. A raspy rush of air in and out of the tube told me I'd hit pay dirt.

"Stop struggling, you dumb fuck," I told the ganger. "Look, you're already the last of the Bloodhounds, if you're going to rebuild the gang and come after me in some sort of strange twisted revenge story, then you're gonna have to survive the night. If you struggle and this pen tube comes out, you're going to drown on the blood that it's keeping out of your lungs."

I shrugged exaggeratedly. "You die, there's no revenge on the *pussy* cop that did this to you."

The air crackled with static electricity moments before I felt the breeze coming off the fan motors of a police drone. "Citizen, I am on site to assist," a metallic voice echoed loudly, rattling my ear drums. "You will surrender all weapons or face immediate repercussions."

I turned and stared down one of the six barrels on the drone's minigun. I'd seen the devastation that the standard police drone's two miniguns could do. I didn't want to spook this thing or I'd be dead before my body hit the pavement. *That would really ruin my day.*

"I'm a police officer," I answered.

"Present your badge and face for scanning."

I angled my mug into the dim street light and smiled at the drone's fisheye lens. The floating monstrosity had settled down onto its thin, spindly legs. I reached slowly inside my duster for my badge and held it up for inspection.

"Detective Zachary Forrest, you have been cleared to conduct operations in the Easytown Precinct. I am ordered to assist as necessary. Do you require assistance at this time?"

"Call an ambulance for this asshole and the morgue for the other three."

"Yes, Detective Forrest." The drone paused and then said, "Emergency medical services are on the way to your location. ETA seven minutes."

I worked a set of handcuffs onto the ganger with the field-expedient tracheotomy and pushed myself up by pushing down hard against his chest. *If I kill the little fucker, he can't testify against me*, I mused.

"You had to fuck up my evening, didn't you, asshole?" I accused the Bloodhound instead of giving in to the urge to finish him off. "I was all set to have a nice cup of coffee and discuss work with my partner. Now I've got a mound of paperwork that I'll have to complete."

I started to walk away, thought better of it and turned back to the perp. "If I miss breakfast because of this shit, I'm going to find you at the hospital and disconnect all the machines they'll have you hooked up to."

He gurgled at me. With any luck, he'd be mute for the rest of his life and become a contributing member of society.

*I'll probably see him again in six months back down here on The Lane.*

By the time the ambulance arrived, I'd gotten into an argument with the club's manager about who was paying to clean up the blood and I'd given a recorded statement on my involvement to the N.O.S.T. courier that the department sent over. As a bonus, I was thoroughly soaked with melted snow from standing outside for over an hour. The novelty of the city's first snowfall of the season had worn off; I was ready for summer.

"Alright, you need anything else from me Fourteen Sixty-three?" I asked the police drone still hovering nearby.

"No, Detective Forrest," it responded. "However, I have been instructed to remind you that the precinct's chief of police, Robert Brubaker, has ordered that all Easytown police officers have drone support when interacting with potential criminals—"

I chortled and then snorted at the end of the laugh. "*Everyone* in Easytown is a criminal, Fourteen Sixty-three. I wouldn't be able to take two steps down here without drone support if I followed the chief's order."

The drone's fisheye reflected the neon from Club Megasonic's sign, distorting the establishment's name. "Every citizen in Easytown is a criminal? What is the nature of their offense?"

I held up my hands. "Whoa! Stand down." *Me and my big mouth.* "It's an expression. Everyone in Easytown is *not* a criminal."

"Understood, Detective Forrest. Do you require any further assistance?"

"No, thank you," I answered "You were a lovely dance partner, Fourteen Sixty-three."

"I didn't dance—"

"It's another expression. Never mind. I don't require further assistance."

The drone's fans engaged and it lifted off slowly, the legs retracting inside its body. I watched it lift off for a moment, then glanced at my watch. I was over forty-five minutes late for my meeting with Drake.

"I should have known you'd found trouble, Detective," Drake's voice boomed through the small crowd of onlookers who'd gathered around to watch the medics clean up the bodies.

Sergeant Greg Drake was a bear of a man at six foot three and two hundred forty pounds of solid muscle. He'd played middle linebacker at Tulane and been scouted by the NFL, but a hamstring surgery during the Scouting Combine had kept him from participating. Then, they'd simply forgotten about him. He joined the police force and was eventually promoted into homicide after several years of walking a beat in Easytown.

"I couldn't help myself," I replied. "It was justified though. They drew on me. Some new type of blast pistol that I hadn't seen before."

"Where was the Paladin?"

"I wondered the same thing," I answered bitterly. "Why is it that the dude can be all over Easytown, but when a cop needs assistance, he's absent?"

"Because he's a goddamned criminal, not the hero that everyone makes him out to be. But, he doesn't want his actions on video," Drake stated, pointing at the street camera.

I nodded in agreement. "Hey, you ever hear of a gang called the Bloodhounds?"

"No. Should I have?"

"That's where these four were from. They were yelling out the name of their gang and they certainly didn't have any qualms about starting a fight right out here in the open."

"We should stop by and talk to the gang task force to see if there's a new gang on the street and what their intentions are. I'll go by tomorrow before my shift," Drake offered.

"Sounds good." I looked at my watch. I was out of time. "Dammit. I'm sorry, Drake. I've got to go meet Avery for dinner."

He held up his hands. "Understood, Detective. Genevieve tells me I drink too much coffee anyways."

"How's she doing?"

"As good as can be expected," he replied. "She's not in the completely uncomfortable stage yet, but she's expanding her nest again. She had three more pillows delivered tonight before I left the house. Before too long, I'm gonna be on the couch."

I chuckled at his situation. His wife, Genevieve, was six months pregnant with their second child. She'd started out with a few extra pillows under her stomach and between her legs. Then she began adding more and more around her body until Drake said he slept on a side of the bed barely wide enough for one of his ass cheeks. The new additions might well push him off the bed until the baby was born.

"Good luck with that, buddy."

"Thanks. Hey, I know you're late for your date. I'll stay on site until everything's cleaned up."

"Are you sure?" I asked.

"Yeah, no problem. I'm probably going to get assigned this investigation anyways, so I might as well start now."

"You're probably right. Cruz would fuck it up somehow and I'd end up chained to a bathroom stall on Sabatier."

"He tries hard, Detective."

"I know." Lieutenant Alfonso Cruz was one of the other homicide detectives in Easytown. He was a nice man with a few annoying quirks, but I thought he was a total fuckup when it came to his job—and Chief Brubaker agreed with me, which is why Drake and I worked the bulk of the investigations. "Alright, I'm gonna go over to Dillard for dinner. I sent a recorded statement to the precinct already, but you can call me in a few hours for more details."

Sergeant Drake raised an eyebrow. "A *few* hours? If I was dating a woman like that—and I wasn't happily married—I'd call out for the entire night, maybe the next day too."

I grinned at his statement. "I'll see you tomorrow."

# THREE: FRIDAY

I looked at my watch again and then took a sip from the three fingers of bourbon the waitress had brought. *How many is this?* I wondered idly, relishing the warmth of the drink spreading from my belly and up my neck to burn my ears.

Or was that the heat of embarrassment?

I downed the drink and motioned for another, which appeared quickly, unlike my date. I'd been sitting by myself at a candlelit table set for two for almost an hour. Avery was a no-show and wasn't answering her phone. A quick check of her car's GPS data showed that it was still at her house over in Slidell, making my thoughts alternate between several scenarios.

Was she standing me up and not answering her phone, or did she forget? Was she in trouble? Maybe her house had been broken into and she was being held hostage—or dead. Or was she screwing some other guy while I sat like a chump in a nice restaurant waiting to ask her an important question?

We'd been seeing each other since I met her at the awards ceremony in November when the governor awarded me the Louisiana Medal of Valor. She was a State Police officer who worked a hundred-mile area to the east of New Orleans and was often brought in for local events as a public relations tactic. The message was that stunningly beautiful women could be cops too, visit your recruiter today.

Sexism was alive and well in the south.

Avery and I had a whirlwind relationship of sex, drinking and more sex over the last four months. She was insatiable, often wanting to go two or three times a night. I'd even considered picking up a prescription of Amplify just to keep it up, but hadn't taken that step.

For the twentieth time, I slid the ribbon off the rectangular box I'd placed on the empty dinner plate and opened it. Inside was a diamond tennis bracelet, something that she'd mentioned offhandedly once or twice that she would like. I'd planned to give it to her tonight and ask if she would consider an exclusive relationship with me, give what we were doing an official title.

I was already exclusive—easy to do when you don't have any other prospects—but I didn't know if she was. We lived and worked in different cities, at least an hour apart with no traffic and only met up for dinner and sex about once a week. For all I knew, she could have a full-time boyfriend and I was the guy on the side. She could be with him right now.

*Am I the fool who thinks this is going somewhere?*

"That's pretty," the waitress interrupted my melancholy thoughts.

"Thanks." I snapped it shut and tapped my glass. "Can I get another one?"

She tried to be discreet, but I noticed her glance at the vacant seat across from me. "Sir, are you sure you'd like another one? You've already had three. If your friend shows up, you might—"

"Please just bring me another one," I mumbled, my tongue feeling thick in my mouth.

"My manager says you're cut off. I'm sorry."

I pulled out my badge and slapped it angrily down on the table. "I'd like another one. Please."

The waitress looked over her shoulder out of my line of sight and a man walked up quickly. "Sir, I'm sorry. It's time for you to leave. The city of New Orleans won't allow me to serve more than twelve ounces of liquor to an individual."

"Dammit, I'm a cop. I know the fucking law."

He cleared his throat. "Then you'll realize that you're putting me in a very difficult position, sir."

The waitress retreated to another table and I ogled her tight behind in the modest skirt she wore as she bent over the guests. I was in the mood to take anyone home.

*If I can't have Avery, that pretty little thing will work. I wonder what that blouse is hiding.*

"Sir, please."

I tore my eyes off the waitress' ass and stared balefully at the manager. "What?" I shook my head. That last drink was hitting me hard.

"All of these other customers came to have a nice, peaceful dinner. Please don't make a scene."

I tried to push my chair away from the table, but my weight kept it in place and the table clattered away loudly. Every head in the restaurant turned toward me.

"I'm going to be leaving now." I snatched my badge and the box with the bracelet off the table, and then dropped a couple hundred bucks in cash on the plate. "Thank you for a lovely evening."

"Thank you, sir," the manager sighed.

The roll of the waitress' eyes as I approached told me that I didn't have a shot with her. *Shaved or not?*

"Thank you," I managed to choke out, keeping my thoughts to myself.

I accidentally stumbled into the hostess stand on my way out the door, knocking the collection of pens to the floor.

"Detective Forrest. Nice to see you again."

*That voice.*

I turned to see Tommy Voodoo standing beside the desk I'd bumped into. He had two stunning women on his arm, one of whom looked familiar.

"Mr. Ladeaux," I greeted him.

He stuck out his hand and I shook it. "You'll remember Anastasia, I'm sure," he gestured toward the redhead.

"Ana—? *The clone?*"

"Yes, although we prefer to be a little more discreet in public, Detective," Ladeaux replied in his weaselly voice. "And this beautiful blonde is Greta."

"Stop, Tommy!" Greta pleaded as she stuck out her own hand. "Nice to meet you."

"Are you a clone too?"

Her smile faltered and she dropped her hand. "No. I'm one hundred percent real woman—and you're drunk."

"Yes, I am." I peered over my shoulder at the manager. "And I'm leaving. Nice to meet you."

"Detective, we need to talk," Ladeaux called after me. "I've made a little business arrangement that will likely bring us back together."

I ignored him and stumbled to the parking lot.

I had no clue where my Jeep was parked. It'd dropped me off at the door when I came in. "Dammit, Andi," I cursed into my phone as I fumbled it from my pocket.

"Yes, boss?" her voice came from the small speaker.

"Where's the goddamned Jeep?"

"It's forty-three feet from your current location. Turning the lights on now."

A pair of headlights came on to my left and I stumbled my way to the Jeep. When I got there, I sat heavily in the front seat.

"Are you coming home, Zach?"

I opened the box once more and stared at the bracelet. *What the hell.*

"No. I'm going to Slidell," I replied as I snapped the box closed and tossed it down on the passenger floorboard.

"Zach, is that—"

I disconnected Andi's feed and punched in Avery's address. The Jeep started to pull out of the parking lot and I typed in a nearby liquor store as a waypoint.

⚜ ○ ⚜ ○ ⚜

My trusty Jeep dropped me off at the walkway to Avery's townhouse in Slidell. The lights in the front room were on, but the rest of the house was dark. I tried to see through the heavy curtains, trying to see if anyone was home—or worse, if she wasn't alone.

I couldn't see anything worthwhile. There was no movement of any kind to give me an indication of the situation. The snowflakes that made Easytown look almost civil had turned to sleet, making the roads treacherous and my spying job more difficult.

I took a long, final pull straight from the bottle of cheap whiskey I'd bought and then set the empty container on the sidewalk.

"I came all this way to get an answer," I mumbled to myself. "By God, I'm gonna get one."

The walkway was much longer that I remembered it and I congratulated myself for remembering to step over the loose paving stone. I'd tripped on it the first time I came here.

The applause hadn't even ended in my head when my toe caught on the edge of the paver and I tumbled to the sidewalk. "*Goddammit!*" I hissed.

Apparently, I hadn't made it past the obstacle. I examined my palms. Both of them throbbed slightly, but the lighting was too shitty to see much of anything. I had an itch on my nose and too late, I remembered that my hands were bloody. I lay on the icy sidewalk, and rubbed at the blood with my jacket sleeve.

"That'll have to do," I giggled, imagining Avery's reaction.

I pushed myself up and rubbed at my right knee, which had also hit the walkway. My finger disappeared in a hole in my pants. I'd ripped my damn suit in the fall. *Great. Just great.*

I limped the last few feet to the front door and leaned drunkenly against the doorframe. Her home didn't have an overhang of any type, so I was still getting wet—and smearing blood on her white doorframe like an ancient Jew at Passover.

The sound of the door unlocking surprised me and I squinted at the sudden rectangle of light coming from inside the home.

An angel materialized before me. A beautiful, blonde, buxom angel.

"Oh for Christ's sake, what the fuck are you doing here, Zach?" Her hand flew to her mouth. "What happened to you? Did you get mugged?"

"I missed you," I slurred. "We had a date and I was going to ask you something really important and you didn't show up. I called and called…and called," I sighed. I knew I was drunk, but I couldn't get my mouth to stop making sounds. "But you never answered, so I didn't know if something happened and I wanted you to be okay and I also thought that maybe you were with another guy and I was worried that you'd moved on and that we were over and that—"

"Zach, shut up. Jesus, how much did you drink?"

"Yes," I smirked.

"Figures," she said, crossing her arms under her breasts.

"Can I come in?" I ventured.

"No, you can't come in."

I stood on my tiptoes and started to lose my balance as I tried to peer around her. I caught myself before I tumbled off the porch into the bushes.

"I'm alone. You're a mess; I'm not letting you inside."

I grinned mischievously. "You're alone? Want me to make you *not* alone?"

Her frown told me that what I said out loud wasn't quite as eloquent as I'd thought it would be. "Why are you here?" she asked.

"I was worried about you. You didn't answer the phone when I called."

"Yeah, twelve times in two hours. Little excessive, don't you think?"

I shrugged, wincing at the stiffness between my shoulder blades. "Sorry?"

"Zach, we're through. I can't do this."

"Huh?"

"Look at you. You're a mess. You're a drunk. You're rarely in a good mood. Most of the time, you're a downright asshole—probably because you can't disassociate yourself from your work. You eat like shit. Besides one guy and your partner, you don't have any friends, which is unhealthy. Oh, and don't even get me started on that Andi thing. It's weird. What kind of grown man has a twenty-four-seven computer program that runs his life, watching everything he does? It creeps me out."

"I—"

"I thought it was cute that you were inexperienced with women at first," she continued. "But the more time I spent with you, I realized that it was by choice. You are so focused on your job all the time that it consumes you. I can't do this anymore. I thought you'd be able to change once you realized how much *fun* life could be, but you just can't do it. There's more to life than being a cop, Zach. Goodbye."

She closed the door quietly and turned off the porch light. My angel had retreated back to the depths of hell from whence she came.

I chuckled at my mind's attempt to turn a witty phrase until I remembered why I was standing in the icy rain.

My finger hovered over Avery's doorbell and then I pulled it back. I may have been three sheets to the wind, but I was still a cop. I knew better than to keep harassing her. Maybe she'd be ready to talk about it rationally in a couple of days.

I turned and made my way carefully down the walkway. All of her excuses about my failures were covering something up. *She must be seeing someone else*, I told myself.

*Why else would she make that stuff up about me? Of course I take my job seriously, I had to. Being a cop was all I knew.*

"The Jeep is on its way, Zach."

"Thanks, Andi," I muttered glumly.

As I stood on the curb, waiting for the car, I hoped Avery's list of my shortcomings was her attempt to distance herself from me. If they weren't, I had a whole lot of soul searching to do.

# FOUR: SATURDAY

"Zach."

"*Ungh.*"

"Zach, it's time for you to wake up."

"Wha?" My face was stuck to my pillow.

"It's almost noon. You should wake up if you're going to make your appointment."

I rubbed my palm across my face and regretted it immediately. Somehow, I'd cut my hand. "Good morning, Andi," I yawned. "How long have I been asleep?"

"Nine hours, thirteen minutes and forty-seven seconds."

I tried to do some math in my head. It hurt too much. "What time did I get home?"

"2:16 a.m."

No wonder I felt like crap. I'd been up all day yesterday, then half of the night after—

"Wait!" I said, bolting upright in bed and then immediately regretting it. "I got stood up by Avery, and then I got very drunk." I examined my hands, both of which had abrasions on the palms, meaning that I'd probably fallen. Come to think of it, my knee hurt too.

"I think... Did I go to Slidell?"

"Yes, you did, boss."

I didn't remember much past buying a liter of whiskey from a random liquor store near the restaurant in Dillard. "What happened?"

"Do you want the long or the short version?"

I vaguely remembered Avery stomping on my heart and saying I was worthless, so I didn't need the full recount of what she said.

"Give me the short version."

"Avery doesn't want to go on any more dates with you and says that you need to take better care of yourself."

"She didn't say that second part, you're just trying to trick me into eating healthier."

"*Oh for Christ's sake, what the fuck are you doing here Zach?*" Avery's muffled voice echoed around my bedroom. Andi must have recorded the conversation.

When the short, one-way conversation was over, I sighed. "I wish I hadn't heard that when I was sober."

"I tried to only give you the highlight reel," Andi stated.

I eased out of bed. "It's *highlights*, Andi. A highlight reel would be video evidence."

Before my foot touched the bathroom floor, I turned and focused on Andi's camera in the corner above the bed. "And she's right; it's weird that you're always around."

"I'm not in the bathroom."

"The *one* place I can get away from you," I said over my shoulder as I walked into the bathroom. I wasn't safe in here either, though. The toilet computer was always telling me what was wrong with my urine.

When I was finished, I walked gingerly to the kitchen for coffee. "Andi, can you order me breakfast, please?"

"You don't have time to wait for delivery, boss. You have a one o'clock appointment."

"What appointment?"

"You agreed to a one o'clock meeting with Internal Affairs at 12:27 last night."

"Goddammit! Text or voice?"

"It's a face-to-face meeting downtown, Zach."

"No, I mean did I talk to IA or message them?" I had no recollection of a conversation with IA either.

"It was an email message. I monitored your progress and cleaned up spelling errors based on your inebriated state."

*Close one.* If IA wanted to talk to me, sending a convoluted drunken message would add fuel to their fire. I grabbed my phone and tapped a few keys. The email message displayed brightly and I groaned at Andi's corrections to my reply:

```
Yes,    I    will    gladly    meet    with
    investigators  from  the  New  Orleans
    Police  Department  Internal  Affairs
    Division.  Out  of  the  proposed  meeting
    times,  the  1  p.m.  time  works  best  for
    my   schedule   since   I   typically   work
    nights    due    to    the    astronomical
    homicide   rate   in   the   Easytown
    district.
On  a  side  note,  I  would  like  to  thank
    the   New   Orleans   Police   Department
    Internal  Affairs  Division  for  their
    hard  work  and  diligence  to  ensure  that
    justice   is   upheld   across   our   fine
    department.    I    look    forward    to
```

```
assisting  with  the  investigation  as
needed.
```
Thank you,
Detective Zachary Forrest, NOPD

"Andi, this doesn't sound anything like me."

"I did what I could. Your final paragraph originally read, '*On a side note, the investigators at IA can go fuck themselves. Hardworking cops are just trying to do their jobs and you assholes are interfering.*' That was not an appropriate response from an officer who wants to remain employed by the police department."

"Okay, fine. You win, that would have looked really bad." I scrolled through the original email, IA wanted to talk to me about the shooting last night at Club Megasonic.

"You need to shave and get dressed, Zach. Traffic is backed up on the highway and current estimates put you arriving at 12:53 p.m. if you left now, which you can't do since you are not ready. We can continue our discussion in the car if you'd like."

"Yeah, okay."

"Oh, one more thing, Zach," Andi said as I rushed to get ready.

"What's that?"

"You accessed the Paxton Himura memory chip again last night."

Tommy Voodoo delivered a copy of the droid's memory chip to me after she committed suicide. I'd been guilty on several occasions of viewing the contents when I was drunk and lonely. I considered destroying the damn thing on multiple occasions, but every time I got close to following through with it, something kept me from doing so.

"Thanks for letting me know."

"You're welcome. Current estimate of arrival is now 12:55."

That was my Andi. Always on top of things, even when my life was a total disaster.

"So you admit to provoking an altercation with the Bloodhounds?" the investigator, Smith or some other equally innocuous name, asked.

"I hardly think that talking to a group of men openly taunting a police officer is provoking," I replied. "It is our job to interact with the public and to keep them safe."

"Part of your job is to diffuse situations and not allow them to escalate beyond the verbal level, Detective."

Smith looked at his partner, Jones, and nodded. These two fuckheads thought they were correct about every piece of drivel that fell out of their mouths. They probably went and jerked each other off after they finished raking good, hardworking cops over the coals each day.

I hated IA. I *really* hated them. It may have stemmed from the fact that they always seemed to be investigating me, but I think it was more likely because I fundamentally disagreed with their entire existence. Cops who investigated cops were scum. We needed to band together and help one another, not seek out ways to destroy each other.

"Have either of you two walked a beat?" I asked.

"We're not required to answer *your* questions, Detective," Jones stated. "Internal Affairs is conducting this investigation into your misconduct, not the other way around."

"So, no. You haven't." I snorted in contempt. "We're at war out there, fighting to protect the innocent and detain the rest. You make these grandiose statements about how cops are supposed to diffuse the situation—or what was it you said earlier, to 'ensure the safety of everyone, regardless of their affiliation.' That's what you said, right?"

"That's exactly right," Tweedle Dee answered smugly.

"That's the dumbest shit I've ever heard. You two always come around, second-guessing what the men and women on the street do, when you've never even stepped foot on the pavement. You sit up here in your nice little office and look down from on high, passing judgement on officers who put their lives on the line."

I made an effort to calm myself. I was in dangerous territory, I could be angry and tell them what I thought, to a point, but if I attacked them or said something that they could latch onto, then they'd fry me. Tweedle Dum's face was already beet red and he looked as if he'd explode.

"Do either of you know how many police officers were killed last week in New Orleans?"

"It was two or three, Detective. Honestly, it's not our place to—"

"Eight," I cut him off. "Eight men and women, fathers, mothers, husbands, wives, brothers, sisters, sons and daughters. They will never go home again because they were out there trying to make this city a better place." I jabbed my finger angrily at the window.

Inside my suit pocket, I felt my phone vibrate two times, then pause and two more times. I needed to go, but I couldn't yet.

"This city is infested with thugs, gangs, organized crime, drug dealers, murderers and psychopaths—all of whom don't give a flying fuck about killing a cop. And there's ten times as many two-bit thieves and criminals that we're trying to deal with to help keep the population safe. You want to go tell those officers' families that they should have reacted differently in the situations that got them killed?"

Smith shook his head, but Jones stared at me, cold. "If they screwed up, then I'd absolutely tell their families that."

I pushed away from the table and stood up, leaning menacingly over the table. "Then you're a bigger asshole than I'd originally given you credit for."

"Hey! Where are you going?"

I pulled out my phone and showed them the screen. "I've gotta go to work."

"Uh, what is that?" Tweedle Dum asked.

I didn't what I'd shown them, but the phone's buzzing pattern meant it was a picture message from Drake, so it was work related. When I turned the phone back to me, I saw three mutilated corpses in what looked like a trash pile.

"Are we done here?" I asked, slipping the device back into my pocket.

"No, we're not. You still haven't addressed the actual events."

"I killed some stupid, fucking gangbangers trying to shoot me. There's street light surveillance video, twenty-six witnesses, and my statement to the uniformed cop on site. Those three things are more than sufficient to determine that I acted both in self-defense and in defense of the patrons of Club Megasonic against the four members of the Bloodhound gang. I even tried to save the life of one of those losers."

I resisted the urge to flip the IA cops off as I said, "See ya next time," and stormed out of their little interrogation room.

"Andi, bring the Jeep around."

"On it, boss," she replied.

I rushed down the hallway and out the front door. IA's position on the first floor illustrated how much the NOPD despised them. Besides a few supply closets, the mail room and building security personnel, nobody else was on the first floor. *Worthless sacks of shit.*

As I stood waiting for the Jeep, a uniformed cop made a beeline across the loading zone toward me. "You're Detective Forrest, right?"

I regarded him skeptically. He was young, early twenties, with a wetness behind the ears that was almost visible. I pegged him for a rookie right away. The kid was just average. Average height, average build, average looks, nothing about the guy stood out to me in any way. If I'd met him before, he'd been quickly forgotten. "Yeah, why?"

"I'm a huge fan," he replied. "That case you worked with the Pope? Wow. Talk about exciting."

"Yeah, it was a big deal for the department."

"We spent two whole days on it at the academy. It's one of the biggest law enforcement success stories of the last century."

"A lot of innocent people got killed and injured. They always seem to leave that part out." *Where's the damned Jeep?*

"Sure, but you stopped the drones from killing more people, then saved the Pope. That's awesome."

"It had to be done. If I didn't do it, someone else would have. I just happened to be at the right place at the right time."

"Hey, can you sign this?" he handed me a citation booklet and a pen before I could answer.

"Uh, I guess."

He tapped the thin brass nameplate on his uniform. "Make it out to Jake Hannity. I've never met a Medal of Valor recipient," he added as I signed my name across the page. "I would love to be able to take out some of these punks like you do. Really try to clean up the streets, you know?"

I knew. "It's a lot more hassle than it's worth, kid. Keep doing your job and go home to your family each night."

"Oh, I'm not married."

"Okay, then do whatever it is that you like to do. Don't end up like me."

I handed him back his booklet and stepped down into the street where the Jeep had pulled up.

"But I *want* to be like you. You're a hero."

"No, I'm not."

The slamming Jeep door saved me from hearing his answer. An attitude like that would end up getting the kid killed and I didn't want any more blood on my hands.

When I glanced back at him while the Jeep waited to pull into traffic, he held the citation booklet almost reverently, staring at my signature. He had the biggest, goofiest grin on his face.

*Goddammit.* The last thing I needed right now was some rookie cop trying to follow me around. I hoped the signature was enough for him, but somehow, I doubted it would be.

# FIVE: SATURDAY

"What've we got, Drake?" I asked, ducking under the yellow police tape blocking the end of the alley.

"Good afternoon, Detective," the former linebacker replied. "Garbage droid was making its rounds when it discovered the bodies. Luckily, the DNA sensors in the containment unit triggered a halt before they were crushed, but—"

"The dump site is contaminated," I surmised, looking at the trash bin still suspended in the air above the truck from when the droid dumped it into the compactor.

"Yeah. Don't know how much evidence there would have been anyways," Drake said. "What there was got dumped into the compactor and mingled with all the garbage."

"There's always something," I muttered.

Ben Roberts and his assistant were already snapping photographs of the inside of the truck. I waved to catch his attention.

"Don't think we'll be long, Detective," Ben said as a way of greeting. "There's only so many ways we can photograph a few bodies piled up on top of each other inside a trash compactor."

I gestured toward the trash bin where I presumed the bodies had been dumped by the murderer. "Please make sure you get pictures of the inside of the bin."

The photographer dropped his camera on its strap where it banged against his chest. "How long have we known each other, Forrest?"

I held up my hands in surrender. Ben was the best forensic photographer I'd worked with in twelve years on the police force. "Sorry, Ben. I'll stay out of your way and get suited up."

"Thanks."

I set my bag down out of the way and opened it. Inside I had all sorts of gadgets that the department had supplied for crime scene investigation and a few others that I'd procured on my own over the years. This would definitely be a low-tech investigation, so I pulled out a set of disposable white coveralls and overshoes.

Before I put the suit on, I placed my hat on top of the bag and folded my jacket over the top of it.

"Hey, Detective, I can go up in there if you'd rather not get dirty," Drake offered.

"Thanks, buddy, but I'm alright. I have absolutely no plans for tonight…or the next three hundred nights."

"Oh?"

"Yeah, things between me and Avery are over," I replied. "She said I was a grouch and too involved with my work. Oh, and that I was a drunk."

Drake looked sidelong at me as he squeezed into his own waterproof suit. "That didn't come as a surprise to you, did it?"

I thought about it for a second. "Probably more than it should have. It's hard to have all of your faults listed out loud and then thrown in your face."

"I bet it is. Are you alright?"

"I'll be fine. It just stinks right now."

"It won't mean anything, but I'm sorry for you. Is there anything Genevieve or I can do?"

I grunted as I bent over to slip the overshoes on my feet. "No, thank you. I'm going to try to eat a little better, maybe try to get in shape."

"Nothing wrong with that," he answered, finishing his own preparations to protect against the filth in the garbage compactor.

"Alright, Detective, we're done," Ben said from near the truck. "I'll have all of these uploaded by the end of the day."

"Thanks, Ben."

I wrapped a heavy piece of leather around my lower leg that reached almost to my knee and secured it with a couple strips of silver tape. I *was* in Easytown after all. There'd been several detectives who'd gotten a nasty surprise wading through the garbage. I didn't plan on catching some exotic disease from doing my job.

Next, I put on a thin pair of disposable cotton gloves to absorb the moisture from sweat and then slid heavy-duty rubber gloves on each hand. The gloves could withstand an accidental needle stick as long as I didn't try to jab my hand repeatedly onto something.

"Alright, let's get this over with," I sighed. "How were they killed?"

Drake, similarly dressed and protected as I was, said, "Looks like multiple stab wounds, but that was just me peeking into the truck before Ben got here."

I grunted in acknowledgement and grabbed onto a rung up high, pulling myself up a couple of feet until my foot found the lowest step on the ladder. I climbed up and stopped when I got to the opening. The smell of refuse and spoiled meat hit me hard, causing me to retch involuntarily. The three bodies were on top of several bags of garbage near the center of the compacting unit.

My foot hovered over the edge as I started to step down, but I caught myself and pulled it back. "Hey, Drake!"

"Yeah?"

"Get the driver over here before you come up."

"Got it."

I examined the bodies while I waited. Two females and a male. Lots of bruises and cuts, some were stab wounds while others looked like someone tried to fillet them.

"Yes, sir?" a robotic voice called from a few feet below me.

"You're going to have two detectives up here in the back of your truck inspecting the bodies. Don't start the compactor—actually, don't do anything."

"Understood, sir. I will remain away from the controls."

"Good. Keep it that way."

I stepped down as lightly as possible onto the first bag and it started to roll under my foot. I had to bend down and steady myself with my hands to climb over the trash. I made my way across the shifting mounds until I was beside the bodies.

Up close, they were much worse than I'd initially thought. These people must have gone through an unbelievably painful ordeal at the hands of one sadistic fuck before they died. Burn marks, abrasions, missing fingernails and broken bones rounded out the list of injuries.

"What happened to these people?" Drake mumbled over my shoulder.

"It's bad. I've seen a lot of messed up shit, but the sheer variety and long-term abuse is almost mindboggling."

"That's some extensive scarring."

I crouched down and spread the male's ass cheeks. Dried blood and tears in the skin surrounded the victim's anus. The women showed the same signs of abuse, plus extensive bruising around their vaginas. The mix of older, green bruises coupled with newer, purple ones spoke volumes. "They were raped, repeatedly, over time. Given the combination of scar tissue and scabs, I'd be willing to bet this lasted several weeks."

"Good God. Could you imagine?"

"Unfortunately, I can," I replied.

"That one's got a fresh rope burn around her neck."

"Good observation. I hadn't seen that yet. There's so much to take in…"

I trailed off as I looked at the female Drake had indicated. The lips, swollen and caked in blood didn't sit right on the woman's face. I stood and pushed my way through the bags of trash to the body.

When I separated the victim's lips I saw a gaping emptiness. "Son of a bitch. This one's teeth have been pulled out. What about the other two?"

Drake made his way to the other bodies. "The male's teeth are gone." More movement. "And hers too."

"Missing teeth *and* missing fingernails. Whoever did this didn't want them to be able to defend themselves."

Besides the obvious torture and rape, something else was going on here.

"You thinking some type of sex slave, slash murder?"

"Exactly what I was thinking," I replied. "Probably more of a BDSM operation and these three were killed when their scarring became too disturbing, even for the normal clientele."

"That means they'll be replenishing their stock. I'll put out some feelers with Missing Persons, see if there have been multiple kidnaps in the past few days."

"Maybe we can find these sickos from evidence they left at the kidnapping sites. Good thinking."

We spent another three hours poking around the dump site, including going through all the bags of garbage, piece by piece. Besides the bodies, there didn't seem to be any evidence. The unlikelihood that we'd find anything of value was reinforced by a call from Chief Brubaker.

"Forrest, it's Brubaker."

"Good evening, Chief. We're on site at the triple homicide in the garbage truck."

"That's fine. You can stop searching through the garbage."

"Come again?" I asked.

"We pulled video footage. A large male pulled up in an unregistered and sanitized car early this morning. He dumped the bodies—no other trash—and then left. Going through the bags will be a waste of time."

I stared at the contents of the fifteen bags of garbage that Drake and I had already sorted through. "We're just getting started on the trash, but we'll stop."

"Good. I need you guys to wrap up down there. We're getting calls from one of the councilmen's offices with inquiries as to why we're detaining a garbage truck."

"Who the fuck cares why, Chief?" I snorted. "Police business and all that shit. This truck is ground zero for a triple homicide investigation."

"Not gonna go over. This particular councilman already has a hard-on to see you suspended—permanently."

I knew who he was referring to. *Jefferson.* "Goddammit! When is this guy gonna give it a rest?"

"Probably when his wife comes back to him," Brubaker stated. "Which means, never. You've got to blend in and swim with the current."

"Huh?"

"It's a fishing metaphor, Forrest. It means that sometimes you need to go with the flow and let events carry you along instead of fighting upstream all the time. I thought you were a fisherman?"

"I've been a couple of times, but I wouldn't say I was a fisherman."

"You need to take some vacation time."

"I had a forced vacation five months ago, Chief."

"And you sat around your apartment wishing you were out on the streets investigating crimes instead of doing anything relaxing."

A muffled conversation reached my ear as the chief talked to someone on the other end of the line. I heard him say, "Yeah, okay," and then there was a rustling noise as he brought the old-fashioned phone up to his ear. "Hey, Forrest, you've got to shut it down and let that truck dispose of the garbage. It still needs to complete the route and there are human workers getting paid to keep the incinerator plant open. Release the bodies to the coroner's office and come on back to the station."

I glanced over my shoulder at Drake, who'd been listening in to the conversation and mouthed the words, "*This is bullshit.*"

He nodded, but remained quiet. No sense getting himself in trouble when I was the one that Councilman Jefferson wanted to see thrown to the wolves, not him.

"I got it, Chief. We're done with the bodies and if you're giving me a direct order to stop the crime scene exploitation, then we'll wrap it up."

"Covering your ass. I like it, Forrest. I knew that you'd be recording the conversation, that's what a good cop does." He cleared his throat and continued in an "official voice," "Detective Forrest, this is Chief Robert Brubaker and I'm ordering you to discontinue site exploitation at the triple homicide dump site on Halperson Avenue. Video surveillance evidence indicates that the bodies were placed in the garbage bin and nothing else was put in with them at that time.

"There, is that good enough for you, Forrest?" he asked.

"That'll do. Thanks, Chief."

"Go home, get cleaned up and take that pretty girl of yours to dinner."

I didn't want to go into the fact that Avery had shit all over my cold heart, so I said, "Okay."

Chief Brubaker hung up the phone and I threw an old hangar toward the back of the compactor. "Fuck! What the hell is this shit, man?"

"It's what happens when we let politics get in the way of good, common sense. Decisions get made to satisfy priorities other than justice."

"Drake, sometimes you're a deep motherfucker, you know that?"

"That's what Genevieve says on Saturday nights," he said with a big grin.

I laughed at his crude sexual humor, if you couldn't joke about the size of your dick, then you had no business being a cop in Easytown. "Alright, let's get out of here. It's almost Saturday night."

"Oh, I know what time it is," Drake replied with another smile.

*Guess I'll be hanging out with Andi once again*, I thought bitterly.

# SIX: SUNDAY

*Paperwork.* I hated paperwork. Everyone who thinks that being a detective is glamorous has no concept of reality. I blame television shows and books—writers are such assholes. Eighty percent of my job is paperwork, whether it's preparing initial reports, filing them with the correct office, drafting up search warrant paperwork for the judges, after action reviews, full investigation reports, conducting the standard monthly computer-based training for all police officers, or preparing correspondence with others, I hated all of it.

When I joined the force, I had visions of always being in the field, protecting the population and taking out the bad guys. In reality, it was a rare occasion that I didn't have a case. When I could, I walked The Lane, maybe drove through some of the side neighborhoods in Easytown, and that was about it. There wasn't much time for anything else.

I'd submitted an initial report on the triple homicide from the garbage truck last night and expected the coroner's findings sometime in the early afternoon. Once I had their identities I could begin the process of putting the victims' whereabouts and circumstances together. Then maybe we could catch the fuckers that did it. Most likely not, though.

Maybe the Paladin was right; police officers couldn't stop this type of brutality. It would take a lunatic in a mask murdering hundreds of thugs to put a dent in the statistics. Arresting the Vigilante wasn't high on my to-do list.

While I waited for the coroner, I went for a three-mile run. In truth, it was more of a jog than a run. Okay, it was a jog/walk, but at least it was something. I'd been woefully negligent with my exercise regimen for the past several years and it was time for a change.

Once I got back from my abysmal run, I had Andi develop a training plan for me that would have me running ten miles by the end of July. I still held my own in short distance sprints after a suspect, but anything more than five or six blocks and I was done for. The perps I chased these days were putting a serious hurt on me when I went after them and it was embarrassing to have to call in a drone to snatch someone because they were getting away.

"New Orleans Secure Transfer delivery is inbound, Zach," Andi stated while I undressed to take a quick shower.

"Thanks. ETA on the N.O.S.T. droid?"

"Seven minutes."

I'd have to hurry to finish and get dressed before the droid showed up. That was the annoying part about N.O.S.T.; if you didn't answer the door within two minutes, they were off to their next scheduled appointment. It worked, though. They remained the most reliable and timely delivery service in the city due to their strict adherence to timelines.

Of course, everything could have been instantaneous if the department would switch from the archaic paper reports and simply send them as an attachment to email. But that wasn't how the NOPD wanted to do business. They'd gotten a bad rap, long before I was alive, for poor digital file management and most of the department was relieved. Since then, it was paper copies for every important case—murders, by definition, were important—and then someone down at the central warehouse scanned them and maintained the files digitally as well. In addition to being a giant pain in the neck for someone to do double work, it was a waste of taxpayers' dollars.

*Don't blame me; I just work here.*

I finished in time to hear the doorbell ring and Andi's voice carrying into the bathroom from my bedroom telling me that I needed to hurry.

"The droid from New Orleans Secure Transfer is the only non-standard object in the hallway," she said as I rushed across my apartment in a towel.

Several years ago, I'd gotten stabbed in the hallway outside my old apartment when some gangers found out where I lived. Since then, Andi religiously scanned the hallway for potential threats. I avoided leaving if anyone was in the hallway. As a result, I had no idea who any of my neighbors were.

I threw open the apartment door just as the droid from N.O.S.T. was turning to leave. "I'm here!" I shouted.

The droid looked me up and down. "We are not that kind of service, Detective Forrest."

"Shut the fuck up." I wasn't keen on N.O.S.T.'s new droid programming. They'd taken tons of criticism that their bots were too mechanical, so they uploaded some new software and now every one of the damn things thought they were a comedian. I'd thought they were too robot-like before, but now I wished for the good old days. "Do you have the package?"

"Yes. Please sign the clipboard to accept delivery.'

I signed and the droid handed me a standard manila envelope. I hefted it. "Hey, this seems really light. Are you sure nothing fell out?"

The droid took the package back and turned it over. "The seal is still intact and the package weighs sixty-three grams. This is consistent with the acceptance data in the system."

I took it back. "Okay, thanks."

"No problem. See you later, alligator."

"Jesus," I muttered and closed the door in its face. *That* would get annoying quickly.

I tossed the envelope on my "desk" which was really the dining room table. I never used the thing to eat at, only work, and since there wasn't an office area in the apartment the table had become my desk by default. I chose to ignore the fact that I wasn't having company over any time soon that would require the use of the table.

With a cup of coffee in hand, I sat down at the desk, not even bothering to get dressed. The lack of paperwork in the envelope intrigued me. Typical coroner's reports were at least twenty pages long, per victim.

I opened the envelope and slid five pages into my hand.

The first two pages were the coroner's findings report, which was usually much longer. The other three were photographs, all close-ups of a series of numbers tattooed behind the right ear of each victim, labeled "**Male**," "**Female 1**," and "**Female 2**."

"What the hell?"

I returned to the coroner's report and read it quickly. "Are you fucking serious?"

The letter was both straightforward and ambiguous with a way ahead. I don't know what I'd been expecting, but it sure wasn't what the coroner wrote. I reread it slowly to see if I'd missed something the first read through.

Report of Dr. Charles Brandt, New Orleans Medical Examiner, regarding the three homicide victims discovered in a garbage bin in the Easytown district on February 7th, 2099.

Patients presented with virtually every type of injury imaginable in an extreme abuse case. DNA and fingerprint analysis inconclusive. During my workup, I noticed a similar numerical tattoo behind the right ear of each victim. I cross-referenced this information with the New Orleans Mainframe computer network and confirmed that these markings are typical in clones. As such, my requirement to examine the bodies ceased. Clones are not human and are not protected under the law in any capacity.

However, I did perform a cursory autopsy on the clones in order to assist the detectives in the case to determine the cause of death. Each victim had deep puncture wounds from knives and some type of round puncturing device, such as a fireplace poker. These deep puncture wounds are the most likely cause of death in the Male and Female 1.

Massive bruising around the neck of Female 2 indicates choking, however cyanosis is not present and a rapid examination of its blood indicate no change to the viscosity of the fluid. Thus asphyxia is ruled out as the cause of death for Female 2. It is most likely that this clone expired due to massive internal hemorrhaging from the volume of fluids found in and around the chest and abdominal cavities. As such, my determination is that Female 2 was beaten to death.

The other injuries, while they would have been extremely painful to a human, especially over a prolonged period of time, are unlikely to have caused death. Current medical science is unclear whether a clone feels pain or if they respond to stimuli as programmed during growth and initial indoctrination.

Vaginal/anal tearing and associated scar tissue in these areas and other parts of the body indicate long-term sexual abuse. My medical opinion is that the abuse occurred over a period in excess of three months, although my training is with humans, not clones. I don't have a working understanding of the regenerative properties of the clone body, so depending on the rate of healing, this could have been much less time—or longer, I simply don't have a reference point with clone anatomy. There is no detectible presence of semen for analysis.

The victims do not appear to be malnourished, a common cause of death in long-term sexual captivity cases. Examination of their stomach contents shows some type of milk-like substance, possibly a nutrition shake.

On a final note, the clones teeth, fingernails and toenails were removed after the body had grown to adult human proportions. This is indicative of a person, or persons, not wanting to be injured while they abused the victims. I've seen medical reports of this type of behavior in other professional correspondence.

This concludes the cursory cause of death examination. The clone corpses are scheduled for incineration at 0900 Monday morning. The destruction will occur as scheduled unless the investigating officer requests a delay.

Signed,

Charles Brandt, MD

Office of the Chief Medical Examiner, New Orleans Parish

"Well, shit."

"You seem distressed, Zach. Is the report not what you wanted to discover?"

I set the letter down on the table so Andi's camera could read it. "Since the victims were clones, you have no legal obligation to investigate further. You can now keep your Sunday night dinner with the Khalil family at 6 p.m."

I glanced at her camera's lens, clearly annoyed. "That's not the point, Andi. Clones may not be protected under the law but I've seen these things close up. There's no way they don't feel pain; they're a copy of us—I mean, a copy of a human. They don't have an immunity to pain. Those things suffered for a long time at the hands of some sick people. I can't just ignore it and say, 'Oh well.' I have a *moral* obligation to find the murderers and put them behind bars."

"According to the law, they have done nothing illegal," Andi countered. "Under current state and federal regulations, a clone is not classified as human, animal or even droid. As such, arresting the perpetrators is not authorized. A clone is considered property, similar to the dining room chair you are sitting on now. If you wanted to break the chair, carve your name into it or any other form of destruction, it is your property to do with as you please."

"These things aren't the same as a goddamned chair."

"However, if the clone is currently being financed and not purchased outright, the perpetrators could be arrested for vandalism of private property."

"That's it! That's my way around the bullshit regulations. Andi, you're a genius."

"I'm a computer program, boss. You tell me that often enough."

"Yeah, and you're only as good as your programmer."

⚜ ⚬ ⚜ ⚬ ⚜

My Jeep dropped me off at the front door of the Pharaoh's Tomb. My friend, Amir, inherited it from his father when he died and turned the place into an Egyptian-themed tourist destination. Even though it was off the beaten track in West Lake Forrest, the Pharaoh was listed as a must-see when in

New Orleans. I liked the food and Teagan Thibodaux, one of my only true friends besides Amir, worked there.

The restaurant was packed with tourists and cops, like always. Over the years, it had become an unofficial hangout for cops looking to get a good, quick, and inexpensive meal with their discount. I nodded to a few officers that I recognized when I walked through the doors.

"Good afternoon, Zach," the hostess said.

"Hi, Karina. You doing okay today?"

She nodded her head and the black wig that made up part of her Egyptian slave costume bounced accordingly. "Your table's open," she stated as she tapped frantically at her computer screen.

"Thanks," I replied. She was busy today, so I wouldn't bother her with small talk.

I'd been coming to the Pharaoh since I was a kid and three or four times a week since Amir inherited it, so I had a routine. I liked to sit at the same table, which afforded me a view of most of the restaurant and the front door, and tended to order the same thing on the same day of the week.

As I walked toward my table, a hand shot up from a booth and a young cop waved. It took me a second to recognize the kid who'd asked me for my autograph yesterday outside of the NOPD headquarters. I waved back and tried to keep walking.

"Hey, Detective Forrest!"

"Ah geez," I muttered to myself. Out loud, I said, "Hey. How are you, kid?"

"It's Jake. Jake Hannity. Remember, we met yesterday?"

"Yeah," I nodded. "Sorry, your name slipped my mind. I'm getting old."

"What does that make me, then?" the uniformed cop he sat with asked. The guy looked to be older than I was, but a single chevron on his sleeve told me that he was only a patrolman. I immediately wondered if this was a second career for the guy or if he'd been busted more than a few times.

"Detective, this is my partner, Liam Tidewell," Jake introduced the older officer.

"Don't be trying to turn Jake into some type of hero, Detective," Tidewell said after I shook his hand.

"I'd never do that. Easiest way to get yourself killed is to try and be a hero."

"Heroes don't live long in New Orleans," Tidewell agreed. "How the hell are *you* still alive?"

Something about this guy immediately rubbed me the wrong way. "Sheer, dumb luck. You gentlemen have a nice lunch."

I went to my table, which was only one table removed from theirs. Too close for comfort. When I sat, I noticed Tidewell looking right at me. I stared back.

After a few seconds Teagan sat down across from me.

"Hey, Zach."

"Good afternoon, Teagan," I replied, still staring at Tidewell's ugly face.

She half turned and then looked back at me. "Is there something going on?"

I gave it another second before tearing my eyes away from the patrolman to look into Teagan's hazel eyes. "No. Everything's fine. Just cop stuff."

She glanced over her shoulder again and snorted. "Yeah, right. What's going on between you two?"

"I honestly don't have any clue. I met his partner yesterday, the kid's a rookie and wanted me to sign his citation booklet. Then today, the older guy got bitchy about me putting thoughts of being a hero in the rookie's head. I didn't do that shit."

"Some guys can't handle being face-to-face with their own inadequacy."

She was probably right. "You know, for a kid, you're smart as hell."

"I'm not a kid, Zach. I'm half a semester away from graduating college." She made air quotation marks as she said, "And then I'll be a certified 'real adult' as you call it."

Teagan and I had had our ups and downs over the years. She started working at the Pharaoh almost four years ago, taking on the challenge of being my daily waitress, and we'd quickly developed a friendship. I was more comfortable around her than any other female in the world—and then the bottom had dropped out of my perception of reality last October.

I found out that Teagan was in love with me. I'd chalked it up to puppy love at first, but it became apparent—after people told me—that it was more than that. She'd planned her immediate future around the chance that we would get together. She was in her senior year at Xavier, studying childhood education, and only put out applications in New Orleans, despite the dangerous reputation of the city's schools and rumored corruption within the school board.

I thought the world of Teagan; she was extremely smart, pretty, athletic, witty, and a genuinely nice person, but she was too young for me. She was twenty-three; I was thirty-four, thirty-five next month. The age difference at this point in our lives was a big deal to me. If it were ten years later, I would probably kill for the opportunity to date a woman who was eleven years younger than I was, but Teagan hadn't really experienced life yet. Besides the one year after high school that she'd taken off to work and travel the states, she'd been in the nest of higher learning, sheltered from most of the real world and our problems.

True, as a mixed kid who lived in the Little Woods neighborhood, she did see more than the rich kids from the west side of town, but I wasn't convinced that it was enough. I needed someone who was world-wise, not just book smart.

And so our delicate balance of friendship and innocent flirting continued.

"You are an adult, Teagan. But, you haven't experienced the real world yet."

"Then let's go on a road trip together," she said excitedly. The enthusiasm on her face reminded me of a child when you tell them that they're going to an amusement park.

"I can't take you on a vacation. I'm in the middle of a case."

"You need a vacation, Zach. You're so wrapped up in being a cop, you can't even enjoy life…" She trailed off for a moment and then said what was on her mind. "Does that cop you're dating like that you never leave work behind?"

I'd learned my lesson about bringing someone into the Pharaoh when I brought the droid Paxton Himura here during the Sex Club Killer case. But, Teagan had learned about Avery a few months ago when she was out with her parents at a restaurant where Avery and I met for dinner.

"She's not gonna be coming around anymore," I stated.

"Oh?" Her eyebrow shot up.

"Yeah, things didn't work out."

"Too much of a grouch for her to take all the time?"

I grimaced. "Yeah, that was one of her complaints. She also said I drink too much and work way too much."

"*Hmpf*," Teagan grunted, leaning back and crossing her arms across her small chest. "Maybe I should have gotten to know her; we both seem to agree on your flaws."

"That would've been fun."

"I'm kidding, Zach. I'd never willingly hang out with someone you were dating…" She trailed off once again, leaving the end of her statement open as an invitation for me to say more.

I cleared my throat. "So, I'm working an interesting case."

"That's it? That's how you're gonna leave it?"

*Oh no.* There'd been a few weeks after the truth about Teagan's feelings for me came out where she went on a full court press to get me to agree to go on a date with her, but once Avery and I became a thing, she slowed down her advances. I'd hoped that we could just stay friends.

"It's an interesting legal and moral debate."

She waved me off. "What about other stuff? Like the fact that you know I like you? We're great together and we have an amazing chemistry that's hard to find. Don't you want to try and explore that further?"

"Teagan, you're an amazing girl—"

"*Teagan*," Regina, the manager's voice cut through the air in warning. The restaurant was busy and she'd been sitting with me for too long.

She stood up quickly. "This isn't over, Zach. You're going to take me on a date. You know what? I know the weekends are bad for you because of your job, so pick me up at my place on Tuesday night at seven."

"I—"

"Dress nice," she said as she spun on her heel to go check on the other tables in her section.

"Dammit," I cursed under my breath. *That girl will be the death of me.*

I hadn't even ordered my lunch. But then again, there was the fact that Teagan knew me well enough to guess what I wanted to eat based on my mood.

*What goes best with irritation?* I wondered.

# SEVEN: SUNDAY

I stopped by the precinct to talk to Chief Brubaker about the clone homicide case before going to my Krav Maga dojo for a workout. The chief was probably the only person in the Easytown station who worked more than I did; he was always at work.

"Good afternoon, Chief."

My boss briefly looked up from a report he was reading and indicated the chair across from him with one hand. I sat down and waited for him to finish.

He jotted a few notes down on a sticky pad and plastered it to the front page before setting the report aside. He leaned back and eyed me questioningly. The ever-present, unlit cigar stuck out the side of his mouth, making me think of those old cartoons where the bulldog had a cigar in its mouth. Except, those things exploded.

"What's up, Forrest?" the chief asked.

"It's about yesterday's triple homicide case."

"The clones? That's not a homicide."

"Maybe not technically according to the law, but—"

"Are you looking for more work?"

"No. I—"

"What about the Paladin? Have you caught him yet? No?" In true Brubaker fashion, he bulldozed along, cutting me off. It was best to let him get his initial statements out of the way, then he'd be more receptive to discussion. "Why are you wasting time thinking about the disposal of a few clones when there's a vigilante murderer running the streets of Easytown? Do I need to put Cruz on the case?"

I waited a moment to let him finish. "Well?" he asked, taking the cigar out of his mouth to spit a piece of the tobacco wrapper onto the floor.

"No, I haven't caught the Paladin. He's gone to ground since Drake and I almost had him the other day. It might be the increased drone support, I don't know. But until he does something, I'm stuck.

"The reason I wanted to talk to you about the clones—"

He sighed loudly. "Forrest, what is it about you and clones, you and droids, you and drones? Everything seems to be an issue."

"Have you ever actually talked to a clone, Chief?"

"What? No. Why would I?"

"Hear me out for a minute. I know what the law says about clones; that they're considered in the same class as droids. Personal property to do with as the owner sees fit. They aren't protected in any fashion under the law. Dogs and cats have more protection than they do. That about sums it up, right?"

"Exactly. The three clones you found in the trash yesterday were disposed of by their owner."

"Well, I *have* talked to a clone before, a couple of them. They may not be human, but they think, they feel, they bleed. They are *not* like a droid at all."

"So they've been programmed to pretend to have feelings. Not our problem, Forrest. Close the case and move on to more important things."

"Chief, the only reason we know about those three is because the human DNA sensor in the trash compactor was tripped by their bodies. I don't know the process, but they're grown from human DNA, an exact copy of us. They're essentially human."

"You keep that goddamned opinion to yourself, Forrest. Those things aren't human. They're an abomination against nature. The same as when that scientist in Japan spliced a dog and a human together to create some type of humanoid companion. That thing ended up going insane and killing twelve people before the police were able to put it down.

"Clones are grown in a lab," Brubaker continued. "They aren't human, they're property and this precinct will not waste time investigating whether someone destroyed their own property."

"You have your opinion, I have mine. What if the clones weren't owned by the person who disposed of them? It would be destruction of private property or possession of stolen goods, or—"

"You want to spend time—and the department's money—investigating a *vandalism* case?" he asked incredulously.

"Yeah. I think there's something else going on. Those clones showed evidence of long-term abuse. There's no way that one person is doing that on their own." I scowled as the images from the compactor came back to me.

"You're my best detective, Forrest. I can't afford to have you off on some goddamned wild goose chase."

*He's coming around.*

"I won't be, Chief," I assured him. "Since this isn't a case that the department is interested in investigating, I don't have a mandated time limit. I'll only look into it when time allows. The only thing I need you to do is request a delay in the incineration of those bodies. They're scheduled to burn tomorrow morning at 9 a.m."

The wheels turned behind Brubaker's eyes. I could tell that he wanted to support me, but also wanted to keep everything within regulation. "Okay. You can pursue this destruction of private property issue on the side, around your primary duties. I'll halt the incineration for a couple of weeks, but if the morgue gets low on space, those clones are the first things to get burned."

"Thanks, Chief." I started to stand and then remembered about the photographs. "Oh, I'll also need Ben Roberts to process the crime scene photos he took. I don't want him to dump them since this isn't an official case."

"Fine. Give him a call and tell him that I authorized him to complete the job at his convenience. No rush job requests from you, do you hear me?"

"No rush jobs," I affirmed.

"If something—anything—comes in, that takes priority over your little vandalism investigation. Do you understand?"

"Of course, Chief."

"Alright. It's Sunday, get out of here and spend it with your friend's family."

"Thanks. You won't regret this."

"I hope not," he muttered and crammed the butt of the cigar back into his mouth.

I took the hint that I was dismissed, excusing myself to call the photographer and the morgue. Even though the chief hadn't put in the call to halt the incineration yet, letting them know that it was coming would ensure that they didn't thaw them out overnight in preparation for the burning.

As I hopped in the car, I asked Andi to set up a meeting with Thomas Ladeaux. He'd said something about investing in a cloning company when I learned that his assistant was a clone, and he'd shone the willingness to use one as a deliveryman. Maybe he could give me some insight into where all of these clones were coming from.

⚜ ○ ⚜ ○ ⚜

"Zach, my good friend. How are you?" Amir asked as he hugged me. His accent was a little thicker than normal, telling me that he'd already hit the bourbon a few times without me.

"I'm good, Amir. What about you?"

"I am feeling fine, my man. So fine!"

"Zach, can you please take this idiot into the study and keep him from breaking anything?"

I turned to see Amir's wife, Amanda. She'd snuck up on us from the opposite direction. She leaned in for a hug and I returned her embrace.

"It smells great. What's for dinner?" I asked.

"Roast lamb with mashed potatoes, green beans and candied yams."

"Wow, Amanda. It's like Thanksgiving around here every week."

Amir waved his hand dismissively. "She's been cooking that poor beast all day. I've been so bored."

"And he's been drinking all day, complaining that football season is almost over since the Saints didn't make the playoffs," Amanda replied with a wink toward Amir. "Can you please entertain him for me?"

"Of course. How long do you think I have to distract him?"

Amir laughed while Amanda said, "Probably thirty minutes or so. Enough time for you to catch up to him."

We went to Amir's study while she went to the kitchen. The house felt like a home once again. Just a few months ago, the suspect in the Sex Club Killer had shot up the house trying to distract me from the case. Virtually every window had been destroyed and there were still several places where the replacement bricks out front hadn't faded to match the originals.

As I sat on the sofa, I looked around our favorite drinking spot. I loved the rustic feel of Amir's study. It reminded me of an old smoking room like they used to have in the last century. The walls had cedar planks on the upper half and dark green wallpaper on the lower half underneath a chair rail. Hardbound books filled the shelves of the room's dominant feature, a massive built in bookshelf.

Amir walked loosely over to the wet bar and picked up a decanter of amber liquid.

"Ah, not tonight, buddy. I'll have a vodka tonic," I stated.

He stopped and glanced up at me. "No more blonde cop with the huge bazoongas?"

"No. No more huge bazoongas for Zach," I replied with an exaggerated pouty lip. "I'm okay with it though. She told me in no uncertain terms what all of my flaws were and I realized that she was right—and that she's not the woman for me."

Amir stared at me with glassy eyes and set the decanter down with exaggerated gentleness. "Are you sure you're okay? Hearing how others perceive you when you're not expecting it can be rough."

"Yeah. I'm good. Vodka tonic, please."

"Alright, my friend! Let's drink!"

We spent the next forty-five minutes discussing the previous week's Super Bowl and what we felt the Saints should have done differently in their loss to the Cleveland Browns. Ultimately, it came down to the cybernetic enhancements of the Brown's safety. They put some serious money into that guy and our receivers couldn't get past him.

I watched Amir slam back another double bourbon and I placed a hand on his wrist as he prepared to stand up to get another drink. "Everything alright, Amir?"

"I'm fine."

*Lie.* I was pretty good at determining when people weren't telling the truth and my best friend was lying to me.

"Amir, I know something's up. One, you don't usually drink this much. Two, you're a bad liar. Three, I noticed Amanda trying to cover for you about why you were drinking. What's going on?"

He slid his hands down his face and then wiped them on his pants. "It's the Pharaoh. We're not doing so well."

"I don't understand," I replied truthfully. "Every time I'm in there, the place is packed to the gills. How are you not doing well?"

"Two months ago, a new investor bought the building. Last month, the building's lease came up for renewal and he tripled our rent. I can't afford that."

"Damn. So what's your plan?"

"Today? Drink. Tomorrow? I don't know."

"I don't know anything about real estate law, but isn't there anything you can do? The Pharaoh has been in that building for twenty-plus years."

"Twenty-two," he corrected me. "I spoke to the new owner last week and he's unwilling to budge on the price."

Amir stared vacantly at the wall. "The bastard even said something about you. Isn't that strange?"

My stomach dropped.

"What was that?" I asked.

"The new owner. He said to make sure you knew that he bought the building."

A fuzzy memory of Tommy Voodoo and two pretty women dragged its way to the forefront of my brain. He said something about a business deal to keep us together, but I'd ignored him.

"Is the new owner Thomas Ladeaux?"

"Yes. How do you know that?"

"*Goddammit!* That guy can't leave me the fuck alone."

"You know this man?"

"Yeah," I sighed. "He's a dirty son of a bitch who owns a bunch of clubs in Easytown and the big shipping company down there at the Dockyards."

"What does he want with the Pharaoh?"

"Who knows? It sounds like he bought it to get leverage over me."

"What am I supposed to do, Zachary? I can't afford to pay that much in rent every month."

"Funny enough, I've got a meeting scheduled with him tomorrow. I'll see what I can do, buddy."

"Thank you," Amir nodded and went to the bar for another drink.

By the time Amanda came to get us, Amir was sloppy drunk—probably like I'd been Friday night. It wasn't a pretty sight. *No wonder Avery doesn't want to see me anymore.* He fell into the side table and his glass tumbled to the floor, shattering into hundreds of pieces.

"Oh, come on, Amir. This isn't going to help anything," she chided.

"Zach, my best friend for my entire life, he is going to fix this," Amir stated, placing both hand on my shoulder and leaning in on me until his forehead rested against mine. "Zack knows Thomas Ladeaux. He'll make this go away. Won't you, Zach?"

"I don't—" I stammered

"Thank you, Zach!" Amanda cried, throwing her arms around us both.

My hands came up, unbidden and on their own. I hugged them back. Somehow, I'd figure out a way to get this straightened out; they were counting on me.

# EIGHT: MONDAY

My Jeep drove between the stacked forty-foot shipping containers that served as the entry point for the Easytown Dockyards. I'm sure it was just a matter of convenience, but the containers seemed to completely surround the waterfront, forming a wall that could be easily defended by the workers.

I shuddered involuntarily and hoped that the police department never had to come down here in force. Inside the perimeter, more shipping containers lined the road, forcing vehicles to follow the path. The containers were easily moved with the heavy equipment the workers used, so they could alter the path, create dead ends or block off the passage behind you after you passed through. This place would be a SWAT team's worst nightmare.

Tractors, cranes and forklifts moved everywhere in a carefully choreographed dance of machinery. Men, women and droids went about their jobs, ensuring goods were either loaded onto barges for transport or unloaded from them for delivery into the city.

Business was good for the King of Easytown.

I was back in the Dockyards to meet with Tommy Ladeaux, aka Tommy Voodoo, the self-named King of Easytown. He was as dirty as they come—the department just couldn't find anything to implicate him. Plenty of underlings had gone down over the years, but nobody would testify against him. In addition to the Marie Leveau Shipping Company, he owned a construction company, and multiple sex clubs, dance clubs and regular bars across Easytown. Now it seemed like the bastard owned the building that the Pharaoh was in; I knew it was another way that Voodoo was using to try to get an edge over me—and it pissed me off.

He'd tried unsuccessfully to get me in his pocket by providing key information on the Sex Club Killer case and with the details about Paxton Himura, whom I hadn't known was a droid when I began dating her, thereby violating the NOPD's Immorality Clause that explicitly forbid physical relationships of any kind with prostitutes—human or robotic. Now it seemed he was trying a different angle to make me obligated to him in some way.

Wasn't gonna happen. I wasn't a dirty cop.

The Jeep stopped in front of the corporate offices of the Marie Leveau Shipping Company and I took a swig of water from the bottle I'd grabbed before I left. Amir and I had stayed up through the night and into the morning drinking and talking. I'd only gotten an hour of sleep before I had to get up for the meeting that Andi set up to discuss the clones. I was tired and hung over, not a good combination.

I checked my surroundings carefully before getting out of the vehicle. The Dockyards were a dangerous place for a cop, even if Voodoo did invite me down here. I didn't see anyone or anything near the car, so I got out and took the steps to the office two at a time.

Inside the building, I was greeted with a clean and modern waiting area. It was sparsely decorated, choosing functionality over comfort. Clear plastic chairs sat in a circle around a low table adorned with a local New Orleans magazine that did a feature on Ladeaux. His picture took up the entire cover.

Two familiar receptionists sat at their twin desks. The blonde was a clone and the black haired one was a reformed sex bot. She'd been recycled from a club, given an AI upgrade and put to work here.

"Hello, Anastasia," I said to the clone sitting at the desk on the left.

"Good afternoon, Detective Forrest," she replied and then continued her data entry.

"You're ten minutes earlier than expected," Betty, the droid, stated.

"One of my tragic flaws," I answered. "So your boss is expecting me, then?"

"I've been instructed to rearrange Mr. Ladeaux's schedule to accommodate you."

I felt eyes on me—okay, to be honest, I *always* felt like someone was watching when I was in the offices of the shipping company, but this was different. I glanced over at Anastasia. She stared down at the paperwork on her desk, but watched me intently through lidded eyes.

"You got a problem?" I asked.

"Yes," she responded. "And so do you."

"What's that supposed to mean?"

"Tommy will talk to you about it."

"Bullshit. You're not a droid; they can't program you to be quiet. What am I walking into here?" Obviously something was amiss if the clone chose to say something to me. *What is it?*

She glanced toward the ceiling. I looked up. A parabolic microphone stuck out from the sound-deadening tiles. They didn't even bother to hide it.

"We're in danger," she whispered rapidly. "I feel like part of me is dying."

"Anastasia, that's enough," Betty chided, standing rapidly. "Mr. Ladeaux expressly forbids us from engaging Detective Forrest in conversation. You are violating direct orders from Mr. Ladeaux and I must report you."

"Go ahead, Betty. I'm worried. Nobody gives a shit about clones."

"I'm hurt, Anastasia." I turned away from the drama unfolding before me to see Voodoo walking into the reception area. Every time I saw him, he reminded of a weasel—if a weasel wore a suit that cost three months' worth of my salary.

"I give a shit about you, dear," he continued. "That's why we're talking to the good detective today."

"Ladeaux," I stated matter-of-factly.

"Detective Forrest, nice to see you again." He stuck out his hand for me to shake. I ignored it, choosing instead to stare at his beady little eyes.

He took the hint and dropped his hand.

"Really? I thought we'd moved past all of this unpleasantness. After all, I helped you unravel the Sex Club Killer case. That earned you quite a bit of local fame, if I recall correctly. Oh, and that state trooper. I bet she was a blast, huh?"

"Are you keeping tabs on me, Ladeaux?"

"No, of course not, Forrest. It's hard not to notice things like that when pictures of the two of you end up on every internet tabloid site. Not very discreet, friend."

"I ain't your friend, Ladeaux—regardless of how hard you try to make it that way." Talking about my failed relationship wasn't getting me anywhere, so I changed the topic and turned back to Anastasia. "You said the clones are in danger. What do you mean?"

She stared past me to where Voodoo stood. Her eyes spoke volumes that her mouth didn't. Voodoo was involved in something, but didn't want me to know about it; something that was harmful to clones.

I glanced at Tommy Voodoo and then back at the clone. "Let me try a different approach. I'd like to ask you a few questions about—"

"That's quite enough, Detective," Voodoo said. "My clone is done talking to you."

"I'm not done talking to her."

"Please, don't make this difficult. The laws regarding clones are few and far between, so the federal government has passed stopgaps stating that the same rules that apply to droids are enforceable for clones. I'm within my legal rights to refuse you access to discussing anything with my property without a warrant."

"Your property? I thought you were different when it came to clones, Ladeaux."

"*I am*. However, I know my rights and if I want the discussion to end, I can do so at any time."

"Are you afraid she's gonna say something to incriminate you? Is that why you don't want me to talk to her?"

"No, I—"

"Do you know anything about three tortured, mutilated—and very dead clones that were dropped off in a dumpster on Saturday?"

"Yes."

"Don't give me that shit, Ladeaux. Wait, what?" Sometimes it took a moment for my mind to catch up to my mouth. I was shocked that he admitted knowing anything about the case—or whatever this little side investigation ended up being.

"Yes, I know about them. That's why I wanted to speak with you today."

"Alright. What do you know about it?"

"Let's go to my office," Voodoo suggested. "If certain associates of mine saw me speaking to you about this, the consequences could be severe."

I laughed at his statement. "Are you worried that your street reputation will take a hit?"

"No. More like I'm worried that I'll become a target. There's a lot of money involved in this game, Forrest. More money than I'm worth; far more than you could ever hope to see in your lifetime. The people making that money don't want it to stop coming in."

I thought about it for a moment. How appropriate that he was afraid for his life because of the type of people he chose to associate with. I didn't have any sympathy for him, but I wanted to get the answers as best I could so I agreed to go back to his office.

He led the way woodenly, nodding his chin only slightly when he passed anyone in the hallway leading to his office. We turned suddenly, going a different way than we'd gone the last time I was here a few months ago. Voodoo stopped in front of a seemingly random panel in the wall and pushed on the upper corner.

I heard a soft *click* and then the side he'd pushed on came away from the panel next to it. He pried it open and indicated that I should go through first. I stepped into a small corridor that ran behind the walls of the Marie Leveau Shipping Company. I felt Voodoo step in behind me, so I moved forward a few feet and turned to watch him close the panel. Complete and total darkness enveloped the passageway.

Movement in the dark told me that he was doing something. I didn't trust the man as far as I could throw him, so I drew my service piece and stepped across the corridor to the other side. A moment later, a small, bright light illuminated the space as Voodoo held a lighting orb.

"You can put that away," he whispered. "I'm not going to try anything."

I relaxed slightly now that I could see, but chose not to let him know that. "I'll keep it in easy reach," I assured him.

"Come on. It's this way. We'll be there in a minute."

We followed the passageway straight for what felt like a hundred feet, then took a right when the passageway came to a T-intersection. Another hundred feet and Voodoo stopped in front of a locked door. He pressed his hand onto a flat scanning panel and then a retinal scanner assessed the retinal blood vessel patterns in his eye. It was a lot of security for a simple meeting.

Voodoo wasn't worried; he was terrified.

The door unlocked and we entered what appeared to be an office space. It looked almost exactly like the one we'd met in before.

"Did we just take a secret passage to get to your office?"

He sat down at the desk and smirked. "Yes—and no. This is my real office. The one we met in last October is a duplicate. A clone, if you will."

"So all that sports memorabilia in the other office?"

"Fake."

"This?" I asked as I gestured around the room at the signed pictures of him with players, footballs signed by entire teams, jerseys encased in picture frames and all sorts of other pieces. I'd say all of it looked like it belonged in a museum or at least a sports bar, but the dedication to Mr. Ladeaux made them worthless in my eyes.

"These are the real ones. Everything in here was gifted to me by the players or their team. It's absolutely priceless in my opinion."

"Okay, so we snuck through your building and we're skulking in a private office. Why?" I asked.

"My other office is being watched."

"So won't they know we didn't go there?"

"Betty has already hacked the security system so the video shows you leaving after your little altercation with Anastasia."

"What? How?"

"Video is easy to manipulate, Forrest. You should remember that."

The last time I'd dealt with Voodoo, he'd shared erased video footage from the sex clubs and droids that he owned. The hacker had made his changes imperceptible to the police techs, the only way we knew anything was different about it was because of the criminal sitting across from me.

"Anastasia is right." Voodoo continued. "She's stupid to say something publicly, but the clones *are* in danger."

"Like the ones in the dumpster?"

"Yes. Have you ever heard of torture tourism?"

I thought about it for a moment before answering. "No, I haven't heard that term before. It sounds like that virtual reality game that swept through Easytown ten or twelve years ago. People got their rocks off by torturing and killing others in VR."

"It's similar to that, in a way," he affirmed. "VR torture made people a lot of money. The levels of depravity in the human soul are truly amazing. But I'm sure you know this all too well, Detective."

Unfortunately, I did.

"So, what is torture tourism and how does it relate to my case?"

Voodoo smiled, reminding me that even though he'd helped me in the past and it seemed like he was willing to help me now, he was still a snake.

"It's a mix of extreme gambling and murder. Clones are brought in and things are done to them—we don't need to go into the details, I'm sure the bodies you discovered had plenty of evidence as to what they are subjected to. Players make bets on mundane things like which one will scream first and it goes up from there, including what it will take to kill the clone. There's really no limit to what they could bet on."

"How do you know so much about it, Ladeaux?"

"Because I sold the clones to the club before I knew what they were going to do with them. Those three you found originated from the company that I own sixty percent of."

"Who'd you sell them to?"

"A broker named Joseph Kleer. I've been told, after the fact of course, that he runs the torture tourism ring. We've looked for him, but I can't find him. He's become a ghost. The best I can tell, he's set up torture houses across the city and the gamblers are told where they will go at the last minute to keep the location a secret."

*Fuck me. It seems like Voodoo has done all the background research... Again.*

"Alright, so they're gambling illegally. *That* I can arrest them for."

Voodoo seemed surprised, for once. "That *would* be a way to put a stop to this. I hadn't thought about that aspect. I wanted to brainstorm with you about how to charge them with murder."

"Can't be done," I muttered. "Clones aren't protected under the law. Like you mentioned earlier, they're property. They can be disposed of at any time by the owner. I couldn't even get an autopsy done by the coroner. Once he found out those three were clones, he stopped working on them."

"That's bullshit—pardon the expression. Biologiqué International has perfected the cloning process. They are exact duplicates of their counterparts, down to the minute they were cloned. With our memory implant technology, they even retain the memories, mannerisms, and personalities. If lawmakers would talk to a clone or spend time with them, they would know that they're just as human as the next person. Maybe more so since all the genetic deformities and undesirable traits are removed before the body is grown."

"So you're on the side of the clones?"

"Certainly. You may think I'm only one misstep away from Sabatier Island, Detective, but I'm much cleaner than you give me credit for."

"*Hmpf.* I doubt it."

He let the insult slide. "My company has been in the development phase for years. Clones feel; they have emotions, they reason and they seek self-preservation. Seems like they're pretty human to me, even if they are grown in a laboratory. Genetically, they are one hundred percent compatible with humans and I believe they are a viable option for companionship for millions of lonely people. Part of that is affording the clones certain rights; chief among those is granting them basic human rights—like protection against murder."

"Companionship. If that takes off, you'd be one of the richest men in America. Maybe even the whole damned planet."

"Yes, I will be. However, as a compassionate person, I want to see the clones treated fairly, but it's not entirely altruistic. We're on the brink of earning billions, maybe even trillions, in the clone industry and I don't want that opportunity spoiled because the government can't see the truth and grant the clones rights."

"*Hmpf*," I grunted again. "How many clones did you sell to this Joseph Kleer?"

"Thirty-eight. Of those, we've recovered the bodies of four more, all of them mutilated beyond belief. Those, plus the three from Saturday still leaves us with thirty-one unaccounted for."

"That's a lot of clones to track down."

"I know," Voodoo sighed, making a face like he'd taken a sip of curdled milk. "I swear to you, I didn't know what these people were going to do when I sold the initial batch. I figured they'd end up as prostitutes or private house servants for people who mistrusted droids. Nothing like this though."

"Since you know so much about this stuff, please tell me you know where they're hosting next."

"I do. And I want you to bring them back to me—alive."

"You're shitting me, right?" I asked.

"No. I know the block where the club is located. It'll be up to you to determine which building it's taking place in."

He'd thrown me a softball. If I wanted to put an end to the torture tourism, it was up to me to hit it out of the park.

"Give me the details," I hissed.

# NINE: MONDAY

The darkness concealed me as I stalked toward what I believed was the target building. Out of the four buildings on the block, the warehouse was the logical choice to host the events that Voodoo described. It was a giant, dilapidated building with roll-up doors that the clients could drive their cars into and be hidden from view.

I'd briefly considered requesting official police backup before going in, but since this was so far outside the realm of my responsibilities, I knew that Brubaker wouldn't authorize it. I settled instead for a drone and my partner. Unfortunately, Drake called out sick, so it was just me and the drone.

"I want you to scan the warehouse," I ordered as I pressed my back against a building to get under a slight overhang. Heavy sheets of cold rain fell out of the sky above, adding to the concealment that I desired, but made for a miserable experience. "Tell me how many people are in there."

"Understood," the drone responded. "Unit One Six Four needs to achieve an altitude of one hundred fifty-seven feet to properly scan the entire building."

"Uh… Sure. Go on, do your thing."

The drone drifted upward slowly, the whirring of its rotors the only thing that gave away its presence in the inky darkness. I watched until I couldn't see it anymore and then slowly continued toward the building.

I didn't know what I expected to find. Hopefully, we'd make some quick and easy arrests and that would be the end of it. Too bad I'm a realist and didn't believe my own line of BS; this was probably going to get ugly. There was apparently way too much money involved for the assholes to just roll over and let me take it away from them.

Angling around to the back side of the building, I did my best to avoid the homeless who sought shelter from the elements under the old awnings. They were mostly harmless, like the thousands of other homeless in Easytown, but they could also be used as an early warning system by the people inside. One guy with a phone could ruin the element of surprise quickly.

I stopped in the shadow of the building next to my destination and looked around. The warehouse was made up of two connected buildings. The first was the large storage building where I'd noted the gamblers' cars could be hidden. Next to that was a small, square two-story building that must have originally been the offices. By Easytown standards, the buildings were ancient; they must have been one of the first attempts at a business in the district when the city built the new levees.

Circling the building was a decrepit chain link fence that had seen better days—I was guaranteed to get tetanus if I even walked near the damn thing. It was down in several places, the fence posts leaning drunkenly and the fence lying flat on the ground. Besides the fear of getting an infection, it wasn't a deterrent for me to get inside.

Small ventilation windows ran the length of the larger building, set high above the ground, so those wouldn't be any use to me. I'd probably have to go in through what I thought were offices, either through the door or through a window.

The drone was high above me. I could barely see the red and white navigation lights on the thing. It was scanning the building as I'd requested, but was taking much longer than I thought it should. I wanted to get in, bust these guys and get out.

I was about to leave the damn thing and go on my own when my phone rang. I looked at the display, the goddamned drone was calling me.

"Yeah?"

"Scan complete, Detective Forrest. There is one human inside the office building on the second floor. No other humans are alive inside."

"What do you mean?" I asked. The way it said that last sentence made me wonder about dead humans.

My phone automatically projected a hologram of the building into the air in front of me. The rain broke up the image and caused a slight distortion that made it difficult to see in some places. Worse, I hated when freaking droids took over my electronics.

"Unit One Six Four detected one human heartbeat on the second floor."

The hologram shifted, rotating rapidly and zooming in on the second floor where a bright red dot pulsed slow and steady in rhythm with a heartbeat. After a couple of seconds, the image shifted and several green circles flashed across the second floor.

"There are eight masses of organic material that may indicate human remains."

"Well shit," I cursed. *I got here too late.* "What else is there?"

The image flashed brightly with more white dots than I could count. "Hundreds of lesser life forms, likely rodents, are now indicated on the schematic."

"Rats. I don't care about them. What else about the building?"

"At this time, there is nothing else significant to report."

"I'm going in," I told the drone. I'd hoped to arrive during the betting and get a recording of it so I could legally bust all of these assholes, but it looked like I was too late. Since there was only one person left inside, I could bust them quickly and then figure out what to charge him with. "I want you to provide overwatch. Continue to scan the building and the perimeter to alert me of any threats. Got it?"

"Understood, Detective."

I put my phone away and inserted an earpiece before running at a crouch from the shadows where I'd received One Six Four's report. As I ran, I noticed a door on the warehouse that I hadn't seen from across the street, so I angled toward it. Entering the warehouse at the farthest point from the person in the attached offices would help me maintain the element of surprise.

The downed chain link fence rattled impossibly loud in the night, making me cringe. *He had to have heard that*, I thought. No time to stop, I had to keep going.

I made it to the door. *Dammit!* A heavy padlock secured the outside, plus it opened outward, so trying to kick it in would be useless. I thought about running around to another door, but decided against it and pulled the Aegis from its holster. The end of the barrel made a slight *clinking* sound as I pressed it against the shackle and squeezed the trigger.

The Smith and Wesson Aegis shot five, tightly-grouped lasers out to one hundred feet. The lasers lost strength over that distance, until they dwindled to a non-lethal effect at max range. Within the first fifty feet, however, the Aegis lasers punched holes through nearly everything in their path.

I caught the padlock before it hit the ground and set it gently on the concrete slab at the base of the door. The door swung outward with only a slight, rusty squeak at the end. When I slipped inside, I saw that the Aegis had melted a thumb-sized hole through the doorjamb and burnt out on the concrete floor.

I slid the laser pistol back into the holster and drew my service pistol as the water sluiced off my overcoat, puddling at my feet. Then, I put on a pair of bulky glasses that amplified the ambient light coming through the high windows to create a visible image inside the lenses. Besides the unnerving sight of near blackness around the edges and to the side, the glasses lit up the room like it was early morning or dusk.

The floor of the warehouse was empty. Long tables, once used to prepare products that came through this place, were shoved to the side against the wall and stacked on top of one another to allow room for vehicle parking.

I wondered where the car was for the man upstairs. It was odd, unless he lived nearby, took a taxi or rode the bus, but the nearest stop was about eight blocks away. None of those options seemed like something a person with a lot of cash on hand would do.

"One Six Four, are you sure there's somebody in here?" I whispered into the microphone on my collar. "The place looks deserted."

"Affirmative," the drone replied in my earpiece. "The human that Unit One Six Four detected eight minutes ago is still in the same location as previously reported."

"Is he asleep?"

"Unknown. The figure appears to be horizontal."

*Even better.* If I could sneak in and get to this guy while he was asleep, I wouldn't need to worry about a gunfight. *Not that I'm worried about it.*

I jogged across the open space to a door leading into the offices and slipped inside. There was barely enough light to see anything, so I switched on a micro infrared light on the glasses' frame. The IR light was invisible to the naked eye, but shown like a flashlight in the darkness when viewed with the lenses I wore.

The first floor of the building was empty, as expected. Whatever office furniture had been here in the past was long gone. All of the refuse I'd expected to see in an abandoned building had been cleaned out; the place looked like it was ready to be used by any legitimate business.

I checked each of the rooms quickly to make sure that I wouldn't have a nasty surprise sneak up on me when I was going up the stairs. It wasn't that I mistrusted the drone's scan, I was a member of the club who followed the old adage: Trust, but verify.

Especially with my life on the line.

The rooms were all empty, except for one which held a trashcan full of bloody bandages, used tubes of antibacterial cream, syringes and empty meal replacement bottles. *I'm in the right place.*

Thankfully, the stairs leading to the second floor were poured concrete, not wood or metal that would have given me away to anyone in the building. I made sure to place my foot firmly on each step before moving up the curving stairs, there was no room for a stupid error like tripping.

A door at the top of the stairs blocked the landing, so I leaned against it and listened. Everything was quiet inside. The person the drone detected must still be asleep.

*Wait!* I heard something.

I passed the SIG Sauer into my left hand and wiped away the sweat on my pant leg. It was useless, my pants were already damp from standing in the rain outside. I transferred the pistol back into my firing hand and placed my palm on the doorknob.

⚜ ∘ ⚜ ∘ ⚜

I stepped into the room, prepared for the worst. Instead, the place felt more like a veterinarian's office than a sadistic torture room.

Large metal crates lined the wall immediately to the left. Each had a blanket or pillow, it was difficult to tell through the night vision, but they were empty. The crates appeared to be clean—in fact, the entire place looked and smelled clean. The odor of antiseptic masked whatever had been in here before and what likely happened here on a nightly basis.

It made sense. To keep the clones relatively free from infection, and to keep the fun going, the people running this place would have to make sure everything was spotless. It probably helped them attract a high-class crowd, instead of street hustlers, as well. I could imagine gamblers and their well-dressed dates sitting around watching the events while they sipped champagne eating heavy hors d'oeuvres. Cleanliness was a must for those types of people.

"Detective."

I paused and backed against the doorframe. "What?" I hissed at the drone.

"When you entered the second floor, an electronic signal began transmitting."

"What's it say?"

"Unclear. It appears to be only a warning alarm."

*Well shit. They know I'm here now.* "Thanks. Keep an eye out for anyone coming to assist."

I pushed away from the wall and advanced rapidly into the room. Chairs surrounded a large circular cage in the middle of the main room. This must have been where the fights, torture, or whatever else those sick bastards had in mind happened. I crept forward into the gloom. Dark smudges on the floor showed where blood had been spilled and then left too long to clear away completely.

I glanced at the inside of the cage. A small table holding an assortment of scalpels, pokers, knives, pliers and a blowtorch sat off to one side. Manacles extended from a metal ring set in the ceiling and two pairs of handcuffs were bolted to either end of a stained wooden block, used to keep the victim's legs spread apart. More handcuffs rested at evenly spaced intervals around the cage, the clones were likely forced to watch what happened to their fellow prisoners, waiting in horror for whatever the sick bastards had in store for them.

Sitting on the floor beside the table was a set of jumper cables attached to a small generator on wheels and several buckets holding different liquids and powders. I wondered which one held the sulfuric acid that had been used liberally on one of the female victims we'd found in the garbage compactor.

"Where is the perp in relation to me?" I whispered, barely audible to the microphone.

"You are in the main space on the second floor. To the north, you should see a doorway. The human is in there."

I glanced around the room. There were three doorways leading off the main room. I'd gotten completely turned around when I entered the building and went up the curved stairwell. "I don't know which way is north. Tell me left or right from the way I'm pointing."

I held out the Sig Sauer with one hand, aiming it directly at the door in front of me.

"To your left is the room where the heartbeat originates from as well as the organic matter which may be human corpses."

I turned left and walked rapidly to the door. The only sound I heard was a ragged breath.

A well-placed front kick right below the handle sent the door flying inward. "*Police! Don't move!*" I shouted.

The wave of odor hit me hard. The small room smelled of raw meat, the metallic odor of blood tickled my nose and made me want to vomit. A naked woman rolled away from me, shrieking. All around her, corpses lay piled up like cordwood, wrapped in plastic sheets. She scooted backward into the corner created by the bodies.

I spun, quickly trying to determine if there was anyone else in the room. "One Six Four, report," I ordered.

"You are in the room with the only human, Detective."

I fumbled behind myself until I found the light switch, then winced at the sudden bright light before taking my night vision glasses off. I glanced at the woman. Blood ran from dozens of lesser injuries and one eye appeared to be swollen shut. Nasty red and black welts shown across her fore and upper arm where she'd likely tried to block an object from hitting her in the head. She'd seen better days and judging by the stack of bodies, was lucky to be alive.

"Call emergency medical services and tell them we have a female clone in need of assistance." I thought for a moment and then added, "Also, secure the perimeter. Nobody comes in until I clear them. I think we hit this place in between events and that signal you detected was an alarm."

"Wilco, Detective."

I holstered my weapon and held up my hands. "I'm Detective Zach Forrest. I'm a police officer. I won't hurt you."

She stared at me, a wild look in her eyes. I didn't know if she wanted to flee or try to kill me.

"Do you understand me?" I asked.

I took a step and she responded by screaming. I retreated once again and crouched down. "I won't hurt you," I repeated.

"Detective," the drone called in my ear.

"Yeah?"

"The dispatcher has denied to support your request for assistance since the patient is a clone."

"*What?*" I yelled, further startling the woman, who tried to bury herself under the bodies. "What do you mean?"

"Clones are not considered human, nor are they legally alive. The city will not expend precious medical resources to care for a clone."

"Fuck. Andi?"

"Yes, boss?" she answered immediately.

"I need you to call Dr. Wellington. He owes me a favor and I'm calling it in."

"You need him to operate on the clone?"

"Patch her up. I don't know if she'll require an operation."

"Understood. Hold on."

While she made the necessary coordination, I tried to coax the woman out from under the bodies. "I'm a cop. You can trust me. I won't hurt you."

I held out my hand. "Let's go. We need to leave this place so I can take you to a doctor."

"Doctor?" a frightened voice asked from underneath the corpses.

"Yes! To put bandages on you. Help you heal. Make you feel better." I was out of nice little descriptors for what a doctor was.

The woman's hands appeared and she pulled her way up from under the bodies. "You... You don't want to hurt me?"

"No. I came here to stop them from hurting you," I responded.

"You won't..." She slapped ineffectually at the plastic-wrapped bodies.

"No, I promise. I need to see something, though. Can I touch your head?"

She regarded me for a moment and then relented. "Yes. Please be careful. I'm hurt."

I reached slowly toward her right side and pushed the wild mane of red hair out of the way. I bent her ear down so I could see the skin of her scalp. A tattooed set of numbers, similar to what I'd seen in the medical examiner's report, stood out against her light skin. She shivered against my touch.

I looked around for any type of clothing, but there wasn't anything in the room so I took off my duster. "You're cold. Put this on."

She accepted it, but wasn't quite sure what to do with the jacket. She was either in shock or she'd never worn clothes before. Probably both.

I reached for my jacket and she flinched. "Hey, I'm not going to hurt you." I opened it and put it around her shoulders. "See. It warms you up."

"Thank you."

My earpiece beeped and Andi's voice filled my ear. "Dr. Wellington is on his way to your location."

"What? No, I need to bring the clone to his clinic."

"He said the favor he owed you wasn't worth losing his medical license, so he wouldn't risk seeing a clone in his clinic. He should be at your location within a few minutes."

"Dammit. Okay, thank you, Andi." I looked at the woman as she pivoted her upper body from side to side, letting the arms fling wide and then slap on opposite sides when she'd twisted as far as she could go. It reminded me of a child playing in her father's clothing—only her father didn't exist.

"Andi, patch me through to Jasmin Jones." To the clone, I asked, "What's your name?"

She shrugged in response. "I don't remember."

"Hello?" Dr. Jones answered groggily.

"It's Zach Forrest. I'm sorry to bother you so late." I glanced at my watch. I hadn't realized that it was almost 2 a.m.

"That's what they pay me for," she replied sleepily.

"No, it's not. Evenings, sure, but not this late. I'm sorry. I didn't realize what time it was."

"It's fine. What's wrong, Detective?"

"I have someone that I need you to talk to." I felt foolish and didn't know if calling her was the right thing to do, but I pressed on. "She's a survivor of torture, probable rape and a witness to at least eight murders."

"Uh…" I could hear her shifting around on her bed and she said something about work to someone. It took a moment for her to return. "That's a substantial amount of trauma for somebody to take. What's her mental state right now?"

The woman had wiggled her arms inside the sleeves and was trying her best to figure out how her body stopped at her armpit and reappeared at her hand.

"She— To be honest, Doc, I don't know what she was like before this, but she's regressed to an almost infant-like state, except she seems capable of communicating."

"That's not entirely unheard of, although most of the time, with a psychotic break, speech reverts to adolescence as well."

"I'm not sure how much of a childhood she had. Her speech patterns could have been implanted during her growth."

"Excuse me?" Dr. Jones exclaimed.

"The woman I want you to talk to is a clone." *I'll just leave that turd right there, see how she reacts.*

"A clone? I could lose my license if I provided any services to a—"

"What is it about everyone in the medical field refusing to help?" I burst out. I was sick of this shit. "You people are—"

"Whoa! Stop right there, Detective. Have you ever heard the phrase you'll attract more flies with honey than vinegar?"

"Yeah, sure. So?"

"You can't always go around acting like a jerk and expect people to bend over backward for you," she stated. "The problem with clones is there's an official directive from the US Surgeon General that states they are not human. As such, clones are not to receive any type of primary care nor acute or chronic care from a medical professional. Anyone who knowingly violates this directive is subject to harsh federal penalties and pressure will be placed on the state to suspend their license to practice."

Dr. Jones took a deep breath before continuing. "Clones are authorized to be seen by veterinarians, but there are plenty of issues with that line of thought since a vet doesn't study human anatomy and like it or not, these things are the same as us in every aspect."

"Why does the federal government have such a problem with clones?" I wondered aloud.

"Because they don't know how to handle them. They're technically human in every way except they weren't grown inside a woman—wait, that's not correct. They've implanted cloned embryos into women's uteruses before, so I guess the real argument is who's responsible for them. They aren't natural humans, so what rights do we afford them? Once we start protecting them under the law, then the next step would be allowing them to participate in elections so they could vote for candidates who support their kind. Can you imagine how easily an election could be rigged if someone cranked out a few hundred thousand clones, all programmed to vote a certain way?"

"That's an interesting theory, Doc. That's probably the closest to the truth about why the government refuses to protect them that I've heard so far." It was a lot to think about, but I could do the thinking tomorrow while I sat at my kitchen table.

"So, are you going to speak to her or not?" I asked.

"Yeah. I'll talk to your clone—off the books, of course."

"Of course. And thank you. That seems to be the general attitude when it comes to anything clone-related. People need to see them and understand what they are before they disregard them completely," I added.

*How can the medical profession completely disregard a human in need of help?* I wondered.

*Because of outside pressure,* I answered myself. *Politicians are worried about the influx of like-minded voters. That scares them.* Then I had a thought about the clones. *Sure, they all start the same, but from the moment they're "born," they have free will. Doesn't that free will cause each clone to act differently?*

"Where are you?" Dr. Jones asked.

I gave her the address to the warehouse in Easytown and she said she could be there in twenty minutes.

"Oh, and Doc?" I asked before she hung up.

"Yes?"

"Do you think you could bring an old pair of clothes? She's about your size, but she's naked as an alley cat."

"Of course. I've got a big bag of clothes that was going to get picked up by a donation droid in a few days. I'll get a few things out of there."

"Thanks, Doc."

I hung up the phone and ignored a message from Andi; something about coordinating a space at a women's shelter. That was step five or six, after the clone's immediate medical and mental health needs.

"Is the doctor coming?" a woman's voice interrupted my thoughts.

"Huh? Oh, yeah. Doc Wellington will be here in a few minutes."

"Is he nice…like you?"

I laughed hard at the question. "I ain't nice, lady. I'm a mean son of a bitch."

"No you're not. You're taking me to a doctor—and you haven't hit me yet. You gave me your coat; you're a nice man."

It angered me that her metric for somebody being nice was *not* hitting her and giving her a jacket to keep warm. *What kind of world do we live in?*

"Look, lady—do you have a name?"

She shrugged again. "I don't remember. They always called me Fucktoy, so that must be my name."

"No, it's not," I countered, exhaling forcefully. "That's not a nice name."

I thought for a minute, staring at her wavy auburn hair and green eyes. Who was the person she was cloned after? Was she local? If I'd brought my fingerprint scanner, I could have easily found out, but it was in the Jeep with the rest of my gear. Although, did it really matter who she was? Maybe. Maybe not.

"What do you think about Lucy?"

She shook her head. "No. I don't know why, but that name makes me think of someone mean."

*Ghost memories from the donor.*

"Hmm, okay. Do you like Sadie?"

"I don't know her. She sounds important."

"Never mind," I sighed. "From now on, your name is Sadie."

"Detective," the drone's voice came over my earpiece.

"Excuse me," I told Sadie and touched my earpiece. "Yeah?"

"A vehicle registered to Dr. Douglas Wellington is on site with a single occupant. Am I authorized to detain?"

"No! I'm coming out to bring him in. There will be another doctor, Jasmin Jones, in a few minutes. Let her in also."

"Understood."

"Sadie, I need to go get the doctor. I'll be right back, okay?"

"Don't leave me with…" She gestured toward the stacks of bodies.

*Goddammit! How could I be so insensitive? I need to get her out of this room.*

"Alright, come with me," I said, gesturing toward the door. "I didn't mean for you to stay in there. Sorry."

She moved awkwardly through the door that I held open for her. "It's fine," she replied.

I gritted my teeth. Normally when a woman said it was fine, they meant things were *not* fine, but I didn't know if Sadie had the mental capacity for that kind of duplicitous speech. I doubted she'd ever had the opportunity to sharpen her witty banter.

The woman limped out into the main room and stopped. She began to shake when she saw the cage. I didn't know whether it was from rage or fear.

I slid up beside her. "Hey, it's okay. You're safe now."

"Are you sure?" She looked up at me, tears welling around the corners of her eyes.

"Yeah, I'm sure," I answered as I guided her by the shoulders around the cage to the stairs I'd come up earlier. "Let's go downstairs. There are medical supplies that the doctor can use."

"Hello?" a voice called up the stairwell as we descended.

*Shit. The old man's faster than I thought.*

"We're coming down, Doc. Sadie just needs a little bit of time to make it down the stairs." I glanced at her; she did her best to negotiate the steps, each one a jarring impact on her battered body.

"I can probably carry you down if you need help."

She stopped once again. "No, thank you. I want to do this on my own."

I respected her wishes and followed along beside her as she made her way down. When we reached the bottom, Dr. Wellington had already set up a table with a blanket and his medical kit was open on one end.

"Thank you for coming, Doc."

The old man regarded me solemnly for a moment. The whites of his eyes were yellowed with age and his light gray hair stood out in stark contrast to his dark brown skin. Then his gaze went past me to where Sadie stood a few steps behind me.

"I do this and the debt is paid, Forrest," he stated without breaking away from the clone.

"Wiped clean," I promised.

"Will anyone ever find out that I helped to patch her up?"

"No. It's totally off the books."

"What about that drone watchdog you've got? You gonna wipe its memory?"

"It's a police drone. I don't have access to that. I'll make sure that you're not connected to this though."

He seemed to consider it a moment and then, "Alright, young lady. Can you lie down on the table here? I'll patch you up and try to make you better."

While she got on the table, Dr. Wellington said, "Why don't you make yourself useful, Forrest, and find me a clean bucket and water. I need to wash away the dried blood to see what I'm working with."

I went in search of a source for water and something to hold it in. It didn't take long to locate the janitor's closet that held a sink, but finding a clean container took a little longer. I had to settle for a large bottle of hand soap that I dumped down the drain and washed out.

When I returned, the doctor had Sadie's feet up on the table. "Er, um… Excuse me, Doc. I've got your water and a sponge."

"Throw the sponge away. There's no telling what these animals did with it. I'll use bandages to wipe away the blood." He turned back to Sadie. "You can put your legs down, sweetheart."

He glanced at me and said, "I don't know if it's medically possible for a human clone to become pregnant through intercourse, but it'd be best if we gave her a heavy dose of Mifepristone—which I've got in my bag here—and then you or someone else will need to administer Misoprostol."

"Wait," I said, holding up my hands. "What is Mifewhatever and Meesoprosle?"

Doc Wellington pulled a bottle of pills from his bag and took off the lid. "Here, swallow this."

Sadie did as directed and put the pill in her mouth. She tried to swallow, but without water, it didn't go down. "*Ugh!*" she coughed, spitting the pill on the floor. "That tastes gross."

The old man sighed and shook out another pill. Then he got a bottle of water from his bag. "Here, now, swallow the pill with a drink of water."

"No way. That was—"

"Just do it," he ordered.

She complied, her face contorting into odd expressions as she worked the pill down her throat.

"Good job, Sadie." He looked over at me. "I gave her Mifepristone, commonly called the morning after pill. Misoprostol is a drug that's inserted into the vagina and causes the uterus to contract. The combination of the two will cause an abortion in human females. Clones? I'm not sure."

He pulled out a tablet and scribbled on it before ripping it off and handing it to me. "Take this to any drug store and they'll give you the Misoprostol. There'll be instructions in the box about how to administer it. Her other injuries seem superficial—painful, but not life-threatening. I'll get her cleaned up and she should be ready to go in ten or fifteen minutes."

"That sounds good, Doc. Thanks again."

"Don't thank me. Just remember that I never saw your clone. If anyone asks, you needed help, and the prescription is for your girlfriend, not her. Okay?"

"Yeah. I—"

"Detective," the drone's voice interrupted me in my ear.

"What is it, One Six Four?"

"A vehicle registered to Dr. Jasmin Jones is on site with a single occupant. Am I authorized to detain?"

"No." *Geez, what is it with this drone wanting to detain everyone?* "I told you earlier to let her enter the facility."

"Doc, I've got a psychologist coming down to talk to Sadie. I'm going to go outside and bring her in."

"That's fine, take your time." He'd already bent to the task of washing the blood away from the clone's body. "I'll be done when I'm done."

I went outside and walked toward the back of the building where a pair of headlights crept slowly down the drive. Doc Jones' BMW stopped twenty feet from the warehouse and I was surprised to see one of the back doors open. Even though the odds of ever driving my Jeep manually were astronomically low, I still sat up front in case I needed to take over if the computer crapped out. Apparently, she didn't have the same type of control issues that I did.

"Zach," she acknowledged and waved her hand at the building. "You sure do know how to impress a girl."

"Thanks for coming out, Doc. I know this wasn't how you wanted to spend your night."

"On the contrary, Detective. I'm excited to speak to a clone in a clinical role. This is unprecedented. Too bad I won't be able to tell anyone about it."

"Come on. I'll take you inside and introduce you to Sadie."

"Sadie? Is she a clone from the Wild West?"

"It was just a name that came to me, so I asked her if she liked it. It was better than what the creeps who owned this place called her."

"Do I want to know?"

"No, you don't. The MD examining her right now gave her the morning after pill and I have to give her another drug tomorrow to make sure she isn't pregnant."

"Can clones get pregnant?" Dr. Jones asked.

"No clue. The doc doesn't know either, but he said he wanted to do it, just in case."

"Certainly seems prudent. So, you said 'suspected rape' earlier. It's confirmed, then?"

I spent the next couple of minutes filling her in about the case, from the three clones we'd found in the compactor, through my meeting with Voodoo and ending with the discovery of the eight bodies inside and the cage where the gamblers watched and likely participated.

"That's disgusting," she stated.

"Just another day on the streets in Easytown."

I pulled open the door to the administrative building and stood aside for Jasmine to enter before me. From behind, I saw her head swivel slowly from side to side, taking in the offices.

"This isn't the bad part," I muttered. "Let's go upstairs first while Doc Wellington finishes up and you can see the cage."

"I'm not interested in seeing any bodies, Zach."

"You won't. They're all wrapped up, ready to go into the next trashcan."

When we went upstairs, she took in the cage and the torture instruments. I could see that it was a lot for her to process.

"Wow," Dr. Jones said, placing her hand over her heart. "This is tough. It looks like they took a page right out of *Slavery 101* from the eighteenth century and brought it right back here to New Orleans."

I didn't really know what to say. How do I, as a white male, comment on the city's history with slavery to a black woman? I couldn't say anything without coming off as a total jackass, so I held my tongue and let her take her time.

"These people are sick. Clones or not, they still have emotions, and they can feel pain."

I nodded. Not much else I could do.

"Alright. I'm ready to talk to Sadie now."

We went back down the stairs. Dr Wellington stood outside the door and Sadie stared out the window toward the street. I wondered if she'd ever had a window to look out of since she'd been "born."

"She's all patched up," Wellington stated. "As I thought, most of them are minor and nonlife-threatening. She should be fine as long as she doesn't have internal injuries that I can't see."

"Detective—"

"Holy shit, One Six Four," I muttered into my microphone. "What is it now?"

"A vehicle registered to Mr. Joseph Kleer is on site with three occupants. Am I authorized to detain?"

"Kleer? That's the fucker that Voodoo said bought all the clones," I stated. If I could get this guy, I may have a chance to end the entire investigation right here.

"Yes, detain him," I ordered.

"Andi, give me the details on Joseph Kleer."

"Joseph Kleer is a white male, five foot eleven and approximately two hundred twelve pounds," she replied. "He works at Carryall International, a company that manufactures exoskeletons for industrial use. He is not legally married and has no children. He spends an average of one-point-six hours per day online gambling and thirty-seven minutes on social media sites. His last online purchase was for a three-gallon tub of personal lubricant. He orders meal delivery two-point-seven times a week, predominantly pizza or Chinese takeout. In the last—"

"That's enough," I said. He didn't seem to have a record, or that would have been the first thing Andi told me. If I hadn't cut her off, she would have gone into every detail that was publicly available on the perp.

"Dr. Jones, I'm going to go outside and talk to Mr. Kleer. According to Thomas Ladeaux, he's the one behind the torture tourism ring."

# TEN: TUESDAY

I walked through the warehouse and out the side door into a standoff between drone One Six Four and the three men from the car it reported as inbound a few minutes earlier. They stood foolishly behind the open doors of their car, thinking they would offer them protection against the drone. I ducked back inside the doorway quickly.

I'd seen the police drones in action and was nearly cut in half by one up close at the Puss 'n Boots when it was protecting me. A few days later, I'd seen several of them tear into a massive crowd of people when their programming got hacked. The standard police drone was equipped with twin 5.56mm miniguns that would tear Kleer's car to shreds.

"Put down your weapons," I shouted, around the edge of the door.

"You ain't stealin' our product, man!"

"I'm a cop, New Orleans PD. Put your weapons down!"

"What are you doing here?" a different male asked.

"I'm investigating an illegal gambling ring. Which one of you is Joseph Kleer?"

"Shut up! Nobody tell that pig nothing," the second person yelled.

"What product are you afraid I'm going to steal?" I asked. "Are you dealing drugs out of this place?"

"No, man," the first guy replied. "I just meant—"

"Shut up, Hector!" one of them said. "You got a warrant to be on our property, cop?"

"You got a permit for those guns?" I countered.

"We ain't surrendering, man!"

"The state of Louisiana does not allow citizens to disobey a police officer's orders to surrender weapons of any type or caliber," One Six Four stated. "You have five seconds to comply with Detective Forrest's lawful order or this unit will render the situation safe for the residents of New Orleans."

The drone paused for a moment and then began its countdown. "Five… Four… Three…"

One of the men opened fire on One Six Four. Bullets ricocheted in all directions as he emptied an entire magazine rapidly into the drone's armor.

"One," the drone continued, unfazed by the hits it took.

"You guys need to put them down!" I shouted over the sound of the miniguns spinning up.

"You have refused to comply with a lawful order to surrender your weapons and opened fire on a New Orleans Police Department drone unit," One Six Four detailed.

It didn't give them a chance for rebuttal. The guns exploded into action, throwing two hundred rounds into the car in five seconds.

"*Whoa!*" I shouted. "Cease fire! One Six Four, cease fire!"

The echoes of machine gun fire faded into the night and the barrels stopped spinning. Then, the call I knew was coming sounded loud and clear from the drone in the newfound silence.

"Dispatch, this is Drone Unit One Six Four. Shots fired, current GPS coordinates are accurate. Two perpetrators dead, one severely wounded. Request EMS. Detective Zachary Forrest is on scene."

*Fuck me.*

"Acknowledged, Unit One Six Four. Emergency medical services have been notified. ETA eight minutes."

"Goddammit, One Six Four! Kleer was the key to this fucking case." I glanced at the bodies. The one severely wounded guy wouldn't last more than a few minutes. I ran back inside, yelling as I went.

"Doc! You've gotta finish up and get her out of here!"

"What's this all about?" Dr. Wellington demanded.

"We've got a whole shitload of cops and EMS inbound. You need to leave if you want to remain anonymous."

"Damn you, Forrest! I knew something like this would happen," the old man accused, rushing into the room where Sadie lay on a table. Bandages covered a third of her body and the rest looked like it was slathered in burn cream.

Wellington grabbed his medical bag, slamming it shut. "We're through, Forrest. My debt to you is paid. Don't call me again."

I watched him strut out for a moment and then turned back to the clone. "Sadie, I need you to get up. If I give you directions to an alley, can you go there and wait for me to finish up here?"

"I think so," she answered.

"Hold up," Jasmine interrupted. "You're not going to send this girl out onto the streets. She'd be nabbed in minutes."

"I don't have any other choice," I replied, adding a note of concern to my voice. I wanted Doc Jones to take the clone with her, but she needed to come up with that on her own so it didn't seem like I was forcing her into a corner.

"Yes you do. I'll take her to my place and you can come get her once you're done here."

"That would be a huge help," I sighed.

"How long until the party starts?" Jasmin asked.

"Less than three minutes," I estimated. "You two have got to go."

I watched approvingly as the psychologist pulled Sadie to her feet and dragged her toward the entrance.

"It's okay, Sadie," I said. "I'll come to Dr. Jones' house once I'm done here."

My approval seemed to unlock her feet and she trudged behind the doctor, who pulled her by the hand toward the exit.

"This night can't get any worse," I muttered.

⚜ o ⚜ o ⚜

*I was wrong.*

The night *could* get worse, and it came in the form of six-foot, two-inch Chief Bobby Brubaker. I didn't know how he got word so quickly, or why he was out at 3:30 a.m., but he showed up within minutes of the EMS.

"Are you trying to give me a heart attack, Forrest? Is that what you want?"

"No, sir. I don't," I replied.

"Then why are there three dead men and one of my drones offline for evaluation after it followed your orders?"

"Sir, I didn't—"

"And why the fuck are you out here in the middle of Easytown at a warehouse owned by a company that contributed a lot of money to Mayor Cantrell's reelection campaign?"

"I was investigating an illegal gambling ring."

"Gambling? That's vice, not homicide. Don't we have enough to keep you busy without you going looking for work?"

"I—"

"I ought to bust you down to walking a beat and take you down a few notches. The fucking union wouldn't allow it, though. I'm sick of this shit, Forrest. What's going on with you?"

I decided to lay it out for him. He'd given me leeway to investigate the clone case after all.

"The gambling was a convenient cover to investigate the clone murders, Chief."

"The clone murders? Are you kidding me?"

"You said if there were other illegal activities going on that happened to coincide with the clones, then you were fine with me investigating it."

"I didn't expect a goddamned drone to turn a few guys into Swiss cheese, either."

"They opened fire on the drone unit first."

"We'll see what the gun camera footage shows. If you're right, that can be defended in court," he admitted grudgingly.

"There are eight more dead clones inside," I stated. It had to be said, even if doing so would make him blow his top.

"You went *inside* this building?" he asked, jabbing his cigar toward the warehouse. "Without a warrant?"

"I had credible information that there may have been more murders."

"It's not a fucking murder, Forrest! They're clones. I can toss my shoe in the garbage and have just as big of a repercussion as slitting the throat on a clone. It's a piece of property, nothing else."

"Chief, these things aren't property. They feel every bit of pain inflicted on them. They can talk, reason, and interact. They're just like humans."

"You've lost your goddamned mind, Detective," he fumed. "I gave you the benefit of the doubt earlier. I didn't expect you to actually pursue this clone bullshit any further, but you have. Nobody gives two fucks about a talking hunk of meat. Drop the issue. If I ever hear you utter another word about clones, you're suspended—indefinitely. Do you understand?"

I wanted to push back, to throw it in his face that clones were one hundred percent human, but it wasn't the time. I'd walked too close to the fire with him and he wasn't backing off the issue. He was firmly in the camp with everyone else it seemed.

"Yeah, I got it, Chief."

"Goddammit, Forrest. This is a mess," he muttered. "You convinced a goddamned drone to accompany you on an unlawful investigation. The police department has had a major problem keeping the drone program open after they were hacked last year. Why would you jeopardize that?"

"I didn't think I was going to get into a fight. The drone was for overwatch."

"The damned thing did *way* more than overwatch. You know what? Forget it. I need a report from you no later than 8 a.m. tomorrow morning. I want every detail—minus anything about clones. You need to lock this thing down tight. Give me a reason that you went inside the building without a warrant."

"Understood."

"You're goddamned right you understand. If that report isn't in my hand first thing in the morning so I can immediately go to the commissioner with the details, there'll be hell to pay, Forrest. I'm talking about walking a beat in uniform for several months. Cruz can handle the workload."

He spun on his heel and walked away from me toward the small parking area. I watched as he squeezed into the police cruiser, which looked tiny compared to him.

I glanced at my watch; I only had about three hours to write the report and get it sent over to the Easytown PD station by courier.

"Andi, we need to start working immediately," I told her over the phone while I waited for the Jeep to pull around the block.

# ELEVEN: TUESDAY

I fell onto my couch after the courier droid left. I'd made the chief's deadline for the report with only moments to spare. The part about the three gunmen was a straight statement of the fact, no big deal. The rest of the report read like a redacted copy of the US Government's files on UFOs, but it was the truth—minus the part about the clones. It was hard to explain why I was there, my reasoning for going inside the building and then what I *didn't* discover inside.

I was exhausted, nearing thirty hours of being awake, and the one or two hours of sleep that I'd gotten after dinner at the Khalil's had been shitty.

"*Fuck!*" I exclaimed loudly.

"What's wrong, Zach?" Andi asked.

"I forgot to ask Tommy Voodoo about Amir's building when I was there yesterday. I got caught up with trying to find the clones and forgot all about it."

"I'm sure Amir will understand."

I didn't need Andi to try to make me feel better. I needed to make it right.

"Andi, call the Marie Leveau Shipping Company."

"They are not currently open, Zach."

"It's fine. I know there will be someone who answers."

A soft static filled the apartment as the phone waited to connect. It rang once and then a familiar, singsong voice filled the room. "Marie Leveau Shipping Company."

"Betty, this is Detective Zach Forrest from the New Orleans Police Department."

"Good morning, Detective."

"I need to speak with Mr. Ladeaux regarding a business transaction that he recently made."

"I'm sorry, Detective. Our offices are currently closed and Mr. Ladeaux is not available to take your call."

"What time does he normally get in?"

"Mr. Ladeaux's schedule is not for public release," she replied.

"I'm not the public. I did him a favor last night, now I need him to return it."

"He usually arrives within the next hour."

"That means he's awake. Connect me to his private line."

"I'm not authorized to—"

"Can it, Betty. Put me through to your boss." I wasn't in the mood for his pet robot to deflect me.

"Please hold."

Silence filled my apartment once again as the droid put me on hold. I didn't know if he'd take my call, but I figured the guy owed me. I put that gambling ring out of business and found eight more of his clones—nine, counting Sadie.

The phone line clicked over and a holograph feed projected into my living room of Thomas Ladeaux in trousers and an untucked shirt. A very naked Anastasia walked across the feed and she waved toward me before disappearing out of the camera's frame.

"Good morning, Detective. You look like you've been put through the ringer."

"Thanks," I grunted, noting his well-rested appearance. "I wanted to let you know that I found nine more of your clones last night at the site. All dead."

His face fell. Maybe he was genuinely concerned for the clones and not just trying to cover his ass if this went south.

"Thank you, Detective. That makes…" He trailed off in thought for a moment. "That means there are still twenty-two unaccounted for."

"Right. Joseph Kleer is dead as well."

"Did you kill him?"

"He got shot by a drone, but yeah, it's because I was there," I admitted. After writing it so many times in the report, I was beginning to think it *was* my fault that those three men were dead—or Ladeaux's. "There weren't any clues as to the whereabouts of the other clones. You got any more ideas?"

"I'll have to do some careful digging; maybe I can find out where they're holding the rest of them."

"Or if there's a second gambling site."

"Yes, that could always be a possibility, I suppose."

"Speaking of sites, Ladeaux, it seems like you made a business investment a couple of months ago."

"Ahh, yes." The bastard smiled. "The Pharaoh's Tomb—nice place once you get past all the gaudy Egyptian baubles."

"My friend owns that restaurant. Said you're tripling the rent on him."

He frowned. "It's barely above the market value for a location like that. I have to charge that in order to get a timely return on my investment."

"He can't afford that rate, Ladeaux."

"Then we'll have to terminate his lease and bring in someone else."

"You know it's going to cost a fortune to demo all the crap out of that place. Even then, you may go months or years without a renter. You're better off leaving the Pharaoh alone."

"I understand you're trying to look out for your friend's best interest, Forrest. But it's just good business to charge what the property is worth. If he can't afford to pay it, then somebody else will."

"Come on. You had zero interest in that property until you found out that it belonged to an acquaintance of mine. It wasn't even for sale when you bought it."

"I suppose I *could* be convinced to keep the rates where they are."

"I'm already saving your ass by tracking down and recovering the clones that you sold without researching your buyer."

"True," he admitted. "It wouldn't take much for me to help your friend out."

"What is it that you want?"

"It's easy. Not even that big of a deal."

I sighed. "What is it?"

"I want to be given space. Your people are always snooping around my companies, looking for evidence of illegal activities. They've never found anything and I'm tired of it; all the constant turning over of my books, property inspections and the like. I'm not dirty—a smart businessman, yes, but a legal one."

"You expect me to believe that shit, Ladeaux? People around you are constantly being implicated in crimes. It's only a matter of time until they get you on something or your iron grip on one of your flunkies lessens and they squeal. Happens all the time."

"So is that a 'no' then?"

He had me over a barrel. I could flat out refuse and my lifelong friend would lose his business. I didn't know if I could face him if there were such a simple solution to the problem. Amir had three kids; it wasn't fair that they were put in the middle of this because of me. Ladeaux bought the building as leverage against me. Helping in a few investigations hadn't won him any favors with the NOPD so he was trying another route to get the space he needed. The bastard had been under investigation in some way or another for as long as I'd been a cop. I wondered what he was up to that he felt he needed the extra room.

"It's not a flat out refusal. I'm a homicide detective, not vice or white collar crimes. I can't influence their investigations."

"I understand. And I'm a businessman, not a charity worker. I can't continue to lose money on the building the Pharaoh's Tomb is in."

"So that's it? You're going to raise the rates?" I asked. "You know how much shit *I'm* taking for following the trail on these clones? I'm risking suspension by trying to help you out. If this matter with the torture tourism goes public, you can kiss that easy money in the cloning industry goodbye."

A hand snaked over Ladeaux's shoulder and Anastasia's face appeared near his ear. A large "**MUTE**" sign appeared over the hologram, blinking slowly as the two of them talked heatedly about something for a full minute and a half.

Then the notice disappeared and Ladeaux smiled like he'd been forced to eat a bowl of shit.

"After careful consideration, I have decided that I won't raise the rates—yet. If you can recover the remaining twenty-two clones before the end of February, I'll sign a five-year lease with Mr. Khalil so he can get his affairs in order. At the end of the lease, the rate will be adjusted to the market at that time. Is that fair, Detective?"

Today was the tenth; that gave me eighteen days until the end of the month. Could I find all of them in time? I had to try.

"Yeah. That's fair."

"Good. Anything else?"

I thought for a moment and then dredged an important fact from my fatigued brain. "Like I said, I'm risking a suspension doing this. I've been officially ordered to stay off any case involving clones. They're off limits to the department, so don't expect any support and everything will have to be off the books."

"Of course they are," Ladeaux replied. "Our lawmakers are so incredibly afraid of new technologies, of their own human frailties, that they're worried that they'll be cloned and replaced." He paused awkwardly before continuing, "It doesn't work that way."

"It *could* though. You said yourself that they are an exact duplicate, including personality and memories. If you cloned someone and then eliminated a life-threatening disease, say cancer, and replaced the original person, wouldn't the clone be in your debt?"

He chuckled. It sounded more like an animal grunting. "You've been reading too many science fiction novels, Detective. It doesn't work like that. What would keep the clone loyal to me? All I'd end up doing is turning someone into a completely healthy individual whose only fear is eventual cellular deterioration and death of old age."

"Fair enough," I sighed. I was exhausted and needed to get sleep. "I'll continue to investigate the clone case and I will find those other twenty-two clones. I'll need you to give me intel on where the torture tourism ring is going to go since their main site is shut down and Kleer is dead."

"I can do that," Voodoo answered. "I'll be in touch by the end of the day; tomorrow at the latest."

He clicked off before I could respond, which was fine. I was tired, and talking to Tommy Voodoo hurt my head, because I knew that he was playing some side game as well; I just hadn't figured out what it was yet.

I stared blankly at my work shoes sitting in the biohazard bin by the door. I needed a new pair, those had been in that bin far too often recently. I considered whether I should have a drink or shower and go to bed. The urge to pour a glass was palpable, causing my mouth to go dry. *I'm not on shift for another twelve hours, so I can have one*, I reasoned with myself. *It's not like I have to have one, it just helps me to relax.*

"Andi, pour me a Scotch," I ordered and pushed myself off the couch.

"Boss, you asked me to work on you with your health choices. Based on your biometric data, having a drink at this time would have a negative return. You need to sleep, introduction of alcohol into your system will hinder that for at least two hours."

"Dammit, Andi," I said, standing in the hallway. To the left was the kitchen where the bottles of Scotch sat, not poured by Andi. To the right was my bedroom and the shower that I desperately needed after wading through clone blood and gore

"Additionally, your drinks contain two hundred and forty-nine calories. The consumption of the additional calories immediately before sedentary sleep is a contributing factor to an expanding waistline in middle aged men."

"I'm not middle aged," I growled.

"You are correct, technically," she agreed. "However, studies vary as to the age at which that moniker is granted. My point is that you don't need to have the drink when you've been awake for thirty-one point two hours. You need to sleep."

I grumbled at her logic and my own stupidity for getting a wild hair about fitness and asking for Andi's assistance. I knew how to take care of myself, I didn't need to have my AI tell me what to do.

"Fine," I relented. "I'll get cleaned up and get some rest."

"That is the optimal choice."

The door to the bathroom closed solidly, giving me a little bit of privacy from Andi's prying cameras. Without her, I'd never get anything done, but sometimes I felt she was more like a nagging wife than a computer program and I needed a break.

I unzipped my pants and stepped out of them before dropping them in the laundry chute. Then I pulled off my shirt and poked at my stomach. I watched the reflection in the bathroom mirror. Sure, there was a little bit of softness to my belly that hadn't been there a few years ago and I could still see the top four bulges of my old six-pack abs, but it wasn't the same. Along with the layer of fat on my lower abdominals, several gray hairs poked their way prominently amongst the black ones on my chest.

Maybe Andi was right. I *could* do a better job of taking care of myself.

I went to the toilet to pee and my annoyance at the intrusion of privacy returned full force when a chime from the speaker above my head rang out.

"Urine test complete. Zachary Forrest, you have elevated levels of protein in your urine. This could be an indicator of kidney damage or the onset of kidney disease. You are dehydrated; optimal levels of hydration—"

"Shut up," I mumbled, flushing the toilet while it droned on about my urine. Louisiana Health Department code enforcement wouldn't allow me to disable the apartment's toilet sensors and it drove me crazy. It said the same thing every time. I had kidney damage from drinking and recommended that I stop drinking. I also had moderate to high levels of sugar in my urine, which could be the beginning stages of diabetes, and the toilet recommended that I stop drinking.

Even worse, Andi *talked* to the toilet computer constantly. I'd told her thousands of times to stop, but it was one of her core processes as a check to keep me healthy. And it was annoying.

Almost immediately after stepping into the shower the overhead light began to flicker, letting me know that someone was calling my cell. I'd purposefully not installed sensors or cameras in the bathroom to keep Andi out of one aspect of my life, but at times like this it would have been beneficial to have the ability to talk to her and let her know to take a message.

I completed showering as rapidly as possible and roughed up my hair with a towel before wrapping it around my waist.

"Andi, who was on the phone?" I asked, opening the bathroom door.

"Dr. Jasmin Jones, New Orleans Police Department staff psychologist."

"Dammit." She probably wasn't happy I'd stuck her with the clone. "Did she leave a message?"

"Dr. Jones said to call her back, that's all."

I unwrapped the towel and finished drying off. Then I put on a comfortable old t-shirt and my sleep pants. "Call her back, please."

Jasmin's face filled the wall screen in my bedroom. "Hello?"

"Hey, Doc. How's the clone doing?"

I watched her eyes wander disapprovingly over my messy bed before coming back to me. "She's doing as well as can be expected. She slept on my couch last night and ate more food than I thought possible for breakfast and now she's laying down on the couch again."

"Yeah, there were a lot of meal replacement bottles at the warehouse. I think that's all they fed the clones."

Dr. Jones nodded and said, "I need to know what we're doing with her. I've got a six year old and a three year old. I can't keep a clone around them—not one that was as abused as this one has been anyways. I'm willing to try to help her, but you know that abuse does some strange things to a person's mind. I don't want her around my family until I have the opportunity to talk to her and see what's going on upstairs."

"I understand. Thank you for taking her last night."

"You didn't give me any other option. I had to get out of there or risk getting caught up in an investigation."

I winced at her choice of words. "I'm sorry about that. I didn't know that the drone would get into a firefight when I called you. If those three guys hadn't shown up, we would have been fine."

"But they did. I know a women's shelter not far from here that would be willing to take her in—as long as she kept the fact that she's a clone to herself."

I couldn't risk her telling anyone who or what she was. I was already in hot water with Chief Brubaker over the clone issue, if it came to his attention that I'd kept Sadie's presence hidden from him *and* that I took her from the warehouse, then I'd get raked over the coals. Everyone considered clones to be property, so freeing her was tantamount to larceny.

"Okay," I replied. "I don't know that trusting her to be quiet is the best plan right now, especially if she discusses how or why she's at the shelter. I'll bring her back to my place until we can figure out what to do with her."

She frowned. "I don't know if that's the best course of action."

"Are you afraid that I'm going to try something with her?" I chuckled uncomfortably.

"No. But now that you mention it, that has to be absolutely the last thing on your mind. Other than some passing conversation over breakfast, I haven't been able to speak to her. I'm worried that there may be some psychological damage and that she wouldn't even understand what's happening. She has lucid memories of everything about the person she was cloned from, except her name or locations of work or home. It's like they've been erased. Bottom line, she could be dangerous to herself—or to you since you're a male—without extensive therapy."

I considered her words carefully. The clone had seemed grateful enough last night that I helped rescue her from the situation. I had to take the risk that she wouldn't murder me in my sleep if I brought her back here. I couldn't risk her talking just yet and I'd kept her a secret from Voodoo because I didn't trust him either. Bringing her to my apartment was the only option I had at the moment.

"Thank you for your help, Jasmine. It means so much to me that you're willing to risk your career to help out a clone."

"I'm not like a lot of others. I don't think the clones are property, they're basically a human—I think. But I am extremely interested in talking with her to see if my thoughts on the subject are correct, once my children aren't around."

"Sounds good, Doc. We'll schedule a time for you to talk to her in a clinical setting. I'll be over to get her in a few minutes."

"Alright, Zach. See you in a little bit."

# TWELVE: TUESDAY

The Jeep pulled up at Dr. Jones' house and I slapped myself on the cheek. I'd almost fallen asleep on the way over and now I needed to be awake. When the car stopped, I opened the door and stumbled wearily down the sidewalk to her house.

"You made good time," she said when she opened the door. I didn't even remember pushing the doorbell.

"Since I'm a cop, my car doesn't have a governor like everyone else on the road. Comes in handy sometimes."

"I sent my husband to the store with the kids, so it's just Sadie and me if you want to come in."

"Thanks," I replied as she held open the door for me.

"Down the hallway here," Jasmin said. "Have you figured out who she is yet?"

I pulled the fingerprint scanner from the pocket of my overcoat and held it up for her to see. "Not yet. You had to leave so quickly last night that I didn't get a chance to scan her. This will tell us who she is."

"Good. I'm intrigued."

I thought back to how I felt last night when I first found her, naked, bloody and scared. Did it matter who she was cloned after? She could be whoever she wanted to be now.

"Does it matter? She's a clone; her fingerprints will only tell us who she was modeled after."

"It matters to me. What if she's cloned after a violent murderer and the geneticists went to prisons to get their DNA samples and brain scans?"

"Hmm. Good point, Doc." I hadn't thought of that. "Voodoo said they retain the memories and mannerisms of the original, right up to the point of cloning, so by figuring out who she was, we'll know what she can become."

"Voodoo?"

"Thomas Ladeaux, Tommy Voodoo, same guy."

"You're working with Tommy Voodoo again?"

I hadn't been shy when I wrote my report on the Sex Club Killer case. I'd said that Ladeaux gave me the information required to figure out that the droids were being hacked.

"His company engineered the clones and he found out what these guys were doing, so he's trying to get them back. It seems like he's being humane and genuinely wants them cared for instead of being treated like that."

"I don't like it," Jasmin stated. "The guy is using you somehow."

"You're probably right. He says he isn't dirty—and after fifteen years of the department trying to pin something on him, I'm starting to believe it."

*Dammit. Did I just defend Tommy Voodoo?*

"Just watch yourself."

"I will, don't worry. But, I need whatever help I can get. I won't get any support from the department because Chief Brubaker forbade me from doing anything else with the clone case and threatened to suspend me indefinitely if I went any further with this thing," I elaborated.

"I don't know who he's protecting, but the whole thing stinks to me. There's the refusal of the medical and legal communities to acknowledge the clones' existence, and Voodoo's 'accidental' sale of them to a group whose forte is torture and murder. Everything is sideways with this and I want to know why."

My therapist stared at me for a moment and then sighed as a sign of her displeasure. "Stay safe, Zach."

She didn't say anything else before turning back down the hall. I trailed along behind her, hoping I was doing the right thing trusting Voodoo's information and in going against Brubaker's direct orders.

Doctor Jones' house was small and filled with lots of little knickknacks, pillows and plants. It wasn't my style, but it did make me feel welcome and I got the vibe that they spent a lot of quality family time together—which was definitely not my style.

Sadie sat on a bar stool at the counter between the kitchen and the living room, doodling on a pad of paper. She looked up at me and smiled brokenly, the scabs on her face pulling her lips askew.

"I'm not a murderer," she mumbled softly. "I ran a business—I think. It's all so murky up here." She poked the side of her head with her index finger. "I remember big meetings and sitting at the head of the table. And I remember seeing families at the park and being sad while playing with a dog."

"Those are memories from the person you were cloned from," I stated, trying to keep my voice even. Doctor Jones and I had already upset her by talking too loud in the hallway. I didn't want to upset her further and even those few words made me think that she'd recovered from her ordeal slightly. I didn't want to push her back to that place.

She nodded softly and then, "They feel so real, though. I remember being there, not like a memory implant or something. I was there."

"It may seem like that, Sadie," Doctor Jones said. "But all of those memories, up until the moment the brain scan was completed, were input into you as you grew. For you, those memories are just as real as they are to the person you were cloned from."

"Do you want to know whose memories you have?" I asked. "Of course, you don't have to know, either. It's up to you."

She considered my words, tracing interlocking shapes on the pad of paper to make the lines darker. After a moment, she picked up the paper and held it so I could see it.

"Does this symbol mean anything to you?" Sadie asked.

The design she'd drawn didn't look like any business logo that I remembered seeing in New Orleans, but after I puzzled out what she'd drawn, I knew what the symbol stood for. It was a capital "B" in block letters with a lowercase "i" beside it. The lowercase letter was filled in and the dot on the top swirled around the capital "B" and finished near the origination point, effectively turning the dot above the "i" into a globe.

"Biologiqué International," I replied. "That's Ladeaux's clone company where you were born."

"I remember seeing it on a white wall," Sadie mumbled almost too low for me to hear.

"Are you alright?" I asked.

"Yes. I just thought that maybe that was a clue as to who I was." She sighed and put the paper back on the counter, then held out her right hand. "I want to know whose memories I have."

"Are you sure?" I asked. "There's no need to know, you can become whoever you want to be."

"I know. I *want* to know who she is and why they did this to me." She gestured vaguely at her face and body.

"Alright," I said, taking her hand gently. I slid the scanner over her index finger and waited for a match.

And then I waited some more.

"What the hell?"

I pulled the fingerprint scanner away and looked at the sensor. It didn't appear to be dirty or blocked, so I put my finger inside.

In seconds, it beeped and "**Zachary Benjamin Forrest**" flashed on the display.

"Let me see your hand," I ordered as I leaned forward for a better view.

Sadie turned her hand over to reveal a patchwork of scars that caused me to whistle softly.

"Somebody's gone to a lot of trouble to burn away the texture on your fingers. Let me try another one."

I tried each of her fingers; all of them gave me the same negative results.

"So what does that mean?" Sadie asked.

"It means that whoever cloned you doesn't want anyone to know who you're cloned after."

I thought back to the report from the coroner on the three clones that started this whole thing. Were their fingerprints burned away as well? The report said the fingerprint analysis was inconclusive, but I'd chalked that up to them being clones so he hadn't bothered to run the prints.

The clone held her hands close to her face and stared at her fingertips. "No. I remember having fingerprints. Tracing the lines. Getting arrested in college for…a protest about beef consumption? I think that's right."

"If you were arrested, then I can do a full DNA workup on you," I suggested.

Jasmin shot me a confused look. "I thought you were told to stay off the case."

"Shit. You're right. I can't run the DNA without giving someone an idea of what I'm doing."

"So that means you are free to be whoever you want," Jasmin told the clone.

Sadie shook her head. "I want to know who's up here." She tapped at the side of her head again.

"I know a way to get some leads, but I'm not entirely sure if the answers are worth the costs," I said.

"What do you mean?" Sadie asked.

"It's something that I've been thinking about for a few days. The idea of clones having fewer rights than a pet turtle bothered me from the moment I found out about it. I have some contacts in the media—real sleazeball reporters—who would love to investigate a story like this. If they could break open a story about the federal, state and local government cover up of human rights violations simply because the *potential* that a company could manufacture a large voting population, then they'd probably be looking at a Pulitzer.

"That's a major incentive for any journalist," I continued, keeping my opinion of the city's reporters to myself. "There is one guy, though, who's decent and I'd be willing to talk to. Plus, it's the breakthrough that he needs to get out of the New Orleans market and onto the national stage, so he may be willing to pursue this story enthusiastically."

Jasmin crossed her arms across her chest. "So, you want to go to the media to find out who Sadie was cloned from?"

"It's an option," I replied. "It's certainly not the most preferred option, but it's an avenue that we could pursue since everything else seems to be closed off."

"And that will end up creating a problem?" Sadie asked.

"Probably. Our population is complacent, easily distracted by the latest trend, and they don't care about clones. They know that we have the technology to clone humans, we've been cloning animals for over a century. But, they've been complicit in the lack of regulation and granting of rights to clones. They don't see the results every day in their vid feeds, so to them, it's easier to pretend that clones don't exist. We put Sadie up on the screens and they can't ignore it."

"What's the down side, then?" Jasmin asked.

"She'll be in danger. She'd be a target for politicians and their lackeys, not to mention the religious hardliners. We do something like that and we might as well paint a bullseye on the back of her head, because that's where the bullets are going to go."

"So it'll be dangerous if I talk to a reporter about who I am?"

"Yeah, sweetie," Jasmin agreed. "I can see what Zach means now. It's too dangerous."

Sadie thought about it and said, "I want to do it. I can't go through the rest of my life pretending to be something I'm not and ignoring what's happening to other clones."

"Are you sure?" Jasmine asked, giving the clone one more opportunity to back out and live a life of anonymity. "It might be too much for you right now. You can always decide to talk later. Even just a few days may make a difference."

She shook her head fiercely, her auburn hair whipping around her face. "No. I want to know who I am and I don't want what happened to me to happen to anyone else."

Sadie touched her bruised and scabbed face. "In a couple of days, the worst of this will be fading. I want the city to see me like this."

I pulled out my phone and tapped the code to unlock it. "Andi, put me in contact with Chris Young."

⚜ ◦ ⚜ ◦ ⚜

I drove Sadie over to a small studio in Milneburg to meet with the only investigative reporter that I knew who wasn't a complete oxygen thief. If I had to put a number to it, I'd say he was only depriving the earth of her oxygen forty percent of the time.

I'd met Chris Young a few days after the Sex Club Killer case came to a head at Jackson Square. He'd obstinately sought me out until the police department finally relented, granting him an exclusive interview to learn the details of the events leading up to that night. We'd struck an uneasy friendship and had kept in touch every few weeks, mostly when Chris was struggling for a story. He'd come down to Easytown and see what smelled fishy.

The problem was that the whole district was dirty and he had a hard time finding just *one* topic to focus on, which is why he needed me.

I didn't want Sadie to feel like a bleeding seal in shark-infested waters, so I'd asked Chris if I could bring her to the recording room in his house. The studio was small, but private and away from the bigger news agencies downtown. He'd agreed to talk to us, even though I was cryptic about who I was bringing because I didn't want to trip any keywords that the government may have been listening for.

Chris was waiting outside of his home when the Jeep pulled up. "Zach," he said when I opened my door. "To what do I owe the pleasure?"

"This young lady right here," I pointed at Sadie as she came around the car. "Chris, this is Sadie."

To his credit, Chris didn't comment on her obvious physical trauma when he shook her hand gently. He glanced around the neighborhood and his eyes narrowed as he stared at a spot off to his left. "I think we should probably go inside. You never know who's out here."

I turned, following his stare, and saw a parked car down the street. It appeared to be empty and I didn't see anyone else outside in the fine mist that fell from above.

"Worried about being scooped?" I chuckled.

"No. I'm probably being paranoid. I've been seeing that car down there for months—since my interview with you went live. I've never seen anyone in it and the homeowners down there don't know who it belongs to. I've asked. The car will show up at random times, but nobody ever sees anyone get out. It just seems like they're watching me."

"An empty car? I'm as skeptical as the next guy, Chris, but if you've never even seen anyone in the car and they haven't tried anything, I wouldn't be too worried. Maybe they're parking the car and commuting in to work with someone, or one of your neighbors has an illicit lover that they're covering for."

"I guess so." He didn't appear convinced. The paranoia in his eyes was evident.

We walked around the back of the house to the separate building where his studio was located. Once inside, he locked the door and flipped the switch on a white noise generator before leading us into the heart of the structure.

The walls in his sound studio were covered with noise-dampening foam, divided into varying patterns to further break up any sounds and eliminate echoing. He sat down in a hovering maglift chair—another innovation to remove sounds from the studio—that was positioned in front of a giant sound board and several small microphones. Chris leaned back in his chair and indicated we sit in the row of chairs spaced loosely in the small room.

"Alright, Zach. What did you bring me?"

"Have you ever seen a clone before?" I asked.

"Yeah, of course. They're not new; been around for as long as I've been alive."

"You're right, but they were always easy to spot. Full-grown adults with a third or fourth grade vocabulary, awkward quirks that most people would have grown out of after other kids made fun of them in elementary school, things like that."

"Sure."

"Well... I don't know," I pretended to stumble. "Sadie, maybe you could explain it better."

"Of course, Zach," she replied with a rehearsed nod. "The clones that are being produced by a company called Biologiqué International are more than exact physical replicas of a human. The company has figured out a way to map the original person's brain and download their memories, personalities, even the mannerisms that Zach just spoke about. That 'human essence' is then imprinted into their exact physical replica. When the full-grown clone is born, it has every memory up until the moment of the brain scan."

"That's impossible," Chris interrupted. "They'd be no different than anyone else at that point."

She shrugged. "As best we can tell, the clones probably think they're the real person—unless some type of trauma occurs and they lose memories."

We'd practiced what she should say on the ride over. While it wasn't exactly what I wanted, it was close.

"Chris, meet Sadie," I said, reintroducing her. "She's a clone."

"No she's not." He looked at me and then back at her. "You're not, are you?"

Sadie pulled down her right ear to show the numbers tattooed there. "Fresh off the production line it would seem."

"But you're so… Human."

"I *am* human, Mr. Young," she replied.

"No. Like a real human. You seem just—"

"Just what?" she interrupted, her fiery temper beginning to peek through. "I have every single molecule that a human grown inside a woman's womb has. The only difference is that my womb was a laboratory."

"But you don't talk like a clone," he countered. "And I assume you have all these memories implanted into you, or else you wouldn't have mentioned them. Those aren't *your* experiences; someone else did them and you got the vid feed."

Sadie's nostrils flared and her eyes narrowed. "Are you willing to help me or not, Mr. Young? If not, I don't want to waste any more of Detective Forrest's time—or mine."

I hadn't seen her upset before now and I wasn't sure if she was preparing to come out of the chair to claw the reporter's eyes out at any moment, or just verbally dress him down. The real Sadie must have been a wildcat in the boardroom.

"I'm not even sure what the story is here, guys. I mean, you say that Sadie's a clone, but the only proof you can offer is a tattoo on her ear. What am I supposed to do with that?

Is this supposed to be a public awareness piece to inform the public of the presence of a new type of clone? I don't get it."

"We want to give you a lot of information in exchange for running a story on Sadie," I answered. "We want to know who she is. Her fingerprints were burned off and I can't do a DNA workup on her, so I think an interview with you will do the trick. Somebody will recognize her."

"Why can't you run her DNA? Seems simple enough to me."

"I've been explicitly ordered off the clone case; if I run a DNA scan, they'll know I disobeyed their orders."

"Wait. What clone case?" he asked, suddenly interested.

"Four days ago, I was called to a dump site for three bodies in Easytown. I don't know where they were killed. They'd been put into a dumpster and the only thing that kept them from being lost forever was the human DNA sensors in the trash compactor that emptied the dumpster.

"The bodies were mutilated. They'd been tortured over a long period of time, suffering terribly in life. Burns, cuts, broken bones, abrasions…those three experienced every imaginable type of trauma that one human being could do to another. When I got the coroner's report back, it was only five pages, including a cover sheet."

"They were clones," Chris surmised.

"Yeah. Clones." I paused and leaned back in the chair so I could dig a digichip out of my pocket. The chip held the entire video that my cell phone recorded at the warehouse last night.

I tossed it at the reporter. "Have you ever heard of torture tourism, Chris?"

# THIRTEEN: WEDNESDAY

I felt like I'd been run over by a truck.

I rolled over and abruptly fell off the couch, jarring my bruised body even further. It took a moment for me to get my bearings and remember why I was on the couch.

*Oh yeah, I got jumped by four ninjas at Chris' house.*

I'd stuck around while Chris interviewed Sadie, checking outside periodically. The longer they talked, the more reporter's paranoia rubbed off on me. The car that he'd mentioned earlier still sat where it had been when we first got there so I walked down the street to have a look at it.

The car turned out to be empty, but by the time I got back to the interview booth, four men were stacked up outside the door, ready to go inside. From my angle to the side of them, I could see that they all had knives drawn. The fuckers meant to kill us inside, but they hadn't expected me to be outside.

"*Hey! New Orleans PD!*" I'd yelled. "Drop your weapons."

The men turned as one, all eerily similar. Then I saw that they were each an exact replica of one another. *Clones.* They were Asian, with short-cropped hair and a thick, square jaw that looked like it could take a few punches.

I'd advanced slowly, thinking I could get them to surrender, but they attacked when I was a few feet from them. I shot two before I had to rely on my Krav Maga to save my ass.

I was a street brawler fighting against two men who were clearly masters in some type of martial art. The first to reach me did some type of fancy flying kick that hit me in the shoulder as I ducked my head out of the way. I elbowed blindly behind me as he soared by and was rewarded with a solid impact against one of his kidneys.

The second man was on me before I could worry about what else the first would do. He threw a flurry of punches, about half of which I blocked, and then kicked me hard in the crotch. I doubled over and fired my weapon blindly into him, the bullet tearing a large hole through his abdomen. He collapsed, screaming in pain.

Then I got a heel kick to the spine from the first guy, causing me to drop my gun. I fought the urge to sink to my knees and surged upward, swinging my arm in an uppercut that caught the man unaware. His jaw *could* take a punch.

After a few minutes of fighting and a nasty cut to my forearm that would have been much worse if I hadn't been wearing my heavy raincoat, I was able to subdue him with an arm-bar that dislocated his shoulder. A black and white arrived to assist, probably alerted by the report from my pistol. They handcuffed the clones while a paramedic bandaged my arm.

Once the officers found out that the four men were clones, nobody asked me anything. It was as if I'd been transported to a strange alternate reality where everyone ignored the clones like they weren't even there. The officers on site threw the bodies and the two live clones into the back of a van and took them to the Milneburg precinct. I'd expected to have to answer a string of questions since I'd killed two of them, but the questions never came. No one wanted to hear my paper-thin excuse as to why I was at Chris' house. Nobody cared that I'd discharged my firearm in a residential neighborhood outside of my precinct. The fact that I'd been injured was swept away with the bodies of the clones.

Even Chief Brubaker avoided the issue when I called, which was uncharacteristic for him. When I'd asked him what was going on, he replied that the mayor had convinced the governor to give full powers to law enforcement officers to eliminate the clone threat that had erupted upon the city. I didn't know what he was talking about and his answers confused me. He ordered me to get some sleep and come talk to him in the morning.

Tommy Voodoo's fear of being overheard came back to me. The men running the torture tourism ring were rich and powerful. They were willing to do whatever it took to keep their multi-billion dollar industry secure, including goading the mayor into wiping out any known clones, no questions asked.

All the while, Chris and Sadie were clueless, locked away inside the soundproofed studio in the shed.

After their interview was over, they'd been shocked to hear my story. In truth, if my coat hadn't had a gash in it and my arm wasn't encased in a layer of rapid-heal bandages, then I might have been convinced that I'd hallucinated the whole thing in my sleep-deprived mind.

Chris said he needed a couple of days to put together the interview and the footage I'd provided him. Plus, he said he wanted to have a geneticist look at a sample of tissue that

Sadie had provided as proof that she was a clone. I cautioned him against staying in New Orleans, and he promised to leave immediately and do the work at his network's sister station in Slidell if he felt threatened in any way.

I guess the four guys planning to murder him in his sound studio weren't enough of a threat to him.

After that, Sadie and I returned here, to my apartment—which is how I ended up on the couch.

"Coffee," I groaned to Andi and stumbled through the bedroom into the bathroom to do my business. A ruffled lump under the covers on my bed and a splash of red hair on the pillow told me the clone was still asleep.

When I was finished, I went to the kitchen to wait for the deep, dark goodness in a mug.

"I'm relieved to see that you're feeling better, Zach. You did not appear well last night when you returned."

"Thanks, Andi. I've had better days. I still need to shower and then go meet Brubaker, but I don't know what to do with the clone."

"I have the ability to restrict access to everything in the apartment except the kitchen cabinets and your closet. All the other doors are equipped with a magnetic lock that I control. She could stay here without any worries of something important being stolen."

I laughed. *God, that hurts*, I thought, holding my ribs where I'd been kicked by the last clone. "I'm not worried about Sadie stealing something from this place."

"Is she going to stay here?"

"I don't know. I'll have to ask her."

"Understood. You have six messages and seven missed calls. I felt it best to let you sleep."

"Six messages? Oh shit."

Last night was Tuesday. I was supposed to take Teagan to dinner on her self-imposed date. I'd forgotten about it and now I was in deep shit.

"Call Teagan Thibodaux," I said, not bothering to listen to the messages she'd left.

"What do you want, Zach?" she asked after answering on the fourth ring. She'd chosen to accept voice only.

"Teagan, I'm so sorry."

"Sorry? Are you kidding me? I went out and spent a lot of money on a new haircut and got my nails done," she exclaimed. Then, in a softer voice she said, "I don't know why I let myself get excited about you."

"I got stabbed yesterday. I couldn't—"

"Oh my God, Zach! Are you okay?"

"Yeah, I'm fine. The paramedic patched me up quick and with the rapid-heal bandage, scar tissue should form in the next day or so."

Teagan sent a video call request and I accepted it. Her face filled the screen. Even the day after, I could tell that she'd gotten her hair straightened as it hung down to her shoulders.

"Where did you get stabbed?"

"Over in Milneburg."

"Huh? No, I mean *you*. Where did *you* get stabbed?"

"In the arm." I held it up for her to see the bandage. "I'm sorry about last night. I wanted to go out with you."

"No you didn't," she replied. "I forced you into agreeing to take me out and regardless of why you didn't show up, I know that you didn't really want to go out with me."

"Teagan, I did—I mean I *do* want to go out with you." *Is that true?* I asked myself.

"You've been one of my better friends for years and I don't want to lose that," I told her. "We should be able to go out as friends, have fun and spend time together socially. You're beautiful; I'd be crazy not to want to go out with you."

She smiled. "You don't need to try to make me feel better. I'm a big girl, Zach. I can handle being told that you're not interested."

"That's not it at all, Teagan. You know that my only hang-up has been our difference in age."

"The difference in our age? We're only eleven years apart. I'll be twenty-four in a few months—but what does that matter? We get along great. I can deal with your occasional grumpiness and you know how to make me laugh without trying too hard." She frowned before continuing. "I'm going to graduate in a few months and once I start teaching, I won't be working at the Pharaoh anymore. I want to see how we'd do together."

"And if we're horrible together, what then?" I asked. "You heard how my last break-up went. Women always think they can change me, but it's not going to happen."

"I don't want to change you. I like you just the way you are—even if you *did* stand me up for some lame excuse like getting stabbed."

*Goddammit, she's right*, I told myself. She was almost out of college and planned on going to work in the New Orleans school system instead of somewhere nice like Baton Rouge, and it was because she wanted to stay near me. That wasn't fair to her; I'd put off her affections and hidden my own for her for far too long.

"Saturday night."

"What?" she asked.

"Saturday night. Let me make it up to you on Saturday. I'll take you to dinner and we'll go out."

"Zach, isn't Saturday your busiest day at work?"

"Yeah, so what? I feel terrible about last night." I paused and then smiled. "It's not like the bodies are going to go anywhere if I'm a few minutes late."

"You know that Saturday is also Valentine's Day, right?"

"No, I didn't know that."

"So you still want to take me to dinner, even though it's Valentine's Day?"

"Yeah. I'm okay with that. Let's go."

"Alright, it's a date," she replied. "It's going to be hard to get reservations anywhere last minute like this."

"You let me worry about that. I'll probably see you at the Pharaoh, but if I don't, Saturday at six. Okay?"

"See you then, Zach."

She hung up and the soft scrape of bare feet on hardwood caused me to turn in time to see Sadie duck around the corner.

"Good morning," I called after her.

"Hmm? Oh, good morning, Zach," she responded, stepping out of the room and stretching as if she'd just woken up instead of spying on me a moment ago.

"You sleep alright?"

"Mmm hmm. Your bed is comfortable."

"Good, I'm glad you were able to get some sleep. Do you drink coffee? I can brew you a cup."

"No, I never took it up… I mean, the woman whom I'm cloned after never took it up."

"It's okay. Those memories are yours. They're as real as if it was your physical body experiencing them."

"I guess so. I'm just so frustrated because I have no idea who I'm supposed to be. I don't even know if she has children."

"That's probably a memory that would transfer over," I said in an effort to ease her upset mind, even though I had no idea if that was true. "If you remembered working someplace, but don't remember children—or giving birth—then it's unlikely that you have any."

"Do you think the interview is going to turn up any clues about who she is?"

"I hope so. There's no guarantees, but Chris has a large local following. He's our best bet at finding out who you are."

She dipped her chin without replying.

"We'll figure it out," I assured her. "I've got to go to work this morning and meet with my boss. You can stay here if you'd like, or I can take you to a park or wherever you'd like to go, and pick you up afterward."

"Are you sure I can stay here? I don't want to go out in public like…" She touched her face.

"Yes, of course you can stay here." My eyes wandered over her bruised skin before saying, "You're already healing. Looks like old Doc Wellington patched you up good. Before too long, it will just be a horrible memory and you'll be able to move forward with your life."

"I can't wait," she replied with a hint of sarcasm.

"Uh oh. I think I heard a bit of your real personality peeking through. Better be careful or you may even laugh one of these days."

She chuckled lightly. "Thank you for helping me out, Zach. I know you didn't have to, clones being property and all."

"Nonsense, Sadie. You're not somebody's property. You're a human being."

I waited for a response, but she stared at her hands. "Okay. I've got to get ready. Andi can assist you with some juice or food. If we don't have what you want, she can have anything delivered, just make sure she clears the delivery person before you open the door."

"Thank you. I don't know how I'll be able to repay you."

"No worries. That's the benefit of being single, I've got plenty of money for an extra meal or two."

I went to the shower to try and massage away some of the bruises that the clones inflicted, berating myself the whole time instead of relaxing. I shouldn't have said that I had money. The woman was destitute and wearing borrowed clothing. *God, she must think I'm such an asshole.*

*Join the club, lady. Join the damn club.*

"How do you always seem to find a way to get into trouble, Forrest?"

"Chief, this wasn't my fault," I appealed. "I went to speak to Chris Young for another interview and those clones jumped me."

"Any idea if they were there for you or for the reporter?"

"There wasn't a lot of time for talking. I'll interview them and get some answers."

"No you won't," he grunted, chewing harder on his cigar stub.

"What do you mean? I made the arrest, I'll interrogate."

"Mayor Cantrell ordered them destroyed."

"What?" I asked, horrified.

"The clones were euthanized this morning," Brubaker replied. "I don't like it, but the governor's office granted the mayor the power to do whatever he needed to do to confront the clone threat, up to and including mobilizing the Louisiana National Guard."

The floor seemed to drop out from underneath me. "Chief, those were *human* clones. Regardless of how you want to spin it, they were people. The mayor ordered a *murder* and we followed suit."

"Goddammit, Forrest! I know. I don't agree with it. I spoke to the Milneburg Precinct chief about an hour before you got here. Doctors from Sabatier Island injected both of the clones in custody with a lethal dose of potassium chloride. Then they dumped the bodies in the garbage."

"Why the fuck would they kill them? They could have given us information about who ordered them to try and get to Chris. Or maybe they were trying to get to me, I don't know. That is such—"

I stopped. Why would Governor Talubee allow the clones to be euthanized before they could give a statement? Based on the order to police to eliminate the clone "threat," I knew no one had any love for clones, but even then, why would they order their deaths before information could be gleaned from them?

In my mind, there was only one answer: The two of them were part of the torture tourism ring. It was the only explanation that made sense.

*For that matter, why is Chief Brubaker dead set on keeping me off the clone case?*

Shit, I was beginning to get paranoid. The governor had simply granted the mayor of his largest city the power to enforce the law as he saw fit. Governor Talubee—and Chief Brubaker—were more than likely clean.

"Chief, why has the mayor declared a war on clones?"

"I'd hardly call it a war."

"It seems like a war when we forego any attempt to follow due process and begin exterminating prisoners."

The chief stood up and walked around his desk. I watched as he shut the door to his office and followed him as he came back to his seat. He turned on an old radio with a tap on his computer's display. Soft sounds of oldies that my dad listened to filled the small space.

"I don't disagree with you, Forrest," Chief Brubaker said, leaning forward. "*Something* doesn't add up. Lord knows this city already has a hard enough time with public relations. If word of this got out—this shoot first, don't ask *any* questions mistake—then the department would be done for. If that happens, there'll be anarchy in the streets."

"Where are all of these clones coming from all of a sudden?" I asked, even though I had a good idea of the answer.

"Nobody knows. Your buddy Thomas Ladeaux is scheduled to speak with a special prosecutor appointed by the state later today. One of his subsidiary companies grows clones, maybe he's got some info."

"He's not my buddy," I reminded my boss. "I know his company Biologiqué International is in the clone business, but I thought they were in the early stages of development, still experimenting with prototypes, not full-on production."

"That's the official story coming out of the company. Word on the street says that isn't the case, which is what the prosecutor is going to try to get to the bottom of."

I knew in my heart that Voodoo was dirty, but I'd believed him when he looked me in the eyes and said there'd been a mix-up when the company sold those thirty-eight clones by mistake. If he was lying, then he was the best liar I'd ever met.

"How bad is the surge of clones, Chief?"

The older man shrugged. "There's no telling. The feds are scrambling to develop some type of clone detector. Nobody has much faith that it will work though, since they are genetically the exact same as us. I mean, what do we test for?"

Brubaker glanced at the thick wooden door to his office and turned the volume up on the music. "A clone tried to infiltrate the mayor's staff last week. The only way they knew to check into it was because the staffer's wife noticed that a large scar on his backside was missing and he couldn't explain it. She talked to a few people and hired a private dick that was able to pull security tapes showing her husband going into a club in Easytown a few weeks ago and then banging a hooker in the alley.

"We got lucky with the camera angle and saw a couple of thugs hit him over the head *while* he was fucking the hooker. They connected a bunch of leads from some type device in a briefcase to his head while the hooker took strands of hair and scraped some skin cells into a bag. The whole thing took less than a minute, then they left him there."

The chief sighed and continued, "That's why I changed my directive mid-stream about investigating the clones, Forrest. The feds are all over this, they want to find a scapegoat, so the more distance we can put between ourselves and the investigation, the better."

I felt relieved. The fact that I'd suspected Brubaker was involved was ludicrous. He and I had known each other for a long time; he was a straight arrow. He gave his officers a certain amount of leeway and I didn't want to screw up the good thing we had going.

I decided to come clean about the conversation Voodoo and I had about the torture tourism and the mission I'd undertaken to help find the missing clones.

"Chief, there's a reason I was at that warehouse Monday night. It's probably why those clones showed up at the reporter's house yesterday."

He leaned back and took the cigar out of his mouth, tossing it carelessly onto the surface of his desk. "Spill it."

# FOURTEEN: WEDNESDAY

"I don't know what the hell to think of this one, Detective."

"What do you mean, Drake?"

"I could tell you, but you wouldn't believe me, sir. It's best if you get down here and have a look for yourself."

I glanced at the Jeep's readout. It was only an hour after sundown. Was it going to be a crazy night?

"Alright," I sighed. "Send me the coordinates and I'll be there as soon as I can. I just left the precinct headquarters about ten minutes ago, so it shouldn't be too long."

A set of coordinates flashed on the readout and the Jeep's nav system asked if I wanted to go there. I tapped the "**YES**" key and felt the car's speed ease up as it prepared to turn around to head back to Easytown.

"Andi, are you there?" I asked aloud.

"Of course, Zach."

"How's Sadie doing?"

"She's a much better conversationalist than you are."

"Thanks. Can you put her on the phone?"

"You're being broadcast across the apartment now. She's currently in the living room, laying on the couch."

"Uh… Hey, Sadie. It's Zach. Are you there?"

"Oh! Hi, Zach. You startled me. I wasn't expecting you to call."

"I was on my way home, but got called in to a murder investigation. I'm sorry."

"It's fine. You're busy, I get it."

"Are you doing alright?"

"As best as can be expected, I guess," she replied. "Your friend Jasmine called to talk to me today, so we spent about thirty or forty minutes talking. It was therapeutic."

I shook my head at her use of the word. The advancements made in the cloning industry were amazing. Twenty years ago, the first adult human clones produced were like infants mentally and had to be taught how to do everything from going to the restroom, eating with utensils and how to speak. It was unsettling. Now, it was plug and play. They could insert *anyone's* memories into any clone body and it seemed like they were a normal person.

That's probably how the latest version of torture tourism came into being. Torturing, maiming and killing something that only knows how to scream probably became boring quickly. Now, the clones could beg for mercy and offer everything they could to end the suffering. It was sick—like the people who engaged in that lifestyle.

"I'm glad you were able to talk to her," I replied. "I meant to have you spend some time with her yesterday, but I think talking to Chris will be better in the long run."

"We're going to talk tomorrow morning also and work on a plan to find me a place to stay."

"You're welcome to stay with me for a bit."

"Thank you, Zach. I appreciate it, but it's not a long-term solution. If I'm going to move past this and become a functioning member of society again—I mean, like the person I was copied from is—I need to have my own place and earn my own money."

"I can respect that. The offer still stands though."

"Is it okay if I stay tonight? I'll go out looking for something tomorrow. Andi told me about your date with Teagan on Valentine's Day, so I don't want to screw things up for you if you bring her back here."

"What? Teagan's just a kid—" *Besides, I don't know what I want with her*, I finished my statement internally. "Yes, of course you can stay tonight."

"Thanks. I'm also going to pay for a DNA analysis once I make enough money."

"Are you sure you want to do that? I want you to be happy and all, but moving forward, don't you just want to be you? Forget about everything that happened to that other person."

"It's easier said than done," Sadie answered. "I have all these little islands of memories and the only thing missing is personal information. Her name, where she lives, where she works—all of those connecting lines between the dots are gone. But if I can learn who she is, maybe it can help me become who I'm going to be."

"I hadn't thought of it like that," I admitted. "Maybe we'll get some leads from Chris' story."

"I hope so."

There was a slight pause that I took as a point to end the conversation. "I'm almost to the crime scene. I'm gonna go and quit bothering you."

"You're not bothering me. Stay safe, I'll see you when you get back."

As I hung up the phone I wasn't entirely sure I liked having someone in my home, expecting me back at a certain hour and saying things like, "I'll see you when you get home." It seemed unnatural for me. I adored women, but I also enjoyed my space. The two seemed at odds with one another, did that mean I was destined to be alone? Was that even a bad thing?

Sometimes I hated not being able to drive myself so I could just concentrate on the road instead of thinking about all of the shit that seemed to circle around me like a hurricane.

The Jeep pulled up to a Synthaine house seven blocks from Jubilee Lane. Boarded up windows and heavy, soaking wet blankets across the door greeted visitors from the street. A large doghouse sat prominently near the structure with no sign of the animal that it housed. The lawn was a patchwork of mud and rock, transitioning to overgrown crabgrass beyond the limit of the dog's chain.

The smell of rotting garbage, feces and God knows what else hit me the moment I slid the blanket away from the doorway with my probe. The lighting was poor inside, barely lit from the streetlamp on the corner. From what I could tell, there were bags of garbage, piles of old clothes and food wrappers of every kind strewn about the inside.

Peaking amongst the refuse were several children's play toys. An infant swing. A baby walker. An overturned bassinet. Dirty diapers. All of it pointed to a ruined childhood—if the kid didn't get sold off for a couple of hits of synthaine.

I finally got sick of trying to pick my way along the "path" and stuck my hand inside the kit bag, searching for my flashlight.

The light didn't help at all. It made it worse. The garbage was piled higher than anything I'd ever seen outside of web vids. The walls, once painted a tan, or possibly white, were covered in bloody handprints and various messages that only made sense to a synth-head. I'd seen *that* a thousand times. There wasn't anything left of their brain except what told them to eat every once in a while and to defecate once the stuff moved through their systems. Often it was a combination of both at the same time. Hence the smell.

Flashes from a forensic cameraman's camera helped guide me through the rubbish toward the back of the house.

"Drake?" I called.

"Back here, Detective. Watch your step coming into the back room."

I followed the sound of his voice and saw a body lying across the threshold. "Watch your step," I muttered to myself as I lifted a leg over the bloody mess.

My foot hovered in the air above the corpse. The thing that lay at my feet was *half* of the torso. Something had ripped the victim in half, except it wasn't the easy way, at the waist. One side had been separated from the other.

"Ah?"

"The other half of her is over here," Drake answered my question.

"What the hell did this?"

"The tweaker they found here said it was a giant human octopus, with glowing eyes and the hands of a crab."

"A droid?"

"Probably. The dude was so high when they arrived, there's no telling what he really saw versus an image that the synthaine produced in his mind."

"Sounds like the legend of Cthulhu to me," the cameraman interrupted our conversation.

I glanced at the man. It wasn't Ben Roberts, our normal forensic photographer. "What's that?"

"The Cthulhu. It's an old legend about the end of the world. The creature is the destroyer of worlds. He's gigantic, man-shaped with an octopus face and the wings of a dragon."

I snorted in derision. "Where's Ben?"

"Ben's sick, so they had me come over from the Lower Ninth for the evening. I'm Teddy."

I shook the photographer's hand and said, "Nice to meet you, Teddy. Were you drinking a little bit before you came to work?"

"I'm not saying I believe in it," he defended. "I had to learn about it in college. There are a lot of people who prescribe to a supernatural being of some kind that will destroy the world. In fact, all major religions do. This one is just one of many of the pantheon of gods who's supposed to do it."

"I can't put that stupid shit in my report. Thanks anyways," I stated, glancing back at Drake. "So this was a female?"

"Yeah. Hard to tell until you look at both parts. Whoever—whatever—did this ripped off her arms and legs while she was alive according to the tweaker, then her head, and finally it ripped her right up the middle."

"That's a gruesome way to die," I said, eyeing the blood splatters on the ceiling. "Wonder what she did to deserve it."

"Mmm hmm," Drake mumbled. We had differing opinions about violence. I prescribed to the belief that truly random acts of violence were far and few between. There was usually some type of connection between the perpetrator and the victim, or at least a motive as to why the perp did what they did. My partner, on the other hand, believed that random violence was the majority of humanity's problem. I was right in about seventy-five percent of our *solved* cases, whereas his theory took up the rest. We still had a metric shit ton of unsolved cases.

"So, there was a kid that lived here. Any word where they are?"

"No sign of them." Drake pointed at the garbage. "But he could be right here and we wouldn't know."

"The tweaker give any motive for why someone would've done this?"

"Nope. He kept screaming about the octopus demon until they shot him up with tranquilizers and he passed out."

"They take him to New Orleans East?" I asked, referring to the nearest hospital.

"I'm not sure."

"Hey, fellas," Teddy the photographer interrupted. "What do you take this for?"

I pushed my way through the garbage, wishing I'd taken the time to put the thick leather armor on my lower legs. I didn't need to get tetanus, or worse.

Teddy used the blue laser pointer on his camera to circle a spot on the wall. The spot became clearer as I got closer and I realized it was some type of metal imbedded in the wall, only allowing me to see less than half of it.

"What the—hey, Teddy, make sure you take pictures of this before I contaminate the scene."

The camera flashed repeatedly as I dug in my bag for a pair of needle-nosed pliers and an evidence baggie.

"Alright. I got it," Teddy said.

I switched the flashlight and baggie to one hand and used the pliers to dig the metal out of the wall. When I had it free, I held it up in the glow from the light to examine.

It looked like a miniature circular saw blade. The thing was less than a half an inch across from tooth to tooth and solid metal of some kind. I twisted my wrist a few times, turning it over, and then dropped it into the baggie. It was much heavier than I'd thought when it was clasped in the pliers.

"What is that thing?" Drake asked over my shoulder, startling me.

"I don't know. I've never seen anything like it." I paused, thinking for a moment. "Hey, Teddy, are you done photographing the torso halves?"

"Yeah. I'm basically finished here, Detective."

"Help me out for a second, Drake."

I knelt beside the half of the body I'd stepped over earlier and had Drake hold the light. Four small rectangular wounds ran up one side and I held the baggie with the miniature saw blade next to each of them.

"Son of a bitch. This is a weapon of some kind."

I pulled on a pair of gloves quickly and pried open the top wound. I wasn't exactly shocked to see the dirty carpet underneath the corpse; the wound went completely through the body.

"Let's go to the other half," I suggested.

There weren't any exit wounds where the blades came out. I flipped the meat over and checked inside where they would likely be, but there wasn't anything inside.

"The killer tore her body apart to collect the blades," Drake said.

It made sense. If I had some new type of ammunition or weapon that gave me an edge over the competition, I'd probably try to keep it hidden for as long as I could as well.

I held up the baggie and looked at the disc inside. "Why were you left behind?"

"Probably ran out of time to find it," Drake answered. "It'd take a while to tear that body apart searching for all of the blades. The police showed up and ruined the killer's search. He had to go."

"I need to talk to that tweaker."

"Shouldn't be a problem. Depending on how much of that shit he used, it could be a couple of days until he comes down."

"I can wait," I murmured while I sealed the baggie and placed it in a lined evidence box.

Not much else of interest came out of the site, except for a few bottles of a liquid that field-tested positive as synthaine and several eyedroppers that they used to administer the shit. Everything went into the box with the disc. Add a shredded corpse and an odd tweaker sighting of an ancient mythical god and this scene was a wrap.

I wondered what the part about the creature meant. It was likely a mask of some kind, but without talking to the guy, I could only imagine what he thought he saw. As I packed up my kit and Drake finished securing the back door from the inside, my eyes wandered over to the discarded children's toys.

Where was that kid?

# FIFTEEN: THURSDAY

It was another night on The Lane, walking slowly, trying to lure the Paladin out of hiding or be lucky enough to be in close proximity to him when he made his move. The uneven sidewalks were unusually crowded due to a break in the rain. The lines outside of the thumper clubs stretched for hundreds of feet, while men, and the occasional woman, stood in gaggles waiting for their turn in the pleasure clubs.

Nearby, a shout of alarm rose from several throats as a hovering police drone electrocuted a pickpocket in the middle of a crowd. Men and women edged as far away from the writhing kid as they could. The drones were good for killing and subduing, but not at arresting, so it gave a small jolt every few seconds to keep the suspect down while a call went out to any uniformed cops in the area.

I sighed and pushed my way through the crowd until I stood on the inside of the circle. Thin wires snaked down from above and imbedded into the youth's pale skin. Two blossoms of red marred the back of the brown coat he wore where the barbs disappeared into the fabric.

"Citizen, please stand back so you are not harmed," the drone stated.

I took off my hat and pulled my badge out of my coat. "Detective Zach Forrest," I answered. "I'll cuff the suspect and wait for transport."

"Detective Zachary Forrest, you have been cleared to arrest the suspect on the charge of larceny. I am ordered to assist as necessary. Do you require assistance at this time?"

"Stop juicing him and let me put the handcuffs on," I ordered.

I waited until the hair on my arms stopped tingling and knelt on the kid's back while I wrenched one arm up to slap the cuffs on his wrist. Once he was cuffed, I pulled the barbs out of his back and the drone retracted the wires back into its body, causing more gasps from the crowd.

"What were you thinking, kid?" I asked.

"That I'm hungry and all these rich bastards waiting to spend their money to fuck a tin can had enough cash to go around."

"There are programs—"

"Don't, man. Just don't. You don't know what it's like down here on the streets. Fucking creepy things are happening."

"Creepy things are always going on in Easytown," I scoffed as I pulled the perp roughly to his feet. "Now you don't have to worry about it. You'll be nice and warm on Sabatier Island before the sun comes up tomorrow."

"They're probably already there."

"What are you on?"

"Nothing. I'm clean. I don't use that shit," he protested. "There are machines hunting the alleys for the Paladin. They turned *people* into machines to find that guy, except their brains can't handle it and they're going fucking crazy, man."

"What? Who's turning people into machines?"

"The dealers. They dumped a ton of tech into their top soldiers, now the damned things have gone nuts."

"Humans with tech? Do you mean *cyborgs*?"

"I don't know what they're called." The boy shrugged and then winced when the cuffs cut into his wrists. "They kill whatever comes across their path."

The tweaker's words from the night before came back to me. "What do they look like?"

"They're all different. They got outfitted with whatever tech was sitting around."

"Do any of them look like an octopus?"

"Octopus? Nah, man. Hey, since I'm helping you, are you gonna let me go?"

"Nice try…" I thought about how a cyborg would appear to someone high on a drug that is administered by dropping liquid chemicals onto their eyeball and came up with a question. "Do they have wires and things like that sticking out of their heads?"

"I guess so? I've only seen one of them closer than a block away. Most people avoid them because they are so messed up."

It was the first I'd heard that the crime lords were building some type of cybernetic-enhanced hunter to take out the Paladin. Maybe the guy was doing more good than we gave him credit for.

The circle of the crowd around us had collapsed, so I pulled him hard through the people until we stood on the outside.

"Hey! My wallet!" a man shouted.

I reached inside the kid's jacket and produced two wallets and a nice watch. Inside one of the wallets was an ID of the man who'd called out. "Over here, Mr. Stensen."

He rushed over, thanking me profusely and talking about pressing charges.

"He'll be booked within the hour, sir. You can go down to the NOPD Easytown Precinct station and file a complaint against him."

Mr. Stensen mumbled something about being in town for business and faded back into the crowd. He obviously didn't want it documented that he was in line at a pleasure club.

"How long have these *hunters* been around down here?" I asked the kid.

"I saw the first one a couple of days ago— Maybe Monday or Tuesday?"

"Where have you seen them?"

"They're all over the alleys at night looking for that Paladin guy. He's been cutting into the profits and making a lot of drug runners scared to go out at night."

A cop car pulled up to the curve and the officer flipped on his lights. The red and blue strobes added to the garish scene as the lights from the clubs shone brightly in the rare clear night.

"This the larceny perp, Detective?" the uniformed officer asked.

"Yeah. The drone, uh…" I glanced up and read the service number. "Zero Eight One deployed electroshock wires and apprehended the suspect. I happened to be the nearest officer on The Lane."

"Got it. I'll take him off your hands, sir."

"Thanks." I released the pickpocket and waited while the other cop put new handcuffs on him so I could get mine back. "Hey, kid. Stay safe out here once they release you. Alright?"

"Man, as long as it's outside of Easytown, I'm staying wherever they drop me off."

The uniformed cop handed me my cuffs and I watched him put the kid in the car with disinterest. He'd given me a lot of information and I wished there was a way I could assist him, but the drone camera footage was all the evidence they'd need to put the kid away for at least a year.

Come to think of it, maybe that was best for him. I had the feeling that Easytown was about to become a war zone.

⚜ ◦ ⚜ ◦ ⚜

After the pickpocket was safely in the car and gone, I began the steady, meandering walk that I'd developed over the years as a plain-clothes detective. It helped me to get a feel for the population and customers of Easytown. More times than I could count, I'd gleaned information just from walking around. Sometimes, it was the clarity of being outdoors, other times it was the human interaction and overhearing people say things when they thought nobody was listening.

Lieutenant Cruz, the second homicide detective in the Easytown Precinct, thought I was crazy to walk around like I did. The residents knew who I was—or at least the ones who were up to no good did. He said it was a pointless endeavor and stuck to informants coming to him in the safety of the police station or what the forensics lab told him. There was a reason my arrest rate was higher than his, by a wide margin.

I stayed close to the lines of people, avoiding the street side when possible. An enterprising ganger could do a snatch and go on a cop paying more attention to the people than the rest of his surroundings. The murder rate for officers was already high enough, no sense in making myself an easy target.

Of course, having an increased presence of police drones hovering twenty feet off the ground helped to ease my fears of a kidnapping. I'd be more likely to die in the drone's gunfire as it attempted to stop the vehicle than by the gangers in the van. The drones were both a godsend and a problem for officers. The fear of getting completely obliterated by the guns had helped to drive the crime further away from the parts of the city where the drones patrolled, but any time those guns spun up, we were almost guaranteed to have collateral damage and sometimes innocent deaths. Each casualty resulted in more paperwork and less trust in the police force.

A familiar voice stopped me in my tracks. Chris Young's manicured southern accent announced over the megavid screens above that his feature story was so shocking that the network had granted him five entire minutes on the big televisions normally reserved for advertising and national news broadcasts.

I tilted my head toward the nearest megavid screen and saw the words, "**BREAKING NEWS**" blinking in red over the black screen while Chris spoke the voiceover. Then Sadie appeared, her unkempt auburn hair framing the bruised face and her eyes staring hauntingly into the camera. Murmurs of curiosity erupted from the crowds, who weren't used to the unscheduled interruption in their daily lives.

"This is Sadie," Chris said. "That's not her real name, that's the name she was given by the city's hero police officer, Detective Zachary Forrest."

The screen cut to a vid feed from Jackson Square when I fought against the drones that the Sex Club Killer had hacked. I flipped up the collar on my coat and scrunched my hat down closer on my head. The fucker was supposed to keep me out of this.

Sadie reappeared and Chris continued the voiceover. "Detective Forrest rescued Sadie from the most hellish conditions known to man. She, along with eight others—and countless more that we may never know of—were beaten, tortured, burned, raped, sodomized, and abused in every imaginable manner. All of it was for the enjoyment of gamblers, betting on the outcome of whatever horror the captors inflicted. It's called torture tourism and the industry is worth billions—and our politicians know about it. More on that in a moment."

The video synched up with Sadie's voice as she described, in detail, some of what she'd endured, things that made the weaker-stomached patrons in the crowd blanch.

She ended her story with, "I am the only survivor. All the others were already dead by the time Zach found me."

"Dead." Chris let that word hang for a moment as the camera zoomed in on Sadie's haunted eyes.

The video reset and the symbol that Sadie had shown Dr. Jones and me a few days ago faded in over her face, then cut to the outside of a building somewhere on the southwest side of town that boasted the same symbol.

"This is the headquarters for Biologiqué International, a company that specializes in genetic engineering and is majority-owned by Thomas Ladeaux, who also owns the Marie Leveau Shipping Company and approximately half of the businesses in Easytown. Biologiqué International is the world's leading researcher for human cloning and they have perfected the technique. Sadie is a perfect example; she's a clone."

The murmurs rose to shouts of anger and rumblings about people playing God. The crowd was not happy about what Chris said as Sadie dipped her ear for the camera, showing the serial number printed there.

"Biologiqué's clones are so advanced," Chris continued, "that they are indistinguishable from humans. In fact they *are* human."

A man wearing a suit replaced the image of the headquarters building. "This is Dr. Henry Grubber from Scitech Engineering, a nonprofit laboratory that conducts medical research. Dr. Grubber is the world's leading geneticist who isn't on a corporation's payroll."

"I've examined the DNA sample sent to me of the Sadie subject," Dr. Grubber said. "And she is completely indistinguishable from a human, everything about her is an exact replica. In fact, if I hadn't been told that I was looking at a clone, I would have assumed she was simply another sample, like what I see hundreds of times a day. The clone may have been grown in a lab, but Sadie is human."

"So you disagree with the government's current stance on clones?" the reporter asked on screen. "Right now, in the eyes of the law, a clone is property that can be bought, sold, treated as the owner wishes and disposed of at any time."

"I disagree with it one hundred percent, Mr. Young. I'm a scientist. I tend to see the world in absolutes. Any harm done to that woman, or others like her, should be prosecuted under the full extent of the law—just as we do for humans carried in a woman's uterus and born through various means."

Sadie reappeared, discussing her childhood. Chris' voice once again came over the speakers, "Biologiqué International has discovered a way to transplant entire brain scans from the original human into the cloned human. As far as the clone knows when she opens her eyes, today is just another day in her life."

That sent the crowd over the edge. People who'd been lined up to fornicate with droids and human prostitutes screamed obscenities about the wrath of God and Judgement Day. The edge of my collar stirred in a sudden wind, causing me to look up further and see the drones descending. They would quell a riot before the first rock was even thrown.

"We've contacted both Biologiqué International and Thomas Ladeaux for comment. Neither have accepted our attempts to discuss the matter with them."

Several still pictures flashed by faster than my eye could distinguish who they were. "We said earlier that our politicians were involved in torture tourism. Sadie originally came to Channel 34 News to get help discovering who she'd been cloned from—the folks who made her conveniently wiped away all memory of personally identifying information and stripped away her fingerprints. She remembered being a businesswoman of some type, so we started showing her pictures of prominent New Orleans businessmen and women to give us a lead on where to start. You'll never guess where we ended up."

A picture of a black man appeared and Chris asked, "Do you know this person?

Sadie's eyes grew wide. "Yes! He was with me the night I was rescued—they dismembered him."

"Excuse me?" Chris asked in the video, not as a voiceover.

"He was tortured and killed in front of me while people took bets on what it would take to make him bleed out."

Chris' voiceover returned. "That man was prominent New Orleans business owner John Handy. Handy made a public appearance yesterday at his hotel in the French Quarter."

Several pictures flipped up with the names of business people and politicians. "In the interest of time, Sadie's reactions and statements on each of these New Orleans public figures won't be shown in this broadcast, but they can be seen in their entirety on our website. The final picture we showed her will shock you."

A picture of an older white male filled the screen, blurred at first and then slowly coming into focus. "Do you know…this man?" The video version of Chris asked hesitantly.

"Yeah," Sadie replied as the camera zoomed in on her face. "He raped me. He cut me. He was the one who used the blowtorch and did this." The shot panned out as she stood, lifting her shirt up. She pulled away the bandage on her stomach to reveal a puckered, oozing collection of burn scabs in the shape of a happy face. "He's pure evil."

"That man," Voiceover Chris stated, "is the Mayor of New Orleans."

"Boss, your phone is going crazy."

"I know, Andi. I already saw the shitstorm on the megavids." I paused to catch my breath. "I'm headed back to the station now."

"I'm tracking your movement. You appear to be making good time."

She was right. I'd only been running for a week, but her training plan of steadily increasing the daily distance was already paying off. I wouldn't have made it more than half a mile before walking just last week. Good thing too, I still had ten blocks to go.

"You have received multiple calls directly from the Mayor Cantrell's office, the reporter Chris Young, Chief Brubaker and Thomas Ladeaux. There have been forty-three one-time calls from others. Primarily news agencies and vloggers asking for comments."

"Patch me through to Brubaker on a secure line."

He picked up on the first tone. "What the fuck were you thinking, asshole? The mayor has already demanded your resignation and wants you brought up on charges."

"What charges?" I scoffed, slowing slightly. "I didn't say that stuff, Chris Young and Sadie said those things."

"They said to make up something. You ain't recovering from this one, Forrest. I need you to come in."

I stopped running and started to walk slowly to where the Jeep was parked. "This is a secure line, Chief. No one but you knows I called."

"So this conversation didn't happen," he said, catching on. "And you're still acting with the authority of a cop."

"Exactly," I replied, adjusting the sleeve of my duster as rain began to trickle down the sleeve while I talked. "How bad is this going to get?"

"Like a gator getting stuck in your swimming pool."

"Okay... So, that means this isn't going to end well, regardless of what happens, right?"

"When the mayor asked for your resignation, he also demanded that I issue a shoot on sight order for Sadie," Brubaker explained. "If she shows her face anywhere in New Orleans, she's done for."

"Damn. I'm worried for Sadie's safety at my place. I need a safe house for her."

"Good luck. There aren't any places that the mayor's staff doesn't know about."

"I know of one." I stated, dreading that I would once again put my friend in danger. I felt like I didn't have a choice, though. At least not anywhere fast, like I needed.

"Once I have her safe, I'm going to visit Ladeaux. He owes me an explanation."

"Is that a good idea if he's involved?"

"I don't know that he is, Chief. I told you yesterday when we talked about the warehouse that I think he's clean in this one."

I heard banging on the chief's door. "I've gotta go," he said. "Good luck."

The phone clicked silent and I punched the air in frustration. If they got to Brubaker, I was truly on my own for the moment. I needed to get off the grid and I was uniquely aware that the security cameras tracked my every movement, so I pushed my hat down on my head and flipped up my collar.

As I neared the Jeep, I saw Karen Goldman, a uniformed cop who patrolled in The Lane. We knew each other fairly well, having been working the same area for about four years. I pulled out my phone again and placed it to my ear to help hide my face, regardless of the feedback between the earpiece and the phone. "Andi, turn off all tracking and nav systems in the Jeep. I'll drive myself."

"Is that a good idea?" she asked.

"Just do it."

"You're the boss."

"Tell Sadie that I'll be there in a few minutes to get her," I said as I passed by the female officer.

"May I suggest an alternative?"

"I'm all ears," I replied, not looking back at the cop as she continued on her way toward the livelier part of Jubilee Lane.

I unlocked the car and sat heavily inside, buckling the seatbelt that I'd never worn since the vehicle was normally under robotic control.

"Give Sadie access to the GoPhone and the lockbox," Andi suggested. "Have her leave the apartment immediately on foot. I can guide her to a rendezvous point."

"Uh..." I hunted for a moment for the start button and found it under the dash. I wouldn't be able to use my credit chip, so I'd need the cash in the lockbox, even though I wasn't a fan of the clone taking all of the money that I'd set aside for an emergency like tonight.

"Alright," I relented. "Give her the phone and I authorize access to the lockbox. There's a duffle bag inside that she'll need to grab. Map out a route to where I can pick her up and then tell her where to go."

I shifted the car into drive and it jerked forward in the parking spot, ramming the vehicle in front of me.

"Goddammit!" I yelled in frustration.

I wished I'd paid closer attention to the theory of manual driving classes they gave us at the academy. Hell, I planned to suggest they implement a practical exercise portion of instruction when this was over.

Through trial and error, and more damage to both the front and rear bumpers, I got the Jeep out of the parking spot. After a couple of blocks, I made an effort to restrain myself. The police transponder was off, so I was fair game to any officer patrolling. If I got popped for speeding, it was game over.

I resisted the urge to ask Andi to put me through to Sadie as she fled my apartment. It would have upset her even more, so I forced myself to be content in the knowledge that Andi said she made it out of the apartment safely and was moving toward the linkup site.

With Andi's help, I navigated the car through the streets of Village de L'Est until I saw a woman walking with a phone up to her ear. I recognized one of my coats and the hat she wore was mine as well.

"Tell her that I'm pulling up behind her."

The woman turned and I brought the Jeep roughly to a halt beside the curb. "Get in," I ordered.

"Oh, thank God, Zach!"

She sat inside and looked questioningly at my hands on the wheel, following my arms back to my body where the seatbelt rested. "What are you doing?"

"It's the only way to disconnect the GPS tracking," I replied. "Buckle up."

By the time we made it to Little Woods, I'd gotten the feel for driving. The front tires up on the curb outside of Teagan's apartment, however, indicated that I still had a ways to go on learning how to park.

"I couldn't risk calling her," I told Sadie as we walked down the steps to the front door. "We were encrypted for too long trying to get away from my apartment, any longer and someone would have found the signal."

"So your friend doesn't know that you're stopping by at one in the morning?"

"No. And she's probably not going to be happy about it."

I rang the buzzer outside her door twice without an answer. Then I knocked loudly and waited. No response. I knocked again, this time I saw a light come on through the window.

"Who is it?" a tired female voice came through the speaker by the doorbell.

"It's Zach. Is Teagan home?"

"Zach? Zach who?"

"Is Teagan home?"

"Yeah, she's in here with her boyfriend," the girl replied, sounding more annoyed now. "So go crawl back under whatever rock you crawled out from under and leave her alone, creep."

*Boyfriend?*

"Can you just tell her that Zach Forrest needs to speak to her?"

"Wait, the *cop*?"

"Yeah."

"Hold on. I'm buzzing you in."

The door opened and I saw a familiar, thin blonde girl. "Hello, Rebecca."

"Hi," she raised her hand quickly and dropped it. "Who's she? Oh wait! You're the clone from the vids."

"That's me," Sadie answered.

"Can I touch you?"

"Do you want to get slapped?" Sadie asked, cocking her hip out and resting a hand on it.

"You're right," Rebecca said. "Sorry. I'll go wake up Teagan. She could sleep through an earthquake."

"I don't want to interrupt her and her boyfriend," I said.

"She doesn't have a boyfriend. I just thought you were some creep at our door, so I was trying to get you to leave."

"Alright. I guess I deserved that."

Rebecca disappeared down the hallway and I looked around Teagan's place. I hadn't ever been there before. From what I could tell, the girls were clean and everything seemed to be in its place. I doubted they had a maid service like I did, so that made the fact that the place was clean when someone dropped in unexpectedly even more impressive.

Teagan's roommate reemerged from the dark and crossed her arms across her chest. "Hey, I'm sorry about that time on the phone. We were *really* drunk."

"It's okay," I chuckled. "It's funny now." It hadn't been funny at the time. Teagan and Rebecca had been out at a football game until very late and decided to call me so Teagan could profess her undying love. The problem was that Rebecca had a different idea about how things should go—and so did I. In truth, I was surprised she was still speaking to me after I called a cab for Teagan and left Rebecca stranded at the stadium.

Teagan came around the corner rubbing her eyes. "Good morning, Zach." Then she yawned. "Whatcha doing here so late?"

"My place isn't safe right now, so we needed a place to go." Like a bandage, it was best to just rip it off quick.

"*Hmm*... Um... Who are you?" she asked, pointing at Sadie.

"Sadie. I'm a clone. Zach rescued me. Didn't you see the news broadcast?"

"No. I was at work until eleven. Clone? Like what Zach told me about?" she asked, showing remarkable mental agility for someone woken in the middle of the night.

"Yeah, same thing," I answered. "It would probably just be easier for you to watch the vid feed and then ask any questions. It's only five minutes."

We pulled up the vid on Rebecca's screen and watched in silence as the facts were laid out quickly by Chris Young. The blonde girl kept looking back and forth between the screen and Sadie.

Teagan sat quietly until the final part about the mayor's involvement and then shouted, "No way!"

I felt the same way when I learned about it by watching the interview on the megavid screen.

"I voted for that guy!" Teagan continued.

"See, that's why I don't vote," Rebecca huffed. "They're all crooked."

"Now, the mayor has goons out searching for us," I said. "I can't leave Sadie at my place or else they'd get to her."

"Just have Andi secure the place like Fort Knox," Teagan suggested.

"It doesn't work that way. They'd be acting under orders of the Mayor of New Orleans. Dirty or not, he hasn't been charged with a crime, so Andi *can't* ignore their legal orders to open the door. He has the judiciary in his corner as well, so it won't be long before they have a warrant to search my apartment."

"That seems stupid," Rebecca said. "You should tell your housekeeper to only open the door for you and nobody else."

"I wish I could, but city code mandates that all AIs follow the law to the letter. Without extensive reprogramming, that's what Andi will do."

"Oh…" Rebecca replied, likely feeling stupid that she was the only one who hadn't known Andi wasn't a physical person.

"Is it safe for us here?" Teagan asked.

"I wouldn't have came here if I thought there were any danger to you."

"Okay then. You guys can stay."

"Thanks," I replied. "I just need to catch a quick catnap on the couch, and then I need to get back out there to find some answers."

"You don't have to sleep on the couch, Zach."

"Nah, I just need about an hour or two and I'll be good to go."

We spent a few minutes going over the ground rules with the girls that they had to keep Sadie's presence a secret and continue to go on about their day like they normally would, then I used the restroom. Their goddamned toilet computer was programmed with a female voice. It didn't irritate me any less than my own.

"Shit! Teagan," I called through the door without flushing.

"Yeah?"

"I need some chemicals. Bleach, drain cleaner, perfume, anything liquid that can go in the toilet."

"Uh… Sure, hold on."

She brought me a bottle of fingernail polish remover that I added liberally to the contents of the bowl. It sent the toilet computer into overdrive, citing a string of problems that someone who had acetate in their urine could have. Then I flushed the contents down the drain.

"Information from every flush is sent to the Louisiana Health Department for population monitoring," I explained. "It's for trend analysis and helps keep track of where certain diseases are concentrated, but it could also be used as a way to track somebody. If they took my profile from the toilet at my apartment and then searched for similar data across the city, they'd be able to narrow down the places to look for me."

"Wow. That's really scary, Zach."

"It's an interagency trick that we use to our advantage that most of the population doesn't know about."

Teagan excused herself to give me some privacy. A quick scrub of my teeth with some toothpaste and my finger and I was as ready for bed as I was going to get.

I walked out into the living room to see Sadie already stretched across the sofa, asleep. I checked to ensure the locks were engaged before sitting in the recliner. The girls were already in their bedrooms with the doors closed. I hoped that I made the right decision to come here.

I sighed and leaned the recliner back all the way, getting as flat as I could to try and get a little bit of sleep.

The small *tchk* of a door latch made me drop my hand to my gun until I heard the soft padding of feet on carpet from the hallway. I pretended to be asleep, watching Teagan's lithe form standing at the corner of the room through lidded eyes.

She seemed undecided about what to do. Finally, Teagan tiptoed across the living room to where I lay and she climbed up onto the chair with me. She curled up beside me, pressing her body into mine as I continued to feign sleep.

"I love you, Zach Forrest," she murmured into my chest.

I waited until her breathing became even and peaceful to adjust my arm enough to allow circulation back into it. Pins and needles exploded across my skin as the blood rushed in.

*What a fine mess I've gotten myself into*, I chastised myself silently and pulled the girl closer to me, relishing the feel of her warm body against mine.

# SIXTEEN: FRIDAY

I overslept, enjoying the comfort of Teagan's body next to mine. I ate breakfast quickly, sharing what felt like an awkward meal with the three women. One of them was enamored with me, one was annoyed that she was in this situation and wanted to fight, and the third kept trying to find ways to touch the second one accidentally. When it was time to go, I was thankful to be able to leave.

"Take care of each other—and remember: don't go outside the apartment today," I added for Sadie's benefit.

"I don't want to stay inside and miss everything that's happening," the older woman answered and then quickly held up her hands to ward off my protest. "I'll do it for today, but I'm probably going to go crazy if it's any longer than that."

"I can't risk you getting picked up. If the mayor's people pick you up off the street, we're both done for. They'll make you talk, and that puts both Rebecca and Teagan at risk as well."

She set her jaw and nodded. Staying inside and out of sight was no longer simply a matter of personal preference for her. Now *our* future was in Sadie's hands.

I glanced over at the girls in the kitchen cleaning up from breakfast. "Thank you for letting us stay," I said. "It means a lot to me that I can rely on such good friends."

Teagan smiled, but didn't say anything, which left a gap that Rebecca was more than glad to fill. "You're welcome,

Zach. You guys weren't any trouble at all. Besides, we love having guests over and entertaining."

I planned to go back down to the Dockyards to talk to Tommy Voodoo about why he was cloning businesspeople and I needed to follow up with Chris Young to ask him a few things.

The vid screen in the living room flashed a few times with the words, "Killer Cop on the Loose." The bottom of my stomach fell away and my fears were confirmed when my picture came up. "What the hell? Hey, how do you turn on the volume?"

"Volume on," Rebecca called from the kitchen.

A female reporter's voice filled the room. "Last night, at approximately 1:38 a.m., New Orleans Police Department Detective Zachary Forrest shot and killed another police officer in Easytown. Channel 12 News obtained the following video footage through the Consent to Surveil Act."

The scene switched to street light footage of me jogging through Easytown. "That's from last night," I muttered. I slowed as I neared the female officer and pulled a gun out of my pocket. "That was my phone, not a gun."

"As you can see," the reporter said, "Forrest walked up and calmly shot Officer Karen Goldman, a mother of two, in the back of the head. He can be seen saying something to her, but she doesn't appear to be able to hear him."

"That's because the footage is doctored!" I shouted uselessly at the screen.

Councilman Jefferson's image appeared as he highlighted some of my past misconduct during a press conference. Mayor Cantrell was off to his right, visibly angry that one of his police officers would murder another.

My picture returned and the reporter said, "The NOPD has issued a warrant for Forrest's arrest. Anyone with any information is requested to call…"

I turned back to the women. The looks on their faces must have mirrored mine. Shock. Anger. Disbelief.

"You guys know I didn't do that. I was here for Christ's sake."

Rebecca was the first to speak. "I can't believe they would do that. It's *illegal*. We can all testify that you were here in the apartment after midnight."

"Zach, what are you going to do?" Teagan asked.

"I've got to try and clear my name."

"You can't go down to the police department," Sadie cautioned. "They'll arrest you and put you away without any type of trial. You'll be out on that island before the day is over."

"I can handle myself inside Sabatier," I responded. "But I'm not going to turn myself in. I know a witch hunt when I see one. I've got to get to the bottom of this and it looks like my timeline just sped up."

I put my Oxfords on and slid my arms through the sleeves of my coat.

"Zach?"

"Yeah, Teagan?"

She came around the kitchen island to the little square of tile by the front door where I stood. "Be safe. Please."

"I always am."

"No, I'm serious. You've always had support from other officers in the police department. You don't have that right now. Your chief may be on your side, but he's got a career and a family that he has to worry about."

"Chief Brubaker would never do anything to hurt me."

"Maybe he wouldn't, I don't know him. What about all the others; the ones who don't know the truth and think you're a cop killer? Will they protect you?"

"I'll watch my back," I replied, opening the door and ignoring her question. What did the damn kid know about anything out there in the real world? I'd proven myself time and again to the other cops; they knew that I didn't do what the video showed me doing.

*Geez, I can't even explain it to myself without sounding guilty.*

Teagan grabbed my arm and pulled me back inside, wrapping me in a hug. For the first time, I didn't hesitate when I hugged her back.

⚜ ◦ ⚜ ◦ ⚜

I tried to get in touch with Andi, but there wasn't a response from her. They must have already went into my apartment and shut everything down. I hoped that she'd deleted the files from last night where she told me how to get to Teagan's house. I just needed her to remove the reference to where we were going, anything else about Sadie's escape or me driving manually wouldn't matter.

The drive to the docks went slowly as I sat in morning traffic. The Jeep had deep tinted windows, but I still tried to sink low whenever I passed by other cops. I hated doing it because it wasn't like me. I was used to being the guy in charge of the situation, not an accused murderer slinking from place to place.

After what seemed like hours, I finally reached the headquarters building for the Marie Leveau Shipping Company. I parked the Jeep out front and rushed inside.

"Detective Forrest! Tommy isn't expecting you," Anastasia exclaimed, jumping to her feet.

"Well I'm here," I retorted. "If he's really as innocent as he claims, he needs to talk to me. Now!"

"I—"

"Don't give me any shit. I know the way."

I stormed down the hall toward the secret passageway. The unmistakable *click* of a safety being released on a weapon made me stop and raise my hands.

"You are not authorized to see Mr. Ladeaux this morning."

I turned slowly back toward the receptionists. Betty stood behind her desk and held a giant pistol in her hand. The damn thing was pointed at my forehead.

"Whoa! Let's take a step back from the situation, Betty," I said coolly, and then felt like an idiot. The droid didn't need to be calmed down; she was simply following her programming. I took a few slow, tentative steps back toward the desk and when I passed whatever line she'd been instructed to guard, she sat back down and began typing once again. I had no idea where the gun went.

"So, what am I supposed to do?" I asked, ambling slowly the rest of the way to the desk.

"You may have a seat in our waiting area, sir," Betty responded. "I will attempt to find space on Mr. Ladeaux's calendar this morning."

"Let me call Tommy," Anastasia suggested. "I'll let him know that you're here."

With nothing better to do, I sat in the waiting area. The vid screen showed me killing Karen Goldman repeatedly. It was horseshit. I'd pulled my phone out of my pocket when I passed her last night, not a gun, and they killed her because she was in the video. That poor family.

How many more people had died because of this torture tourism ring? Voodoo said it was worth billions, but there were some hefty players involved here, was the money worth it to them? What did the mayor—a rich man by all accounts—have to do with this? Was it purely that he liked to torture people or was there something else, something even more sinister than that going on?

A pair of long, cream-colored legs invaded my line of sight as I stared blankly at the floor in thought. "Mr. Ladeaux has graciously made room in his schedule to see you, Detective," Anastasia said. "Please follow me."

I stood and followed her, glancing back at Betty when I crossed the point where she'd drawn on me before. The droid typed merrily away at a document, not paying any attention to me whatsoever.

"This goes deeper than just torture," Anastasia mumbled.

"What was that?' I asked, catching up to her.

"I said you're lucky that Mr. Ladeaux could see you. He's a very busy man."

*Did I hear her right the first time?*

"No, the other part."

She looked at me and shook her head. "I don't know what you mean, Mr. Forrest."

I knew what I heard, but she wasn't going to say it again. She had the one opportunity to pass along a short message and I'd received it. What did she mean that it went deeper than torture? Who was she afraid of? Was it Voodoo or someone else?

We went to Ladeaux's decoy office.

"Good morning, Detective Forrest," Tommy Voodoo greeted me when we arrived. "I hear you've been a busy man."

"Not half as busy as someone wants people to think."

"Anastasia, please bring the detective some coffee. I believe you take it with cream and sugar, correct?"

"I'm not going to be here long enough for a drink," I replied. "I need info and I need it quick."

Voodoo leaned back and put his hands behind his head. "You see, we have two problems with your request."

"What's that, Ladeaux?"

"One, you're no longer on the force. The mayor had you kicked off when you shot that other cop."

"It wasn't me. Anyone with even half a brain knows that."

"They only know what the vid feeds tell them. It's too hard for the masses to form their own opinion. With 'indisputable' video evidence like the news showed this morning, you're already guilty."

"*Hmpf*," I grunted. It was bullshit, but essentially true. It seemed like hardly anyone researched topics for themselves or thought too hard beyond what the media spoon-fed to them and public opinion was easy to manipulate.

"The other problem is that you lied to me. You told me you found nine dead clones. Who is this Sadie person?"

"She's a clone."

"I know that. The original version of her runs my company. What I want to know is why you kept her a secret from me. We were supposed to be in this together."

"Wrong. We aren't in anything together, Ladeaux. I'm trying to recover your prop—No, that's not right. I'm trying to find missing *persons* and you're the one giving me the information in exchange for keeping my friend's rent affordable."

He picked at a piece of lint on his tailored suit. "You see it one way; I see it another."

"So Sadie *is* a businesswoman? She said she remembered being in board meetings and speaking in front of large groups."

"She's modeled after Kelsey Bloomfield, the Chief Operations Officer of Biologiqué International. No children. Has a few animals—maybe a dog? I can't really remember."

Voodoo leaned forward once more. "There, I just told you exactly what you wanted to know when you went to the media to ask for their help. If you'd simply come to me with the truth that the clone was alive, we could have avoided this disaster."

"Well, shit, Ladeaux. You don't have the best reputation. And to be honest, I'm still not entirely sure what your role is in all of this. Your company made these clones, they got away from you somehow, inexplicably, and instead of going public with the info, you wanted to keep it quiet that there's a multi-billion dollar torture industry in New Orleans. Add to that the fact that you coerced me into finding the clones by purchasing the building where my lifelong friend's business is located... Do you think I can trust you?"

"Please, Detective. Let's be civil," he protested against my questioning of his credibility. He squirmed in his seat for a moment before turning to the computer screen and tapping a few icons. The familiar absence of noise descended upon the office as a white noise generator enveloped the room.

"Have you ever stopped to wonder why the bodies of clones are destroyed immediately?" he asked. "Why the mayor is explicitly clear when it comes to clone politics, and not much else?"

"I think it's complete and utter bullshit. You don't destroy evidence, *ever*. And doing so before a case is closed makes me think they're hiding something—like being involved in the torture tourism that Sadie accused him of. But I'm not sure I'm following you on the politics piece," I admitted.

He nodded. "You're exactly right. It's all about the destruction of evidence. Covering up the lie."

He adjusted in the chair once more and pointed at the sound-dampening equipment in the corner. "Do you *really* think I'd be concerned about gamblers and two-bit street thugs? There's more security in this building than you could imagine, I'm quite secure against common criminals. This goes much higher than you're thinking—and they're certainly willing to kill a few cops and sweep aside investors like me to make sure they keep a good thing going."

"Do you mean the mayor is involved like Sadie claims?" If I could get a second person to come forward, we might have a chance of opening an actual investigation against him.

Voodoo tapped the side of his nose. "More than involved, Forrest. Mayor Cantrell is the architect of this scheme. When it all started out, he commissioned a clone of himself. It was supposed to be used as an organ donor in case he ever became ill. I knew about it and I even agreed with it. Then, about a month ago, I learned that he'd made an arrangement behind my back with Kelsey Bloomfield. She began cloning government officials, businessmen and women, and influential people in the state. They weren't willing participants."

"What do you mean?"

"She sent me a few documents, trying to play both sides I imagine. Her paperwork told me about the thirty-eight clones—but there's probably more. Then all communications from Bloomfield ceased. I didn't know what they were truly after by cloning those people until I watched the video of Sadie. Now I know."

Everything clicked in my mind. "Kleer didn't buy the clones from you," I interrupted him. "He took them. This isn't about recovering the clones for humanitarian reasons. This is damage control. You're worried that this is going to get out and then everything will come crashing down. Billions in potential revenue, gone."

"Of course it is," he snapped. "I think it's despicable what they're doing to those poor clones, but people get murdered all the time. I told you, this is worth *trillions* of dollars, I'm not going to let some fucking piece of shit mayor ruin this deal because he wants to increase his local power base."

"Your true colors are showing."

"Don't fuck with me, Detective," Voodoo sneered. "We both know that I need this to go away quietly, you need your friend's business to remain affordable *and* we get to save the lives of clones. What else do you need from me for your investigation?"

"First off, why does she remember everything except personal details? Can they selectively upload the brain scan?"

"It's because her memory's been wiped," he replied. "And then there's Dr. Grubber, the geneticist that your reporter friend interviewed. He stated that Sadie was an exact match for a human. My clones aren't *exactly* the same as you or I. We clean out any resemblance of any type of disease or malformity at the cellular level before they're grown." He paused once again. "We also keep a close eye on our clones by making them chemically dependent on a compound to stave off rapid cellular deterioration. Within five days of not getting the compound the clone begins to die. They're dead by the end of a week or two without the injection."

"And that is noticeable in a DNA test?"

"It's crystal clear if you know what you're looking for—and Dr. Grubber is the best in the business. I checked into him."

"So all this means?"

"That Sadie is not a clone. She's Kelsey Bloomfield. Why they swapped her out, I don't know, but I bet it has something to do with her trying to blackmail me. She probably tried the same thing with the mayor."

"It also means that the dead clones I've been finding…"

"Were likely the original people, not clones," Voodoo finished. "Think about it, tattoo a few numbers on their ear, make sure the coroner or investigator notices the clone serial number and couple that with the state's harsh penalties against those who choose to assist a clone and we've got a coup that was staged by the top people in the government."

"And the clones are loyal to the mayor since he has the juice to keep them alive."

"Exactly," he shouted, slapping the table in his excitement. "Of those that I know about, the mayor seems to have set himself up to run the city for a long time. My information is dated, but there are a few state officials and one federal judge on Bloomfield's list. He's going to make a play for something bigger."

The implications of what he alleged were enormous—and totally unprovable without isolating the potential clone for several days. The only way I would even be able to begin the conversation would be to bring in the double, dead or alive, and compare them to the person living and working in our society. How would the average citizen view *that*?

"Why is it that every time I talk to you, I get into deeper shit?" I mumbled.

"It must be my good reputation with the city leadership," Voodoo answered with a sly grin.

I regarded him for a moment before answering, "You coulda fooled me."

⚜ ○ ⚜ ○ ⚜

"Not exactly laying low, are you, Chris?" I asked as I stared out over the wrought iron railing of his hotel balcony across Frenchmen Street toward the French Quarter.

"What can I say? I enjoy fine hotels, fine dining, and fine women."

"I can say that you've got a target on your back because of that story you ran on Sadie."

"Just like you do, eh?"

I leaned back and sipped the Brandy Crusta that the hotel's bar staff made. It was good, but not like the one they served over at the Carousel Bar. I was glad that the reporter had decided to leave his house for a few days, but he was taking a chance by flaunting his newfound fame at the Frenchmen Hotel.

"Yeah, I guess you could say that," I replied. "It's more like a death sentence."

"You're officially on the outs, my friend." He leaned over to me and whispered, "But I don't believe them. I'm still in communication with a lot of past informants. *Somebody* has put a price on you and Sadie both."

My arm stopped midway, the drink hovering in the air on its way to my lips. I set it down slowly. "What?"

"You heard me. You've got a price on your head; two hundred and fifty grand. Sadie is closer to a five hundred. They're not leaving it up to the police to find you."

I grunted and then slammed the rest of my drink. "I guess I should be flattered. Most of the time, when gangers put out hits on me, it's only a couple of G's. This means I've made it to the big time."

"You may think it's funny, Zach, but this is serious stuff."

"Ten to one I know who it is that put the hit out on me."

"You think Mayor Cantrell is behind this, don't you?"

I grimaced and pointed toward the empty glass. "Think we can get another round?"

"Of course," Chris replied, tapping a few times on the display set into the table. "You got something you need to get off your chest?"

"If I tell you this, you've got to keep me out of it. I'm still fucking pissed at you for naming me in your original story. I could have continued the investigation without all of this sneaking around if you'd just kept me out of it."

"I'm sorry, Zach. I was trying to give you the recognition you deserve; I didn't know it would backfire like it has."

"Yeah, second and third order effects are a bitch," I grumbled.

"I should have asked your permission to use you in the story. I rushed to get it out and into the spotlight. As a result, I forgot to run the traps and do a few things—like get your permission to name you in the story."

"Your news vid accomplished its goal. I know who Sadie really is."

Chris choked on the final sip of his gin and tonic. "Excuse me?"

I nodded. "Sadie, or should I say 'Kelsey Bloomfield,' runs the day-to-day operations at Biologiqué International, the company that perfected the cloning process."

"Wow, man. That's... That's crazy. How did her clone get tied up in the torture tourism bit?"

"I don't know. To be honest, until I saw it firsthand, I didn't even believe that it existed. And, come to find out—"

The hotel room's door chime interrupted our conversation and a servant droid brought the tray of drinks out to the balcony. The droid was shiny stainless steel; the hotel hadn't seen the need to pay an extra hundred thousand for the synthetic skin that would have made it look human. Can't say I blamed them. I was more than a little sick of droids at the moment.

Once the droid departed, Chris took a huge gulp from his drink and set it carefully on the table. "Before we got interrupted, you were going to tell me something you found out about the story I ran."

I could tell that he was questioning why I'd risked coming to see him instead of telling him on the phone. He probably thought that he'd staked his entire reputation on the Sadie story and I was getting ready to tell him it was a fake.

I sipped my drink, staring at him over the rim, relishing the warmth spreading through my limbs from my stomach.

"Sadie isn't a clone. She's the real deal."

I cringed as the reporter's glass crashed to the balcony floor.

"But, her clone *is* running Biologiqué," I amended.

"Go on," he snapped, punching the display angrily to order a replacement drink.

"She was replaced by her clone. My informant didn't know she was the original woman either. Once he heard Dr. Grubber's report that she was genetically *exact*, he knew. Apparently, the clones they produce are all chemically dependent on a compound that Biologiqué makes. If they don't get it, they die within a week. Keep's 'em loyal—and it can be detected in a DNA scan."

"A failsafe," he nodded, finishing his order. "It makes sense. If they're out running around, away from the parent company's influence, this is a way to keep control over them."

"You're taking it a little better than I thought you would," I said.

He hunched his shoulders. "To be honest, I'm *not* surprised that they replaced someone with a clone and then sent them off to be raped and murdered. Probably because on some level, I knew that was a possibility. I mean, it makes sense, right? Why else would they create clones?"

"So you're not going to be stunned when I tell you that they've replaced the heads of several corporations and local government officials with clones, even a federal judge, and it's entirely likely that the people who are getting killed in these torture houses are the originals?"

"Hmm... It's a great way to get rid of your opponents," Chris admitted. "Kidnap 'em, clone 'em, and send the clone in to do the work that you want them to do. Sounds like a decent way to ensure your policies are embraced by industry, too."

"Yeah, I guess that's one way to look at it," I replied.

The droid returned with his new drink and *tsked* us for breaking a glass, which it promptly cleaned up before leaving.

"Alright. I can work with this," Chris announced. "Never let a good crisis go to waste, you know."

"*Hmpf*," I grunted. "Is that some sort of journalist's motto or something?"

"No—well, sort of, I guess. Winston Churchill said it during the Second World War."

I tried to remember back to my recent trip to the local World War Two museum, but the name didn't ring a bell. "Churchill? Like the cigars?"

He laughed. "One and the same, Zach. They named the size after him because he always had an oversized cigar in his mouth."

"Yeah, I know the type," I replied, thinking of Chief Brubaker. "So you can still use this information, then?"

"Most definitely. I'll have to be careful how I present it, and I'll probably have to talk to your source and get them on camera before the network will run the story. It'll be difficult without more corroboration than one woman and a fugitive detective."

I frowned at the word "fugitive." How had it gotten to this point?

"I'll ask my source," I responded. "He's probably not going to discuss anything with you. In fact, I can almost guarantee it."

"So we need more proof, then. Sadie is great and we can attempt to find her counterpart at Biologiqué International to get evidence that one of them is a clone..." He paused, thinking through our next steps as he took a sip. "Can you find more clones? When we talked the other day, you said there were about forty of them that your source knew about and you'd found some of them. Can we get the coroner to give an opinion about those bodies? We'd need a clone for comparison. With a larger sample size, we should have some evidence."

"I know a clone that we can talk to."

# SEVENTEEN: FRIDAY

"Damn," I croaked, my mouth dry from the cognac in the drinks I'd shared with Chris Young.

The road was blurry and it was difficult to drive the Jeep. Two days ago, I'd never attempted to drive a car. After drinking, the task was monumentally more difficult. Maybe it wasn't the best idea to operate a vehicle manually after three of the strong drinks.

I saw a side road and turned onto it.

The front tire slammed into the curb, jostling me and throwing my head against the window. I pressed the brake to slow down and the Jeep limped a few hundred feet down the side street. The tire was blown, causing the car to lean awkwardly to the right and rumble as it rotated.

"*Mother fucker!*" I shouted after I brought the Jeep to a halt. How'd I screw things up so badly? I should have known better than to drive drunk. Now I was really screwed.

"Andi, how do I change a tire?" I asked.

She didn't respond. *Oh yeah*. I'd forgotten that she was offline.

I almost used my phone to search online, stopping myself as the light illuminated the interior of the Jeep. If I popped up online, they'd know where I was instantly. It was up to me to figure this out on my own.

Through trial and error, skinned-up knuckles and a lot of sweat, I figured out how to jack up the Jeep and get the tire off. Luckily, there were instructions inside the compartment where the tools were kept that helped me figure it out. By the time I was finished, the alcohol had worn off and I felt safe enough to drive.

"You'd do better to tighten those lug nuts a little bit more," a synthesized male voice said from behind me.

I whirled around, falling into the side of the Jeep and rocking it on the jack. My pistol was in my hand as I pushed myself off the car.

"What are you doing here, Paladin?"

"Observing. What were you thinking, driving after four liquor drinks?"

"Three," I countered. *I think.*

"I watched you and the reporter drinking on the balcony from the rooftop across the street. It was *four*. Pretty stupid for the two of you to be out in the open where a sniper could snap off two quick shots and be done with you both."

I slid the pistol back into its holster under my armpit. "I didn't know you'd taken such an interest in my personal life."

"I haven't," he replied. "You've been singled out by the police as a cop killer and a rogue. Seems like you're my kind of guy."

"I'm not a cop killer," I retorted, turning my back on the dangerous vigilante. I picked up the tire iron and wrenched the lug nuts tighter. Two of them rotated another complete turn.

When I was finished, the Paladin said, "I know you're not a cop killer. Just like I'm not a bad person. We both want justice and are willing to make the hard choices and do things that people aren't comfortable with to achieve it."

"We're nothing alike." I inserted the tire iron into the jack and began turning it to lower the Jeep back onto all four wheels.

"More than you know," he chuckled. "We have a problem in this city. A major problem."

"I know," I grunted, picking up the ruined tire and fitting it on the mount on the back of the Jeep.

"I didn't know all of the details until I listened in on your conversation with Young. The regular police force won't be able to do anything about this, and you know it. It'll be up to you and me to find a way to get to the mayor."

"So not only were you watching me, but you were spying on me as well? And you want me to work with you, are you kidding?"

"I had to know the truth in case you get arrested or killed. This way, there are two of us searching for clues."

"I'm not going to get killed. I'm going to find the rest of those missing people and bring them to the public. I'll expose the mayor and clear my name."

"All noble gestures, Detective Forrest, but without me, your chances of success plummet. You don't have the police drone support this time like you did at the warehouse. They'll be hunting you instead. Your partner is officially on the lookout for you as well. You're all alone in this."

*Dammit.* He had a point.

"I know how to get around the drones, the security cameras, the beat cops, and the crowds of people," the Paladin continued. "I *want* to take out those sickos and free the clones—or whatever we find."

"How do you get around the cameras?" If I could figure that part out, I could bust him once I was back on the force.

"I'll let you know once we have a target. Has Ladeaux contacted you yet?"

*Son of a bitch! What else did this guy know?*

"Why would he contact me?" I asked.

"Because he's your informant," the Paladin replied. "You may be fooling most everyone else, not me. You spend enough time in the shadows, listening and observing, you see things. Hear things. Word on the street is that Ladeaux's been spending a lot of time with a cop and people don't like that—especially not the mayor, who has a lot invested with the King of Easytown.

"You're not the only one with a target on your back right now, Detective."

"The guy may be sleazy, but he isn't involved," I lied. I needed to feel like I was in control in some aspect. If it had to be information, then so be it.

"Hmm... I'll have to think on it," he challenged. "So has your *informant* told you where we need to look next?"

"No. They said they'd poke around and try to find the next site."

"Alright. I'll keep an ear to the ground and see what I can dig up. I'll be in touch soon."

He spun on his heel and began walking toward the wood line. *What the hell is he going into the park for?* I wondered if he left his vehicle at the parking lot there.

Then I remembered what the pickpocket told me about the ganger's creations when I busted him. *Damn,* I thought, *was that yesterday?*

"Wait! What do you know about the cyborgs that are hunting you?"

He turned slowly. "I've heard rumblings about a new kind of creature haunting the alleys of Easytown. I didn't know that they were coming after me, though."

I relayed to him what the kid had told me about the mechanical monstrosities allegedly arrayed against him. I also told him about the disc ammunition we pulled from the synthaine house. "I guess I'm just warning you to be careful out there."

"Oh, *now* you want me to be careful?" he asked. I could hear the amusement in his voice, even through the voice synthesizer. "Two weeks ago, you threatened me with kicking my teeth in. Something about shitting enamel if I remember right."

I chuckled slightly. It had been a good one-liner and the video replay got me lots of laughs from the guys down at the precinct. "Of course I want you to be careful. When this is all over, I'm going to arrest you and send you out to Sabatier."

He gave me a two-finger salute, his fingers touching where I imagined his eyebrow to be and jogged toward the park. I watched him until he disappeared into the trees before making my way around the Jeep to the driver's seat.

"What a weird son of a bitch."

Teagan slept in the chair with me again that night. She invited me to her bedroom to share her bed, but I'd declined for some reason. The girl nodded her head sadly and went into her room while I stared blankly at the ceiling trying to understand why I wouldn't allow myself a bit of pleasure from such a beautiful, willing woman.

She returned, once again, and curled up with me, attempting to draw some sort of strength from me—a strength I wasn't sure that I possessed any longer.

I figured it out in the middle of the night, with Teagan's small body weighing me down, pressing my lower back deeper into the cushion. I finally understood why I'd been adamant that we not date and had made up silly excuses like she was too young for me and hadn't experienced life yet. I didn't want to hurt her.

I was a major fuck-up in every way when it came to women. I didn't let the ones I cared about get too close because I didn't want to disappoint them. The disappointment almost always led to resentment and eventually outright hostility.

Teagan didn't deserve that. She *was* young, but she'd set me up on some sort of pedestal and expected me to be this perfect man for her. I knew that wasn't me. I would screw up and end up hurting her. I always did. Being an unrelenting dick to perps and ruining relationships, *that* was my M.O.

In the morning, she'd kissed me, grabbing a handful of my hair as she rubbed her body along mine with a hunger I hadn't seen from her before. She bit my earlobe and whispered into my ear that she had a Valentine's Day surprise for me after she got off her shift at the Pharaoh's Tomb.

Of course, I told her that we had to stop; that the timing wasn't right, but that didn't deter her.

"You promised that you'd take me out on Valentine's Day. That's today," she replied to my protest. "I know that we can't go to a restaurant right now because of what's going on, so I'll bring home some food from the Pharaoh and we'll have a picnic."

"A picnic? I don't do picnics."

"You do now, buddy," she answered and kissed me again.

My erection threatened to become downright inappropriate, so I pushed her away gently. "You don't want to be late for work."

She smiled sadly. "You're gonna love me back one day, Zach. I know it."

Then she disappeared down the hallway and I heard the shower turn on. I tried to adjust myself without waking Sadie, who slept on the sofa a few feet away. *Funny, you didn't seem to be too concerned about her hearing anything a few minutes ago,* I chastised.

"I thought I was going to get a show there for a minute," the woman's voice drifted from behind the arm of the couch.

"Uh… I'm sorry, Sadie. Dammit, I mean Kelsey." I'd told everyone the news that Sadie wasn't a clone last night after I returned from the strange chance encounter with the Paladin.

A wild, disheveled mass of deep red hair appeared. "You can still call me Sadie. I don't know who Kelsey is. Plus, I kind of like it."

"I'll try to remember. So, what's on your agenda today?" I asked, half-jokingly.

"Let's see. I think I'll watch some more vids, maybe shower and wear more of Rebecca's clothes… Maybe I'll watch a few more vids after that. This house arrest stuff is really wearing on me, Zach."

"I know, and I'm sorry. I just want you to be safe."

"You're going out there," she countered. "You're probably more recognizable than me right now; your picture is all over the vid feeds."

"Don't think for a minute that Mayor Cantrell's thugs aren't looking for you. They'd kill you in a heartbeat to keep you silent."

"I know, it's— I can't live my life like this, Zach. I thought I was a clone, that I was beaten and abused because of that. But then you tell me that you found out I wasn't a clone. Then why did they do those things to me?"

"I don't know. I wish—" I stopped myself. Trying to understand why they'd done what they did to her was pointless. I understood killing. If they'd replaced her and then simply killed her, it would have been much easier to handle. This? I couldn't wrap my head around why they did it.

Sure, it brought in some extra cash to the operation, but in reality, it couldn't have been that much. The real answer had to be about power—power over the individuals who'd wronged Mayor Cantrell or who hadn't agreed to be a part of his scheme. It was sick.

"You know what? It doesn't matter what I wish," I growled. "The fuckers did what they did to you and I'm going to make them pay for it."

"Yeah, but why me?" she continued to press. "If I ran the company, why did they clone me? I'd think I was an asset."

"More importantly, why'd they wipe your memory before putting you through all that? Why were you still alive when the others at that location were dead? What is it about you that made them want to spare you?"

The shower turned off, plunging the small apartment into complete silence for a moment until Sadie spoke.

"Because they wanted me to suffer," she whispered. "I know something. I can feel it. There's something locked away up here that will put an end to this whole mess."

I watched her finger tap softly on the side of her head. Maybe she was right. The problem was trying to figure out how to unlock the secrets buried inside her tortured mind—if that was even possible anymore after they'd wiped her memory.

# EIGHTEEN: SATURDAY

The mournful echoes of bagpipes bounced off the concrete crypts. Fitting, since the rain fell in sheets this morning. The wind played havoc with the huge drops as they whirled in all directions across the cemetery, blowing alternatively between sideways and straight down the collar of my jacket.

I was in a newer part of New Orleans, on the northeast of Easytown, known as Coastal Flats. The land here was less stable than the reclaimed land in Easytown and subject to floods as Lake Pontchartrain's filth overflowed the boundaries seeking a way to the sea. Few people called the neighborhood home after the massive flood in '84.

Since then, Coastal Flats had become the city's last remaining active cemetery. All the others were tourist destinations, filled to capacity with no further room to expand. Most people in New Orleans were cremated these days, their ashes placed in one of several large memorial mausoleums built for that purpose. Only a select few could afford a stand-alone crypt and yet somehow, Karen Goldman's family had enough money for one only two days after her murder.

Less than a hundred yards away, a small gathering of friends and family did their best to huddle under the canopy the groundskeepers placed over the site. A line of seven police officers stood in the rain off to the side, their ceremonial dress uniforms visible under the clear rain slickers they wore. A lone bagpiper squeezed the bladder of his instrument as Chief Brubaker knelt in front of two small children, presenting them with a folded American flag.

The tune "Amazing Grace" was familiar, yet haunting, and it had far more of an impact on me today than ever before. I'd known Karen for years, our paths often overlapping as she walked her beat in Easytown while I made my way to various places across the neighborhood. She was a single mother of two, her husband had passed away of a heart attack in his late thirties before she joined the police force.

Now those two children were on their own, and they thought I was the man who'd killed their mother.

I watched sadly as the little boy cried, sobbing into his sister's shoulder as she tried to be brave. She gripped the flag closely to her chest, jumping as the first volley of shots rang out from the officers off to the side.

When the three volleys were complete, I saw an older woman, hunched in the shoulders, but similar to Karen's build otherwise, usher the children away from the tomb. The three of them followed behind a man in a suit who held a large umbrella overhead. He led them to a black Mercedes. Once they were inside and the car was pulling away, the man returned to the canopy to direct the sealing of the crypt.

I made my way around the back of a large stone tomb, using it to shelter me from the driving rain. I waited for a full twenty minutes until the sound of the retreating groundskeeper's vehicles told me that they'd completed their task.

After ensuring that they were truly gone, I walked down the muddy gravel road to Karen's new resting place. The crypt was one of the prefabricated kinds; small, white, with an angled roof to help keep the rain from leaking inside. A small metal Jewish star emblem on the door completed the structure. There were five more like it within walking distance, the only variations were the religious symbols on the door. That explained how they'd gotten it so quickly, but didn't explain how they'd been able to afford it. I didn't know her well enough to have any insight into their financial situation, though, so maybe I was reading too much into it.

I wasn't the praying type, but I felt compelled to mumble a few words. Karen had been a caring, compassionate police officer, and now she was dead because someone was trying to frame me. She just happened to be at the wrong place at the wrong time and paid the price for it.

"I'm sorry about what happened," I said. "An apology doesn't do your children any good, though. I'll find the motherfuckers who did this to you and make them pay. They'll wish they never laid a hand on you, Karen."

My thoughts turned darker than they'd already been. The shit these people did to others would be revisited tenfold on them. I'd make sure of it.

⚜ ◦ ⚜ ◦ ⚜

The phone felt odd in my hand. I was used to my small, handheld device, not the large clunky throwaway that I'd picked up off Tyrone, one of my contacts in Easytown. I hefted its weight, thinking the damn thing would make a good weapon in a pinch.

I activated my phone and copied the number into the throwaway. I paused for a moment before placing the call. If my gut was wrong on this one, it may very well unravel all of my hard work, and turn one of my seeming allies against me for sure. Unless I could work a miracle, I needed to make the call.

I pushed the hardwired button to connect.

It rang once and then Betty answered, "Marie Leveau Shipping Company."

"Hi, Betty. This is Jack Arnold," I stated. "I was working with Anastasia the other day on a shipment issue. Can I speak to her, please?"

"Of course, Mr. Arnold. Please hold while you're transferred."

The phone clicked over and Anastasia's voice answered tentatively, "Hello?"

"Hi, Anastasia. We talked the other day about some parts of the company that were dying off and premature shipments. Do you remember me?"

"I'm sorry. I don't," she replied.

*Shit.* I hadn't thought beyond that little coded message. I thought she'd be able to pick it up from that.

"Uh... When I was in there yesterday, I accidently tripped the droid defense—"

"Oh! *Mr. Arnold.* I'm sorry. I forgot to process that order. Can you remind me what it is again?"

"Yeah, I'm missing about twenty-two items from my order. I'd like to know how to get them."

"Sure, I'd love to help you," she replied. "Is there somewhere I could meet you to discuss the options on replacement?"

I looked at my phone—the one that wasn't connected to the network. It was early, before lunch. I needed a place to talk with her where it wouldn't matter who I was; where nobody paid attention to who came or went and one person was as faceless as the next.

"Can we meet at Whispers?" I asked.

"Yeah, that will work. What about noon?"

"Alright. I'll meet your there."

❧ ◦ ❧ ◦ ❧

The girl's hips moved slowly in perfect time with the music as I sipped on a beer. I'd learned my lesson about drinking hard liquor and driving. She twirled her back to me and bent her knees, rapidly dropping her rear end to eye level. The thin piece of gossamer thread she wore left nothing to the imagination as she thrust backward toward me.

The club had several small stages, each with a ring of chairs around it. There weren't any tables off to the side. The proprietor designed the place for maximum viewing pleasure for every patron. The setup also removed the anonymity of a crowd. In the other clubs along Jubilee Lane, someone could go in, watch the dancers and not pay them anything. Not in Whispers. I relied on the overall anonymity of the strip club to keep anyone from recognizing me.

The dancer lifted a leg out to the side and swung it up, using the momentum to turn herself over onto her back. Both of her legs were in the air as she patted her crotch in rhythm with the song's bass drum. Then she put her feet on the stage and her hands near her head, arching her back upward impossibly high.

The girl had talent. I'd give her that. I started to swipe my credit chip and pulled back. That mistake would have been an easy locator beacon for the cops to find me. She noticed immediately.

"You didn't swipe your chip, baby," she purred, cupping my chin in her hand.

"I remembered I don't have enough money in the account," I replied, tossing a twenty dollar bill on her small, mirrored stage.

"Cash works too, doll," the dancer said, gripping my wet shoulders to draw my head between her large breasts. She rotated her torso so they slapped against either side of my face.

"*Ahem...*"

I pulled away reluctantly and turned to see Anastasia. She was stunningly beautiful, even in the strip club lighting. Her smile seemed to take up her entire face as the subtle blacklights accentuated her lipstick against her skin.

"Enjoying yourself?"

"Just passing the time until you got here," I replied.

"Who's this? Is this your girlfriend?" the dancer asked with a smirk of amusement.

"I'm Ana. And no, I'm not his girlfriend."

"Cassadie," the girl replied. The two women exchanged a soft handshake before she began dancing again and we sat down.

I placed my face close to Anastasia's. Her hair brushed against my cheek and the aroma of flowers enveloped me, replacing Cassadie's scent of vanilla sugar that all dancing girls seemed to wear.

"So, do you have any leads on where I can find the rest of the clones?" I asked into her ear.

"Yeah. Tommy wants you to pick away at the edges, finding the one or two here and there. For him, it's all about damage control. That's why he sent you to that warehouse."

"Is there someplace better to look?" I asked.

"Are you—" She stopped as the dancer's butt pressed against her chest and began sliding sensuously up and down.

"Want a private dance, baby?" the girl asked.

"No, thank you," I replied.

She laughed. "I wasn't talking to you, man. Your lady friend is hot."

"Not today, sweetheart," Anastasia answered.

"Suit yourself," the stripper shrugged. "I do *way* more in the Joy Room than I do on stage. You're missing out."

"I'll have to remember that," the clone responded and swiped her credit chip to tip the dancer.

"I'll have to remember that too," I mumbled aside to Anastasia. "You know, when I'm a cop again."

"Oh, leave her alone. She's just trying to earn a buck," my co-conspirator scolded. "Where were we? Oh yes, Tommy is covering his ass by having you clean up the clones that were accidentally sold. That's all good and we need to rescue them, but you're going to find the answers in the Biologiqué International headquarters."

"What answers?"

She pursed her lips. At first, I thought she was thinking, but I started to get the feeling that she was flirting with the dancer as her eyes followed the girl's movements closely.

"Hey." I snapped my fingers in front of the clone's face. "Earth to Anastasia."

"Hmm? Oh, sorry. What was your question?"

"Jesus… What answers do you think I'll find at the lab?"

"For starters, Tommy's in over his head. He'd never admit it to you, but he got taken advantage of. They took his money and then excluded him from everything. That's how we got to the point of the clones being tortured for fun. He has less idea of what's going on over there than he lets on."

"Why didn't he go to the police if he thought they were doing something illegal?"

Anastasia blinked vacantly at me.

"Oh, right. He came to *me*."

"You're the only cop he trusts."

I felt like an ass going behind his back to speak with Anastasia.

"Where are they, exactly?" I asked. "I mean the headquarters—where is it?" I knew from Chris' news feature that it was on the southwest side of town, but there were a lot of neighborhoods and I was driving myself, so I needed to narrow it down.

"The headquarters is in Black Pearl, near the river. The cloning process requires a steady flow of energy into the growth vats. That's provided by hydroelectric generators on property."

"So, your recommendation is to go for the head of the beast and infiltrate the headquarters," I summarized. "What should I be looking for when I get there?"

"I don't know, Zach. Maybe you could start by getting evidence of them cloning influential people in the government."

"Sure. That's a given," I stated. "But first, I need a live clone that would be willing to undergo testing with a geneticist. I need to prove that the chemical dependency exists in clones, which would be a way to determine who is and who isn't a clone."

"And you want me to be your guinea pig?"

"You're the only clone I know," I replied without elaborating. "Unless I can capture the clone of Kelsey Bloomfield and somehow get her DNA tested. Of course, that's kidnapping and wouldn't fix my record if she pressed charges."

She shook her head slightly, eyeing the dancer as she shimmied up the pole. "I don't know. I took a big risk coming here. I'll have to think about it."

"What risk?"

"Tommy gives me an incredible amount of freedom. He treats me like a woman, not like a clone. If he knew I was going behind his back, all of that could change. Heck, if he wanted to, he could beat me or kill me and the law wouldn't care."

"That's because the mayor is behind all of this. He's the problem. We can work on getting the laws changed once he's behind bars."

"No," she shook her head again. "It's an issue with federal legislation. Louisiana isn't the only place with clones. Maybe the techniques that Biologiqué International uses are better than other places, but there are plenty of clones running around. This has to be a national discussion."

The dancer hooked her legs around the pole above us and turned upside down. Her breasts fell toward her face. The sight of them flopping side-to-side made me appreciate Teagan's small chest. Cassadie swung around, using the momentum to carry her down the pole slowly.

"It may be a national issue," I replied, returning to the conversation. "But it needs to start somewhere. Look, Anastasia, you don't have to do much besides go speak to the geneticist that the reporter, Chris Young, is working with. He'll draw your blood, take a few hairs, and maybe scrape off some dead skin cells. That's it. You could be in and out in ten minutes. Shit, you could do it on the way back to the Dockyards."

"I don't know," she replied.

"If you want things to get better for clones, for you to get actual rights and protection under the law, it has to start somewhere. Maybe the doctor won't even need to take blood if you're worried about Ladeaux finding out. I'm sure they could get the same results from a swab of the cells inside your mouth."

The club's neon lights reflected in her eyes as she thought about it. In my periphery, I could see the dancer once again on her knees, crawling toward the edge of the stage. Anastasia smiled and I felt the girl coming closer. The clone caressed the dancer's tits as they kissed deeply beside me until I began to feel awkward.

"Okay," Anastasia said when they broke apart. Her lipstick was smeared and she breathed heavy. "Give me the address. I'll go today, as soon as Cassadie and I finish in the Joy Room."

The song ended and I passed her a slip of paper that disappeared into a small clutch. Then, Anastasia helped the girl off the stage.

Cassadie patted my crotch as she walked by holding the clone's hand. "You sure you don't wanna come back too, baby? It'll be an hour you won't ever forget."

"I'm fine. Thank you."

"Suit yourself. I'll try to bring her back to you in one piece. No promises!"

I watched the two of them walk hand-in-hand to a closed door beside the bar. Cassadie typed in a code on the keypad set into the wall. The door opened and they disappeared inside.

I'd love to be a fly on the wall in that room.

# NINETEEN: SATURDAY

I left Whispers feeling hopeful that Anastasia would follow through with her commitment to visit Dr. Grubber so we could get at least one verified sample from a clone for comparison. If we could get that, and he could identify the chemical dependency at the cellular level, then we could develop a way of screening whether someone was human or a human clone.

The problem was that a type of test like that could also lead to further discrimination and subjugation of the clones without a change to the legislation. I wasn't sure if we wanted that type of knowledge to go public until they were protected in some fashion under the law. To do that, I needed to bust the mayor and get support from the state to recognize them as human. Well, *almost* human.

I believed that Anastasia was correct about the headquarters building. That was the ultimate goal. But I wasn't as convinced as she was that it should be my next move. I wanted to find as many of those missing clones as I could. I felt that finding them would help on several levels, not the least of which would be figuring out who the mayor and his cronies had tried to replace—or had already done so.

On the drive back to Teagan's apartment I decided to call Voodoo. Maybe he'd found out something since I talked to him yesterday and since my phone was off the network, he didn't have any way of contacting me.

"Marie Leveau Shipping Company. How may I direct your call?" Betty asked.

"Betty, its Zach Forrest. I need to talk to Mr. Ladeaux."

"Mr. Ladeaux has tried to reach you several times, Detective. Your phone appears to be offline."

"Yeah…"

"I'll transfer you now."

"Thanks." I breathed a sigh of relief that her software hadn't recognized my voice from the last time I called.

The phone clicked over and Voodoo answered.

"Forrest. Betty tells me you called earlier."

*Shit.*

"No," I lied. "I haven't called."

"You didn't call and try to play spy about three hours ago? Anastasia went to Whispers after you *didn't* call. She's still there, though."

"Hmm… Whispers, the strip club on The Lane?" I asked. I'd already started playing dumb, might as well carry it through to the end.

"Yes. *That* Whispers, Detective," Voodoo sighed. "I know you met with her. What did you discuss?"

"Ladeaux, I don't know what the fuck you're talking about. I was at the funeral for Officer Goldman this morning. I'm still soaking wet to prove it."

"I'd hoped we could be honest with one another," he stated. The distain in his voice was clear. "I suppose you want to know whether I have any leads on the location of the clones."

"Among other things. I've got some questions about Kelsey Bloomfield."

"Fine, but first, I want to know about my *missing* clones, or people. We won't know which until they're tested."

"Gotta start somewhere," I agreed.

"I don't know where they are at currently. However, I know where they'll be tomorrow night."

"Damn. I hoped we'd be able to get moving on this today."

"Believe me. If I knew where they were, I'd send you over there right now," Voodoo replied. "The longer those damn things are on the street, without protection, the worse off it is."

I thought about what Anastasia had said about him being taken advantage of. She was probably covering for Ladeaux somehow. I couldn't help but feel that he was more involved than they both let on, but I didn't have any proof of that. It was prejudice developed after a lifetime of being a cop.

"Where will they be tomorrow night?"

He gave me the address of a small theater out in Slidell. That was *way* outside of my nonexistent jurisdiction. My notebook was on the passenger seat and since I was driving, I didn't have many options to record the address, so I wrote it in the fog of the Jeep's windshield. Once it was safe to pull over, I stopped, put the car in park and grabbed my notebook to copy the address before it faded away.

"Alright, I'll check them out," I assured him. "Now, what about Kelsey?"

"What about her? Like I said, she's the COO of the company. I don't know her well enough to give you any pointers about her if you're looking to get lucky."

"Funny, Ladeaux. The mayor and his people ensured it would be a long time before she would be able to be with anyone intimately again."

"I'm sorry, you're right. My joke was in poor taste."

"Damn right it was," I agreed. "If she's the chief operating officer of the company, why was she cloned?"

"Hmm… Ahh, well. I'm not really sure. I—"

"Look, I know that you were marginalized in the company. I need you to get past that and tell me a few things if I'm going to be able to help you."

"How do you—Ana! That little bitch."

"She only told me in order to help you, Ladeaux. I'll do everything I can to get to the bottom of this, but *you* haven't been honest with me, either."

"What the hell did you want me to say?" Voodoo exploded. "That I let that piece of shit, Mayor Cantrell and his goons, steal my money and then take over the company? Is that what you wanted to hear, Forrest? That I can't manage my own fucking business affairs? Or that I should never have tried to get involved with such a political hot-button issue. Is that what you want?"

"Calm down," I hissed. "I wasn't meaning to get you worked up about this. I want to know why you cloned the person who was supposed to be running your company. It seems counterintuitive to me."

"I've been out of the company for months, Forrest," he admitted. "In fact, it was only a couple of weeks after the Sex Club Killer case when the mayor forced me out. He wanted to create a bunch of clones without the consent of the person they were cloning. I refused to go along with it and they pushed me out."

"And Kelsey was okay with doing that?"

"No, she wasn't. She came to me, asking what she should do. We thought it would ultimately prove to be little more than a passing interest of the mayor since the clones would only be replicas of the *body*, not the *person*. We agreed not to disclose the knowledge of how to map the human brain or the process to transfer the info into the new clone.

"Shortly after that, she called me and said they'd gotten to the chief scientist, who told them everything and showed them how to do it Within days, thugs began to show up with unconscious people and they scanned them without their knowledge. Kelsey is the one who gave me the info on the thirty-eight missing clones and then began trying to get me to pay her for more information.

"If I were to guess, I imagine Kelsey opposed them creating fully functional clones and they decided to get rid of her—or she knew too much. They probably cloned her to keep up appearances. I didn't even know that they'd cloned her until that news broadcast."

"Why would Anastasia tell me to go to the headquarters of Biologiqué International?"

"To put an end to the cloning. Until we can reign this in and get the laws established at the federal level to protect the clones, none of them are safe, so she wants the process to end until the laws are passed."

"Hmm…" It was in line with what I'd been thinking. What sense did it make to keep adding more problems to the mix? Make no mistake, every clone on the street right now was a problem.

"What ever happened to that clone you used as your delivery boy? You know, the blond guy who looked like Anastasia."

"Kaine. He had some…issues with the way the mayor handled his clones. Consequently, he was the first casualty in this war as he tried to fight for their rights. Somebody dismembered him and left him to die."

"Do you have any other soldiers in the front lines, Ladeaux?" I asked, thinking of the Paladin.

The tech in his suit alone would have cost several hundred thousand dollars—quite a bit for the average person. If Ladeaux wanted to stay on the top in Easytown, what better way was there than to finance a vigilante to eliminate his rivals?

"I have a lot of people who work for me, Forrest. I wouldn't consider any of them 'soldiers' though."

I nodded my head and then felt stupid since Voodoo couldn't see my movements. "I'm going to go out to Slidell tomorrow to find those clones to keep up my end of the bargain with regards to Amir Khalil and the Pharaoh's Tomb. Then I'm going to put that factory out of commission and find a way to clear my name in the murder of Karen Goldman."

"Godspeed, Forrest. I hope you're able to accomplish all of those things."

"Thanks. Oh, and Ladeaux?"

"Yes?"

"If you lay a finger on Anastasia out of anger because she helped me, then by God, you will regret it."

He chuckled. "You *really* don't understand me at all, do you, Forrest?"

The line clicked dead and I looked out the window, through the faded address of the place where the clones were going to be tomorrow. I wondered about Voodoo's statement. Of course I didn't understand him. Every time I talked to him, I had to drag information from the man because he kept it close to the vest. How could I get to know somebody like that? *Why* would I get to know somebody like that?

Three loud, metallic taps on my passenger side window made my heart jump into my throat. *The cops!*

I turned to see who it was. The Paladin stood outside my car... Again.

"How the fuck do you keep finding me?" I asked after I rolled the window down.

"I have my ways, Detective."

"What do you want?"

"I want in on the action in Slidell tomorrow."

"How do you— You know what? Never mind."

"You need backup and you don't have it right now. I'm your only option."

"Why?" I asked.

"I have my reasons."

I thought back to the night I'd almost arrested him. "That's right, you're looking for *something*. Isn't that right?"

He inclined his head, the dark suit almost hiding the movement. "I told you there was a war going on that you didn't know about."

*War.* There was that word again. Voodoo had used it only a few moments ago.

"Son of a bitch. You and Ladeaux *are* in on this together. I knew I couldn't trust that guy."

"I doubt Thomas Ladeaux cares enough about your actions to bother lying to you," the Paladin replied.

"You really know how to make a guy feel special, you know that?" I thought about it for a moment and then said, "Alright. I'll meet you at the building tomorrow at 2 p.m."

"Uh…"

"You're right. We'll meet a block south at two."

"I don't have a way to get to Slidell."

"What?"

"I don't have a vehicle," he coughed.

"Are you serious?"

"I haven't needed one. I can get almost anywhere in the city within fifteen minutes on my skiff."

*So that's how the fucker moved,* I thought. He was able to fly above traffic, which is probably how he tracked me. He simply shadowed me from above.

"The battery won't support a thirty mile sustained flight without a rest," he continued.

"Yeah, sure. You can ride with me tomorrow. Let's meet at one by the corner of—"

"I can meet you at your girlfriend's house."

"Teagan?"

"Yes, the cute African American girl you've stayed the past few nights with."

"Why the fuck are you following me?"

"Whether you want to admit it or not, we want the same thing, Detective. I can't put an end to the clone murders without help. I had to make sure that your desire to help us was altruistic."

"Us? You and Ladeaux?" I demanded.

"I'll see you at one tomorrow," he replied quickly. "I'll be in your Jeep."

He turned and disappeared quickly into the rain.

"What the fuck did he mean by 'us'?" I mumbled. I missed having Andi's analytical support for the investigation. Maybe transferring her AI into a droid wasn't a bad idea after all.

⚜ ∘ ⚜ ∘ ⚜

"Oh my gosh, Zach! I love it!" Teagan shouted from the seat beside me.

"Huh? What do you mean?"

"You know what I mean! This is the best Valentine's Day present I've *ever* gotten."

I glanced over at her. She held the diamond tennis bracelet that I'd purchased for Avery. I vaguely remembered throwing it on the Jeep's passenger side floorboard after I got stood up, and now she thought I'd purchased it for her.

"Uh… Happy Valentine's Day?"

She squealed and jumped over to hug me. The car lurched dangerously to the shoulder.

"Son of a bitch!" I cursed, struggling to keep control of the Jeep. Thankfully, we were only going thirty miles per hour on a side street and I was able to steer us back onto the road without going into the ditch.

"Oh, sorry. I forgot that you're driving manually."

"No. It's my fault. You've probably never even been in a car that wasn't automated. How would you know what would happen?"

She nodded, placing her hands across her lap. I smiled after a minute.

"You don't have to keep yourself completely still. You can move around."

"Are you sure?" she asked.

"Yeah. People used to drive themselves all the time."

She held up the bracelet again. "It's beautiful, Zach. Thank you so much."

"Ah… You're welcome. I'm glad you like it."

"How did you know that I've always wanted one? Did I tell you that a few years ago?"

"I—"

"Or did you ask Rebecca? Ooh, did she know about this and kept it a secret?"

"No, she—"

"Wait, you can't use your credit chip because the whole fugitive thing. How were you able to buy this?"

"I have contacts," I replied, which was true. I had tons of contacts, just nobody in the jewelry business—or at least not the legal jewelry business.

I risked a quick glance over at her. The smile on her face melted my old, cold heart. *My God, she's beautiful.*

"What is it?" I asked.

"Every time you leave the apartment, you risk getting arrested—or worse. Even though you've been out trying to solve the clone case and clear your name, you took the time to think of me. That means a lot, Zach."

*Well, shit,* I thought. *Should I tell her?* If Teagan ever found out that I'd actually bought the bracelet for Avery, she'd be devastated. It would be easier—not to mention smarter—to tell her the truth now and give her some empty promise that I'd make it up to her. It was the right thing to do. Lying to her would only come back to bite me in the ass later.

"Teagan, I think you should know…"

"Yes?" Her voice was full of expectation. I knew right then that she wanted me to tell her that I loved her too.

I also knew that I needed to burn the receipt for that bracelet.

"I want you to know that you are an incredibly special girl and mean so much to me. I don't want anything to happen to you."

She reached her hand across and gently massaged the back of my head through my hair. "Don't worry about me, Zach. I'll be fine. Nobody knows about me. You need to focus on getting out of trouble."

"Yeah…" I mumbled as I turned the Jeep into a parking lot for the park.

Her assertion that no one knew about her wasn't correct. The Paladin knew about her, which meant that Tommy

Voodoo probably knew about her, too. Those two seemed to share the same information, further strengthening my belief that they worked together somehow.

"Here, can you help me put it on?" Teagan asked, once again holding up the bracelet.

I put the car in park and twisted in my seat to clasp the bracelet on her wrist. She gripped the sides of my face and pulled me into a kiss.

"Thank you, Zach. It's beautiful."

"Not half as much as you are," I replied.

She pushed me back playfully. "Oh my God! That was so cheesy! You are such a goofball."

Her grin made me smile, covering my shock. I thought I'd given her a nice compliment and she threw it back at me. I *really* sucked at this dating thing.

"Come on. I'm hungry," she said.

We made our way across the wet grass to a semi-secluded area and I set up Teagan's canopy while she laid out a waterproof blanket. In minutes, we had a nice little picnic set up underneath overhead cover.

We ate a light snack of olives, cheese, crackers and wine, all from the Pharaoh. It was perfect.

"Okay, maybe I was wrong," I began.

"About what?" Teagan asked, leaning back on her elbows.

"Maybe I do like picnics."

She laughed. "See, I told you. Maybe you hadn't been with the right person before."

I wanted to say something about her being the right person, but held off since that sounded lame—even to me. I settled instead for nodding my chin and smiling.

"This is perfect," Teagan continued. "The sound of the rain on the canopy, the food, the wine...you."

"Teagan, I—"

Her eyes went wide and she launched herself across the blanket, landing on top of me. She kissed me deeply, flattening her body along mine. She was insatiable, practically burying her face in mine.

"Good afternoon, miss," a male voice echoed across the grass, probably from the pathway.

Teagan slid her hand under my neck and pressed my face into her shoulder as she looked up. "Good afternoon, officer."

Through her hair, I could see a young cop on the path with his hand on his weapon.

"You two keep it clean, this is a family park."

"Of course. We're just kissing. There's nothing illegal about that, is there?"

"No, there's not. Don't let it go any farther than that. Have a good day."

"You too," I shouted into her shirt.

"Bye," Teagan added.

She watched the officer depart and then relaxed the pressure against my neck. "That was close."

I nodded, kissing her once again when she dropped her face to mine.

"The fairy tale is over," I stated when we separated. "We need to get back inside. I can't risk anyone discovering that we're together."

"That's fine by me," she answered. "My Valentine's Day isn't over, though."

"It isn't?"

"Not by a long shot."

"Teagan, I don't—"

"Shut up, Zach," she said as she covered my mouth with her hand. The bracelet sparkled in the light. "This is *my* Valentine's Day and we're going to do what I want."

"And what is it that you want?"

She smiled deviously. "I hope you ate enough. You're going to need your energy."

# TWENTY: SUNDAY

I'd done a fine job of ruining the "just friends" relationship that Teagan and I had. For months after I found out about her feelings for me, I'd been adamant that I wanted to keep her safe by keeping my distance from her. Now that had all changed.

"Good morning. You awake?" she asked as her finger twirled slowly in the hair on my chest.

"Yeah," I replied softly.

"How'd you sleep?"

"As good as can be expected." Teagan had a twin bed. It had been a tight squeeze, but more room than the recliner.

"You thinking about what we did?"

"Of course. I've known you for so long. To take that step, it's just..."

"Amazing?" she offered.

"I was thinking more along the lines of problematic."

She dropped her hand down flat on my chest and pushed herself up, giving me a full view down the length of her lithe, caramel body.

"What are you talking about, Zach?"

"We shouldn't have done that," I replied. "I feel like I took advantage of you."

"Don't you make this about you," Teagan scolded. "This is about both of us. I was a *willing* participant."

"You're still in school. You don't even know about the world yet and here I am, some creepy old dude inserting myself into your life."

"What? You—" She stopped and started laughing.

"What's so funny?"

"Your choice of words a second ago."

I tried to remember what I'd said. Something about me being creepy and old while she was inexperienced.

"Oh, *come on*, Zach! Ha! See, I just did it."

"What? Oh…"

She lay back down beside me and I jumped a little when her hand wrapped around my limp dick.

"You didn't take advantage of me, Zach. I've wanted you for a long time."

Her fingers tightened and she began to work new life into me. "I'm graduating in a few months and then I'll be your definition of an adult. Until then, you can be the creepy old guy and I'll be your little student."

"Dammit, Teagan. I'm serious."

"So am I," she replied, sliding toward the end of the bed.

I flexed my stomach and watched the top of her head for a moment before lying back to enjoy what she was doing.

She stopped and looked up at me. "See. Isn't this much nicer than talking about that other stuff? Let's just live in the moment."

I didn't get a chance to respond before she slid up to my chest and guided me inside her once more.

⚜ ○ ⚜ ○ ⚜

*Well, this is fucking awkward.*

I glanced over to the passenger seat where the Paladin sat, softly tapping his fingers on his knees. He was in his full armor, including the facemask, sitting there like it was perfectly normal as I drove across the lake toward Slidell.

In my mind, elevator music played, giving the entire situation a ridiculousness that I couldn't even begin to describe.

"Why are you wearing your mask?" I asked.

"Because I don't want people to know who I am."

"We're going into a potential firefight together, don't you think I should know who I'm going with? Like… Oh, I don't know. What's your name?"

"The vid feeds call me the Paladin. You know that, Forrest."

"Uh, alright. Why do you wear a mask?"

"Because I don't *want* people to know who I am," he repeated more forcefully.

"And the voice?"

"The same reason. If I didn't have my voice disguised, then I could be identified."

This was getting me nowhere so I stopped talking and concentrated on the road, trying to ignore the stares of the people who passed us.

"Jesus. Could you at least recline the seat or something?" I asked. "People are staring."

"Oh, right. Sorry."

He reclined the passenger seat slowly until he was almost horizontal. If it wasn't such an important and dangerous mission, I would have laughed at the absurdity of the situation.

I felt more apprehension about the place in Slidell than I had in Easytown. Maybe it was that I was totally outside of my jurisdiction—not that it mattered, since technically *everywhere* was outside of my jurisdiction now that I was suspended.

I think the real reason I was nervous was because the night I found Sadie I had a police drone as backup. I'd felt entirely safe with one of those things guarding the perimeter. No one could have snuck up on me from outside the warehouse. In Slidell, I didn't have that. Worse, I was going in with a man who'd I'd been actively hunting down a few days ago and I had no idea of his abilities, other than he had a penchant for beheading gangers and drug dealers.

"Oh, I almost forgot," the Paladin mumbled.

"What's that?"

"I almost forgot. Remember that I told you I had my ways of getting around the cameras in Easytown?"

"Yeah?"

"I found something for you." He pointed at the Jeep's computer system. "Mind if I?"

"No, go ahead. Just make sure you don't turn on the GPS or we'll light up like the Fourth of July on the police scanners."

"Sure. No problem."

He pulled a cable from the sleeve of his armor and plugged it into the dashboard. The car projected a holographic keyboard and he typed a few commands.

"You ready for this?"

"What am I supposed to see?"

"Just watch."

"I'm driving."

"Oh, right. Maybe you should pull off."

"Is it that important?"

"For you it is. This is the piece of evidence that will clear your name in that cop shooting."

I sped up to get off the bridge as soon as possible. Three minutes later, we made it off the bridge and I pulled off onto the shoulder.

"Okay, let's see it."

He pressed the playback button and the vid display on the dash began playing the footage from one of Easytown's security cameras. I recognized the background as a stretch of businesses along The Lane. People milled about in the background, huddling under umbrellas and awnings as they went about their business.

Then I ran into the shot. I was on my phone and my face was clearly visible under my hat. The video switched to a second camera as they tracked my movement along the sidewalk toward my Jeep. From the perspective of another camera, I extended my hand for some reason, possibly to adjust my sleeve to keep the rain from getting inside. I slowed to a walk and then punched the air. It must have been when I was on the phone with Brubaker and he told me that I was wanted on nonexistent charges.

Even better, the Paladin found the same images used in the video of Karen Goldman's shooting. When I extended my arm like that, they'd superimposed a pistol in my hand and fed that to the media.

"Good. We can take that and—"

"What do you take me for, Detective? I'm not some amateur. The show's only just begun."

"Huh?"

"Keep watching."

The video showed me walking off the screen and switched to another shot and then another as the camera's recorded my progress down Jubilee Lane. About halfway through the fifth video camera feed, I put my phone up to my ear, crammed my hat down further on my head and flipped up my coat collar as I passed Officer Goldman and then got in my Jeep. There was clear evidence that I passed her without shooting her.

"Here's the best part," my passenger stated.

The video showed me hitting the car in front of the Jeep and then backing into the one behind before finally pulling onto the street and driving away erratically.

Then the footage switched to Karen Goldman walking her beat, the area she was in strangely devoid of people. A large man, his face hidden from view, pulled out a pistol and shot her in the face. Then he disappeared down an alley.

"Notice the timestamp," the Paladin directed.

I watched as the video continued and yet another camera's footage flickered onto the screen as drones pushed the crowds of people away from a row of businesses. The timestamp showed it as happening two minutes prior to the video of Karen's death.

"What am I—" My voice caught in my throat when I saw what happened. "The drones are pushing the crowds back to clear the area of witnesses."

I squinted to see what their public message screen displayed, but I couldn't see.

"That's right," he nodded. "The police secured the crime scene *before* it happened. There were no witnesses to Officer Goldman's murder except for the security cameras."

It wasn't a smoking gun as far as who killed her, but it sure as hell showed that I *didn't* do it.

"Can you send this to Chris Young?"

"I'll do it right after we're done in Slidell."

I thought about the potential for the mission to go bad. I could get killed, never having cleared my name, or the Paladin could get killed, never having sent the videos. I didn't like it.

"I need you to send them now, please."

"Why the rush? If they air it, the vid feed won't start until eight. We've got time."

"No, I need this to get out as soon as possible. If something happens to either of us, the truth needs to be known."

"Then I don't have any leverage over you," he reminded me.

"*Leverage?* Is that what this is about? I didn't even know you had this footage and was still working with you."

"I—"

"*Please*," I said. 'You won't hear me say that often. That's how much this means to me."

He considered it for a moment before answering. "Alright. Do you have his contact info?"

I turned on my phone and found the reporter's personal and work emails.

"Here's where to send them to."

The Paladin typed the information quickly. "Hold on," I said. "Can you send it to this address as well?"

I typed in Teagan's name and then thought better of it. As it stood right now, there wasn't anything linking her with me in any way. I backspaced over her name and instead, typed Brubaker's. Then I showed it to the Paladin so he could email the files.

# TWENTY-ONE: SUNDAY

"What do you think we're going to find in there?"

"I don't know," I replied as I surveyed the two-story community theater building through a small pair of binoculars. "Hopefully, a lot of live clones."

"What if we don't?"

I sighed in frustration. Paladin had been asking the same type of "what if" questions since we arrived at the address that Tommy Voodoo gave me ten minutes ago. My answer was the same now as it was every other time before this.

"I don't know. We won't know until we get in there and see what we've got." I shifted to look at him, but his face was unreadable behind the mask. "Are you nervous?"

"My armor will keep me safe, but I don't want to find a bunch of dead women. Not sure I can handle it."

"Then why'd you come?"

"Because you needed backup."

"No, I didn't," I countered. "I'm glad you're here, but I don't *need* your help."

He was silent, so I thought about the way my words must have come across. I didn't know the guy, so I had no way of telling how he'd interpret my statement. "You can stay here if you'd prefer," I backpedaled slightly. "It's always good to have a lookout watching over your shoulder."

"No. I'm going in with you. I can do things that you can't."

"Like what?"

"See in the dark."

I pulled the aftermarket night vision goggles out of my bag. "I've got that covered."

"I have the ability to provide a smoke screen and the suit can produce both area lighting and strobe lighting. The strobes are set in intensity and frequency to cause nausea."

I knew about the smoke based on our previous run-in, but I didn't know about the other non-lethal defenses. I wondered what else he had up his sleeve.

"Alright, you're in. Stick close to me. We're leaving in a couple of minutes."

I turned down an alley to piss and double-check my weapons. The SIG Sauer .45 had a round in the chamber and another twelve in the magazine. I also had two more full magazines in my duster's pocket that I'd wrapped in paper towels to keep them from rattling against one another when we were trying to sneak around. I was good to go on conventional weaponry.

The Aegis was another story. I'd been out on Jubilee Lane when I learned that Mayor Cantrell was calling for my arrest on nonexistent charges. That was three and a half days ago. I hadn't thought to ask Sadie to grab the charger for it when she fled my apartment either. When I wrapped my palm around the pistol grip, the charge indicator came up as a yellow light. I had one, maybe two, shots left. *Better make them count.*

"You ready?" I asked, almost calling the Paladin a kid. In truth, I knew nothing about the guy. How old he was. Where he was from. What motivated him to stalk drug dealers and gangers in Easytown and murder them in cold blood. You know, the little things.

"Yeah. Let's do this."

It was three in the afternoon. The only concealment we had was the rain coming down in a fine mist. I would have preferred to go when it was dark, but I also wanted to get here before the gamblers showed up. That's all I needed was some rich guy's wife suing the police department because he got himself killed in the crossfire with a renegade cop.

We made our way down the street toward the target building. The only vehicle in the parking lot was a large box truck. No one had entered or left the theater while we watched. Voodoo thought the festivities were supposed to start once the afternoon football games ended. I had no idea what time the security and the torturers would show up.

Paladin jacked into the security system and disengaged the back door lock. It was much quieter than my plan to blast the locking mechanism.

We slipped inside to total darkness. I fumbled for my NVGs, pulling them out of the small case on my belt.

"It's clear back here," Paladin whispered before I could see.

I slipped the goggles over my eyes and turned them on. Green light illuminated everything. Freestanding racks of clothing held costumes of all shapes and sizes, boxes lined several rows of shelving along the wall and cleaning supplies occupied one corner, piled around a small washbasin set low to the floor. We were in a storeroom of some kind.

"You see a door?" I asked.

"Yeah, this way," he replied, leading me to a doorway on the far side of the shelving units. Paladin's night vision was obviously far better than what I had.

He eased the door open a crack. My goggles washed out in the sudden flare of light. I flipped them off and lifted them away from my face. A familiar aroma of antiseptic drifted in from beyond the door to tickle my nostrils.

"There's a camera in the hallway outside," Paladin stated, closing the door and once more plunging us into darkness. "Can you watch the door? I want to see if there's a camera here in the storeroom."

"Yeah. Hurry up, though."

I flipped my goggles back down. Once again, green light bathed the room.

Paladin moved out of my line of sight along the wall. I turned back to the door, taking a few steps back to give myself some distance.

Small scratching noises filled the space, followed by four small clicks. I didn't know what he was doing, but I imagined the clicks were wire cutters as he hacked into the security system again.

He reappeared quickly. "Alright, we're good. They had an almost obsolete hardwired security system. I followed their camera feeds around the building. There's a guard watching a holo-program near the front door. His back is to us. There's another on the second floor overlooking the cages on the far side of a stage. He's facing the doorway, so we'll have to be careful."

"Are the clones here?"

"Yes. I couldn't tell how many exactly, because they're huddled together for warmth. At least ten or fifteen."

*There's a big difference between ten and fifteen*, I thought. Instead, I chose to be grateful that we weren't bumbling around totally blind. "Thanks, that's a big help."

"I also turned off the alarm system and looped their video. Simple tricks that have been around forever."

"Alright, good job. You ready?"

"Yeah. Let's go."

We ducked through the door and the smell of antiseptic hit me once again. Paladin rushed forward down the hallway, he had the advantage of seeing the layout through the cameras that I didn't have. I tried to reach out to stop him, but he'd used the transition time that I needed between night vision and unassisted sight to separate us by a good thirty feet. What the fuck was he doing?

Two jagged blades shot out of Paladin's armor along his arm. I didn't have time to shout out a warning or stop him before he plunged both of them into the base of the guard's neck. He twisted his wrist savagely, severing the spine. The head flopped to the side, barely held on by the skin on either side of the blades.

I dashed forward and jammed my pistol into the joint between the Paladin's body armor and helmet.

"Don't move or I'll spread your brains across this fucking desk."

He raised his hands slowly, the guard's blood dripping down the twin blades.

"What are you doing, Detective?"

"What the fuck was that? You murdered that guy."

"He's one of the bad guys. We're the good guys. It's up to us to do whatever we can to stop them."

If there'd been any doubt about his mental state before this incident, it was gone now. He was a certifiable lunatic.

"We could have subdued him."

"And let him trigger an alarm? I don't think so. If you want to rescue those clones, we've got to be just as ruthless as these people."

I pulled the pistol away. "We rescue them and then we're done. You hear me?"

"That's what we came here to do, isn't it?"

"No, you stupid motherfucker," I shot back. "We'll get the clones out of here and then it's up to you to figure out how to get back to New Orleans."

"How?"

"Not my problem. I'm still a cop, asshole, and that was murder. I'll add another one to your list of crimes."

He didn't respond, so I gestured toward the stairs. A sign beside them indicated that they were the way to the theater. "Stay in front of me. I don't want you behind me."

"I'm not going to do anything to you." I couldn't believe how hurt his synthesized voice sounded, making me question how old he was once again.

"I didn't think you were going to try to cut off the guard's head without any idea if he was going to put up resistance," I retorted. "Stay in front of me."

"I'm wired into the building's network. I can cut the power once we're ready to go in. The guard will be blind."

"I like it. Do that."

I settled the NVGs over my eyes when we reached the top of the stairs. The Paladin counted down from three and then everything went dark.

For a few seconds, then red emergency lights came on and the security alarm began to blare.

"*What the hell!*" I shouted, pushing past my erstwhile partner. "Can you turn that off?"

"I'm trying. It's hardwired, like everything else in this place. It must have tripped when the power went out."

I shoved the door to the theater open and dove inside. My shoulder hit the rigid metal seat frame that held a plastic stadium seat. *Why couldn't I hit that?*

Below me, people were shouting in alarm from somewhere near the stage while others yelled for help. The clones in the cages were still alive for now, and I intended to keep it that way.

Three shots rang out in quick succession from below. I had no idea where the rounds went, so I crawled along on my belly behind the row of seats until I came to a break in the aisle.

"*Mike!*" the other guard shouted over the screams of men and women in the cages. "Mike, what's going on?"

Mike must have been the guard at the front desk.

"Mike's dead!" Paladin shouted from far to the left. I didn't know if he'd already worked his way around while I crawled slowly like the old fucker that I was or if he'd ducked back down the stairs to the lobby and come in a different way.

More gunfire answered him and I peeked down the aisle. The second guard crouched behind one of the cages. Any shots I took at him would probably have a better chance of killing the clones inside than hitting him.

The alarm was sure to bring the local cops or more of the facility's guards. We needed to end this quickly.

The Paladin stood and fired a smoke canister toward the stage. Several wild rounds answered the surprise move and the gunman shifted out of the smoke behind another set of clones, further obscuring him from the Paladin, but giving me a clean shot.

I lined up the Sig Sauer, aiming a little higher than I usually liked to in order to account for the drop of the bullet across the full length of the theater. And then I thought better of it. There was too much of a potential to miss—and the casings would tie me to being here. The Aegis' weak yellow power light stared back at me as I sighted in on the guard. I didn't need to adjust my aim point at all with the laser. I took a deep breath, exhaled and paused. Then I eased the trigger back.

There wasn't a visible light, no sound and no recoil from the Aegis to indicate that I'd fired the weapon. The only way I knew was the neat, cauterized hole in the side of the guard's head. He continued to crouch on the balls of his feet for a moment and then fell forward.

"He's down!" I shouted. "I need the lights back on and turn off that goddamned alarm!"

"Working on it," Paladin replied.

The lights came on and I took the steps two at a time until I stood on stage. There were five cages, all built of pencil-thick metal rods welded in a crosshatch. Each one had a lock on it. I didn't have time to waste.

"Where's the key?" I said loud enough for all of the clones to hear me.

"In his pocket," someone responded.

I dug through the guard's pocket. It was already wet where he'd pissed himself after death. Finally, my fingers wrapped around a set of keys and a rectangular object that turned out to be the key for the box truck out front.

*This just might work.*

"Everyone, calm down!" I said, patting my hands in the air like a football player trying to quieten the crowd.

It took a few seconds, but eventually the voices faded to a low murmur.

"My name is Detective Zach Forrest from the New Orleans Police Department. I need everyone to listen."

I paused for what seemed like the appropriate amount of time. Silence filled the theater as the Paladin got the alarms turned off.

"I'm here to rescue you, but I'm on my own—well, that guy in the black armor is with me too. We are not safe, we need to evacuate this building and get away before your captors come back."

"We're not safe?" a female's voice repeated my statement.

"No, we're not,' I answered. "I'm going to let you out. When I do, I need everyone to follow me to the white box truck in the parking lot. You'll have to get in the back and we'll get out of here."

I began unlocking cages and continued talking. "I know you're all naked. I can see that, but we don't have time to try and find clothes. You've got to ignore it for a while longer and trust me. Any questions?"

"Where's your backup?"

"We're on our own," I replied as I unlocked the last cage. "Come on, let's go!"

I ran up the stairs, not bothering to see if everyone followed. They could do what I told them or they could get left behind, it was that simple.

The truck was empty when we got there and people filed past me. I had to help a few of the older ones up into the cargo area, which was odd if they were clones. They should have been free of any ailments. I was already beginning to suspect that this was a crop of humans, not clones, and they'd already been replaced.

I grabbed one of them out of line and led her to the cab of the truck.

"I'll need you to open the back when you get to the medical center," I told her and then jogged back to the truck's open cargo door.

The Paladin walked out of the building slowly, which I took to mean everyone who was going to come out was already in the inside the truck's cargo area.

"When you get to the medical center, Dr. Grubber will meet you and do some bloodwork on you," I told the attentive crowd. "I'm sorry I can't tell you more right now, but I'll link up with you as soon as it's safe to do so."

I didn't wait for an answer before I jumped up and grabbed the nylon strap affixed to the bottom of the door. I pulled hard and it slid down, latching the door firmly as the people inside began to scream once more.

I dashed up to the cab and threw open the door as I tossed the keys inside. I crowded the woman out of the way, typing the address for Dr. Grubber's lab. Once the system recognized the location, I accepted the GPS coordinates and closed the door.

The truck rumbled off in the direction of the parking lot exit and I began running in the opposite direction toward the alley where I'd parked the Jeep.

The Paladin labored to keep up with my adrenaline-fueled sprint.

My foot crossed into the shadows of the alley and the sound of squealing tires echoed across the neighborhood as several cars full of replacements arrived at the theater.

I slid to a halt by my Jeep and jumped in.

"What about me?" the Paladin screeched.

I started the engine. "I told you that we were done, man. You need to find your own way back."

He slapped an open palm on the hood of my Jeep in frustration. "I can't get back to New Orleans."

"Not my problem. We accomplished our mission, but you're a fucking psychopath."

"Dammit, Detective. I—" He stopped, obviously realizing his situation wasn't going to improve.

"Can I borrow cab fare?" he asked dejectedly.

I dug into the center console and pulled out three crumpled twenty-dollar bills that hadn't found their way into Cassadie's G-string at Whispers the other day.

"Good luck," I said, dropping the bills out the window and shifting the Jeep into drive.

"Fuck you," he answered and scooped up the money before jogging toward the mouth of the alley.

I eased the Jeep past him and then into traffic just in time to see two ambulances, a fire truck and three black and whites roaring toward the theater in my rearview mirror.

# TWENTY-TWO: SUNDAY

"Oh my God, Zach!" Teagan shouted when I returned that evening, throwing herself into my arms. "Have you seen the news vids?"

"No. What happened?" With the car's navigation and autodrive disabled, I hadn't been able to watch any news vids while I drove, so I was clueless as to what she was referring to.

"Undoctored video feeds from the security cameras in Easytown were released. They showed that you *didn't* kill that cop. You've been cleared of all charges against you!"

"That's great news," I replied, hugging her tightly.

"There's more," Teagan said excitedly.

"What else?" I hoped the mayor was somehow implicated in the killing, but there hadn't been anything linking him to the incident in the video the Paladin showed me.

"I'm dead," Sadie replied morbidly from the kitchen.

"Excuse me?"

"Yeah, the news reported that Sadie, the clone who spoke out about the torture tourism and accused several politicians of being involved, was found dead in an alley this morning," Sadie stated. "They killed my clone in a further effort to discredit me. Now that we know I'm actually Kelsey and not a clone, if I go back to the news and say I was confused, it will bring into question everything about my memories and accusations."

"Shit," I cursed, relaxing my grip on Teagan's waist. "They're one step ahead of us—again."

"Did you find any of the missing clones out in Slidell?" Teagan asked.

"All of them," I beamed.

"*What?*"

"I found the remaining twenty-two people. We rescued them and then went out to see that geneticist. Care to venture a guess about what we found?"

"That none of them have the chemical dependency of a clone?" Sadie asked.

"Bingo—well, except one, she really was a clone." I sat down on the edge of the recliner. "It means that they are the original people, not clones, and this is now a massive kidnapping case. None of them can remember anything about who they are, much like you, and all of them have had their fingerprints melted away, just like you.

"Dr. Grubber is working to identify them based on their DNA," I continued. "If I'm really back on the police force, I can give him access to the police DNA database and we'll know pretty quickly who they are."

"What do you mean *if* you're back on the force?" Teagan asked.

"I don't think Councilman Jefferson and Mayor Cantrell are going to roll over that easily. Just because I'm not charged with Karen Goldman's murder doesn't mean that I've got my badge back or that they're not plotting something else against me."

"That's bullshit."

"It is what it is," I replied, meaning I couldn't change the reality of the situation.

"So what's next then?" Sadie asked.

"I need to call Tommy Voodoo and let him know that I found all twenty-two of his missing *specimens*. Then I want to take a long, hot shower followed by some food—maybe some Mexican delivery."

"How can you think of eating at a time like this?"

"We're still in the middle of the ball game. If I don't recharge the batteries and replenish my energy, I won't make it to the fourth quarter."

"I'm ready to go do something, help out somehow," Sadie replied.

"They've already murdered your clone," Teagan reminded her. "If you showed up on the scene, there's not much stopping them from going after you too."

"Teagan's right. We've come too far to get antsy when we're nearing the end."

"I know. I'm just ready. I can feel myself beginning to slip away."

"Do you want me to put you in contact with Dr. Jones? She can talk to you over the throwaway phone as long as you promise not to tell her where we are."

"I think I'd like that."

"We can set it up tomorrow morning. I'm sure she'd be interested to talk to you and hear what you've been doing while the rest of the world thinks you're dead."

I stood up and fished the phone out of my pocket. "I'm going to call Voodoo right now and see what he has to say about all of these 'clones' turning out to be humans."

Teagan's balcony was small, but secluded and sufficiently sheltered from the rain. I stepped outside and closed the door to gain a small bit of privacy, then dialed the number to the shipping company.

"Marie Leveau Shipping Company," Betty answered on the first ring.

"Good evening, Betty. It's Jack Arnold. Is Mr. Ladeaux available to speak?" I was positive that they'd be listening in on all of Tommy Voodoo's lines since Brubaker knew I was working with him on the clone case. It was better to keep the ruse going.

"Mr. Ladeaux does not know anyone named Jack Arnold and is not in the habit of entertaining opportunistic phone calls."

"Is Anastasia there, Betty? She'll remember who I am."

"Yes, she is here. Do you wish to speak to her, Mr. Arnold?"

"Please," I replied.

The phone line clicked over as the droid put me on hold, then it activated once more. "Mr. Arnold. Nice to hear from you again," Anastasia replied.

"Likewise. So I finished my end of that deal that Mr. Ladeaux and I worked up. I found all of his missing product. They were all intact, too."

"You found *all* twenty-two of them?"

"Yes—and they're all alive. Can I talk to Ladeaux?"

"Of course!" The excitement in her voice was evident. "I'll transfer you now. Thank you, Detective Forrest! You're amazing!"

So much for the alias. I wondered if she'd still think I was as good when she discovered that I hadn't rescued any of her clone brothers and sisters. Instead, those clones were probably in the community, living as the people they were modeled after. It probably wouldn't go well for clone rights when that little fact came to light. In fact, it would probably set efforts back by several years.

"Detective," Voodoo answered after a few seconds. "Anastasia tells me that you have good news."

"Yes and no. You've got some more explaining to do, Ladeaux."

"I'm afraid I don't understand."

"Of the twenty-two people I rescued from that theater today, only one of them was a clone."

"Come, now, Forrest. It's impossible to tell a clone from a human without serious, intensive DNA testing. You know that."

"I had the tests done. Only one of them had the chemical dependency that clones exhibit."

"What? That's impossible."

"And none of them could remember who they were, where they worked or if they had a family. Isn't that strange?"

"They probably had a memory wipe. That's easy to do."

"Who's researching how to do that shit?" I asked.

"Biologiqué had a defense contract to test the feasibility of the effort, turns out with a few chemicals, some targeted radiation bursts and you've got a walking, talking, *functioning* person who'll believe anything you tell them."

I stared out into the light rain while he blathered about the practical applications of the science and probabilities of an accidental lobotomy out of a given sample size. The blinking aviation safety lights of several police drones took shape off to the southeast, in the direction of Easytown. As I looked at them, I realized that the red lights were all on the right and the greens were on the left. Remembering back to my fishing trip with Amir, the old boat captain we'd hired explained to me that the lights on the port side of all boats—and aircraft—were red and the green ones were on the starboard.

Which meant the drones were coming this way.

"*Shit.* I've gotta go. Drones are inbound to my location."

"Detective, I haven't had the oppor—"

I clicked the phone off and dashed inside. The drones were still a mile away or more. I couldn't remember how close they needed to be to use their intersecting signal scans to accurately determine where a target hid. I didn't plan on sticking around to find out.

"Everyone, get in the Jeep. Now!" I shouted, startling the two women in the living room.

"What's going on, Zach?"

"Just go, Teagan!"

I pulled her gently to her feet and noted with satisfaction that Sadie was already moving.

"Is Rebecca in her room?"

"No. She's... She's at class," Teagan stammered. "Zach, what's happening?"

"Get to the Jeep."

I made sure to grab Teagan's keys off the counter and lock her door. If they sent black and whites, an unlocked front door was an invitation for further investigation. At a minimum, they could charge Teagan and Rebecca with interfering with a police investigation, possibly even aiding and abetting a fugitive if they found any of my DNA in the place.

The girls dashed through the rain to the upper parking lot where I'd been parking the Jeep and waited as I unlocked the door. I jumped in the driver's seat and made sure the headlight button was turned off before starting the car.

I couldn't see the drone lights anymore and I wondered if I'd been overreacting to a few lights in the sky. I decided to follow my gut and backed out of the spot, then put the car in drive and turned on the lights.

Behind us, the telltale *brrrt brrrt brrrrrrt* sound of the drones' miniguns told me that I hadn't been paranoid.

"Oh my God! My apartment!"

"I can't see. What is it?" I asked, pulling smoothly out into traffic on the first road leading away from the complex.

"They destroyed her house," Sadie stated. "One minute, everything was fine the next minute holes started appearing through the *front* of the apartment."

If that many rounds were making it all the way through the apartment, then they'd used a lot of rounds. They weren't trying to take prisoners. I'd hit them hard with the rescue of all those people and they weren't going to pull any punches.

I considered using the throwaway phone to call Amir and warn him, but decided against it. I'd only gotten about three minutes after Anastasia identified who I was before the drones arrived. Now that they had the IP for the phone, it was basically useless. Next time I turned it on, they'd zero in on me once more.

Time for a new phone.

"I'm sorry, Teagan," I finally remembered to say.

"What am I supposed to do, Zach? They'll probably suspend my classes and accuse me of murder like they did you—" Her hand flew up to her mouth. "Oh my gosh. My mom is going to *kill* me!"

"Let's take it one day at a time. First, we need to find a safe place to stay for the night. Tomorrow night, I'm going to the clone factory to investigate. I'm going to get to this fucker. I promise."

"Where are we going?" Sadie asked from directly behind me.

"We're going to disappear in Easytown."

"Are you sure?" the older woman pressed. "There are so many cameras down there, they'll see us and then kill us like they did that female cop."

"That's just along Jubilee Lane. There's a whole lot of Easytown that people don't know about."

We drove in silence for a while until we reached the edge of Easytown. Teagan's hand tightened on my leg as we passed the first sex club.

"Nervous?" I asked.

She nodded. "I've never actually been in Easytown before. It's too dangerous for a woman."

I snorted. "It's got nothing to do with your sex. This place is just as deadly for a male—if you don't know what you're doing. You're in luck though, because I know what I'm doing."

I was being cocky. That sort of attitude was what got you killed in Easytown as a cop. I needed to reign it back in. I wasn't down here alone, I had two women that I cared for who were depending on me to keep them safe in the armpit of humanity.

The Jeep's tires bounced over ruts in the hastily-laid asphalt as I turned off The Lane down a side street. The denizens of Easytown, the ones who didn't typically venture to the main thoroughfare except to rob the tourists, watched us from dirty, cracked windows or popped their heads out of wherever they'd lain for the night.

The girls were getting nervous with the attention that the Jeep brought.

"It's okay," I stated. "I'll pay a guy at the motel to watch the car. We should be fine."

"*Should be?*" Teagan repeated. "Five minutes ago, you said you knew what you were doing. I've got my purse; we could get some cash here in Easytown, then go to a nicer part of town, or even the next town over. We really don't need to be down here."

I dropped my hand to hers, which was still on my leg, and massaged it gently. "It's okay. This is our best bet to stay undetected now that they know about you... Ah, there he is."

"Who?" Sadie asked.

"Tyrone. It's cool. Just sit back and don't say a damn thing."

I unholstered my Sig Sauer and placed it on my lap, barrel facing out and pulled up to the man I'd indicated, rolling the window down.

"Zach, my man. What can I do for you—and your ladies—tonight?" the fence asked.

"I need another throwaway. The cops tracked the last one."

He held up his hands and said, "Hey man, that ain't my fault! When I sold you that, it was off the registers."

"I know. They tracked it." Tyrone didn't need to know anything beyond his small part. "They tracked the phone after a couple of days of use. I need a new one."

He eyed the ladies in the car. "Sure, I can give you one. Give me ten minutes with one of your girls and it's on me."

"I'm not some goddamned pimp, Tyrone. These ladies aren't for sale. I need another phone."

"You got the old one?"

I reached over to the console and searched for the old throwaway without taking my eyes off Tyrone. I needed his assistance, but I didn't trust him—especially now that he'd shown interest in the women.

Teagan leaned forward and pushed the phone under my searching fingers. I passed it to him.

He reached into his pocket and I picked the pistol up, jamming it through the open window.

"Whoa, man!" he shouted, pulling his hand from his pocket and putting it up in the air with his other one. "See, it's just a screwdriver."

He held a small flat-tipped screwdriver between the fingers of the hand he'd slipped into his pocket. I relaxed and pulled the Sig Sauer back inside the Jeep.

"Jumpy fucker, aren't you?" Tyrone mumbled as he popped the back of the phone off with the screwdriver and then pried out the integrated communications chip. I watched as he dropped it to the pavement and ground it under his boot.

"There, now that one's gone. Time for a new one."

"What's your price this time?" I asked.

His eyes wandered over to Teagan, visually undressing her. "You sure neither of these ladies are for sale? You don't need both."

"Back off. They're *mine*."

"What the fuck?" Sadie objected from the back seat. I held up my hand to silence her. I knew she didn't like being described that way, but it was the only way to get Tyrone to drop it. On the streets of Easytown, friends, girlfriends, even wives were easily traded for favors and drugs. I needed to get the point across to him that the women were not part of the equation.

"Alright, man. I'm just making sure. A man could use a fine lady like that down here."

"I'm sure you would use them," I replied coldly. "How much for a new chip?"

"A thousand."

"You charged me three hundred for the old chip *and* a phone."

"Inflation, Zach. You're a hot commodity right now. If I was a less-loyal friend, then I'd turn you in for the two hundred and fifty thousand going around the streets right now."

"That's all I'm worth?" I laughed. Chris' sources had been right. I couldn't stay in Easytown now that I knew everybody was in on it.

"Apparently," Tyrone answered, his eyes narrowing. "And that redhead in the back seat is worth five hundred—"

I slammed the Jeep into drive and shot forward. "Get down!" I shouted.

Chunks of concrete flew off the buildings on either side as my *friend* Tyrone fired at us. I took the first turn and sped down an even shittier street than the one we'd been on before.

"I thought you knew what you were doing," Sadie shouted from the floorboard.

"I do. That's why we got the hell out of there."

Several men ran into the street, leveling weapons at us. I knew that asshole did something inside his pocket besides just getting the screwdriver.

The men blocking our way expected the Jeep to stop, like all autodrive cars did when there was an obstacle in the way. Too bad for them, I'd turned off the nav system to avoid detection from the police. I gunned the engine. Picking up speed, the Jeep plowed into the men, knocking them over like bowling pins. I grimaced and held on tightly to the steering wheel as the Jeep's passenger side tires chewed through one of them and threw us around the interior.

The car fishtailed and threatened to overturn, but held on somehow. I caught a glimpse of a hulking beast coming out of the alley that startled me. A man, easily close to seven feet tall, wearing mismatched armor of some type stomped forward. I could hear the *clump* of his feet with each step through the Jeep's windows. Arcing electrical wires, some of them emitting sparks from their ends, sprouted from his head and fell around his face.

I realized this was the same creature that the tweaker thought was the octopus god-thing. A goddamned cyborg.

It raised an arm and I jammed the gas pedal to the floor. Several thin, half-inch long holes appeared in the windshield and one of the disk projectiles embedded into the dash. I heard the high-pitched reports from the weapon and the sound of an air compressor refilling a tank.

Then we were running free to the next intersection. I took the turn and made it back to Jubilee Lane and jerked the steering wheel hard to take the ramp to the highway.

"At least we know for sure that there's a price on our heads now," I muttered, slowing the Jeep to the pace of all the other cars.

"What was that thing?" Teagan asked, running her fingers lightly over the holes in the windshield.

The places where the disks went through the glass were clean, not the typical messy spider-webbing that a bullet would produce. It reminded me of a hot knife sliding through butter.

"It was a cyborg," I responded, gripping the steering wheel tightly. "And it's not our problem right now. We need to get someplace safe before we can begin worrying about that."

"Where are we going?" Sadie asked.

"We need gas and then I've got an idea of a place to go. It's over in Slidell…" I trailed off.

"Slidell? Who do you know out in Slidell?" Teagan asked.

"Avery."

"Are you shitting me? That cop you were dating who threw you to the curb because she couldn't handle your personality quirks?"

"Yeah," I acknowledged. "She's a good person, Teagan, regardless of our past. She wouldn't allow herself to get caught up in all the political bullshit and corruption going around."

"Will she let us stay there?" Sadie asked. "Your last suggestion for help didn't turn out so well."

"*That's* the better question," I muttered, ignoring the jab she'd thrown at me.

# TWENTY-THREE: MONDAY

I made the familiar trek down Avery's brick walkway, stepping around the loose paver that had conspired with my drunkenness to make that night a complete disaster. I grimaced as I remembered broken pieces of the event. It seemed like so long ago, but in reality, it'd only been a week and a half.

*Time flies when you're having fun*, I mused.

It was late—once again. I was sure that the time of day would piss her off, probably even more than me asking for help. I reached out to ring the doorbell and paused. The plastic button felt rough under my finger, like it was purposely designed to be unwelcoming.

We'd parted on such bad terms. As I stood there with my finger on the button, I no longer thought this was as good an idea as it had seemed back in New Orleans. Actually, it had seemed like a terrible idea there, too. One born of desperation.

Avery was a state cop. Was I putting us at risk by going to her house?

A small, brown finger settled over mine and pushed down, ringing the doorbell. Teagan smiled back at me.

"We're not going to do anything except raise suspicions standing out here in the dark."

"You're right," I replied. "I was just thinking that maybe this wasn't the best idea."

"I know you were. That's why I took the decision away from you."

"That's not really you're place—"

"Don't start, Zach. I may be all twisted up inside about you, but I'm still a smart and independent woman. You don't get to tell me where my place is when it comes to saving my own life."

I liked the fiery attitude. It was just one of the many things I admired about her.

"You're right. Sorry."

"Yeah, what do—" the intercom crackled. "Dammit, Zach. What are you doing here? I'm calling the local police department."

"Wait!" Teagan answered, pushing me aside. "We're in trouble and we need your help."

"Who are you?" Avery asked. "Hold on. Have the redhead come closer to the camera."

Sadie stepped up onto the townhome's small porch and smiled. "Uh, hello," she said with a little wave.

"You're the clone that they found dead yesterday," Avery accused.

"Guilty—sort of. I *am* the person who gave the interview to the television station, but I'm not the one that the mayor had killed."

"What? Oh, hold on."

Avery's voice retreated from the microphone and after a few seconds, we heard the chain fall away from the door, then the deadbolt twist open. The door swung inward and my former lover stood there in pajama pants and a tank top that did nothing to hide her assets as her arms pressed them together.

My eyes were immediately drawn away from her ample breasts to the pistol she held clasped in both hands near her navel.

"Whoa, Avery!" I said, raising my hands above my head. "We're not here to start any trouble."

"You're not? Is that the same thing you said to that poor woman right before you shot her in the head?"

"He didn't do it," Teagan cut in, stepping close to me. "They released vid evidence today showing that the original feed was doctored."

Avery shifted one foot backward, keeping her body squared up toward us as she assessed the situation.

"I didn't see that," she admitted. Her eyes narrowed. "Who are you, anyways?"

"Oh, sorry. I'm Teagan Thibodeaux. This is Kelsey Bloomfield." She paused after using Sadie's real name and then lowered her hands slightly. "You can keep us under guard, I don't care—but we need to get off this porch before Mayor Cantrell's goons see us."

"What's the Mayor of New Orleans got to do with a fugitive cop and two women ringing my doorbell in the middle of the night?"

"Can we please come inside, Avery?" I pleaded. "We'll tell you our story and you can decide if you want to help us."

I could see that she was considering it. "Give me your weapons, Zach."

"Avery, I'm not—"

"Then go someplace else."

I frowned. This wasn't going like I thought it would. I thought that once Avery saw Sadie alive, it would have changed things, but she hadn't seen the report exonerating me from Sandra's murder so she wasn't open to helping.

"Zach, please." Teagan said. "You know the longer we stay out here, the more likely somebody will see us. The vid of the undoctored footage didn't get nearly as much airtime as the original cop killer vid. There are probably a lot of people who haven't seen it and still think you killed that woman."

All it took was one call to the police with my name attached to it and Cantrell's computer programs would pick it up. He'd have people here within an hour.

"Fine," I relented. "Here's my pistol."

I pulled the Sig Sauer from its shoulder holster, careful to keep my fingers away from the grip. Once it cleared the leather, I grasped the barrel with my opposite hand and passed it over to Avery.

"The laser pistol too," she directed.

I lifted my suit jacket to expose my belt line and spun slowly, showing her that the paddle holster wasn't on my hip.

"It's out of juice, so I left it in the car."

"Lift up your pant legs too, Zach."

I complied. "I don't use an ankle holster, you know that."

"I also didn't think you made a habit of getting yourself in *this* much shit." She looked over at the women. "You two have anything?"

"Nope, I don't have a weapon," Sadie replied.

"Nothing," Teagan affirmed.

"Alright, you three. Come inside, sit on the couch and don't make any sudden movements."

We followed her directions and filed dutifully into the townhouse. Once we were all lined up on the couch, Avery sat across from us.

"Okay," she said. "Tell me what's really going on."

I brushed my teeth with my finger. Avery had graciously allowed us to stay the night once we told her the entire story. She even let me have my gun back.

A soft knock on the bathroom door made me turn slightly. "Come in," I said, expecting it to be Teagan.

I was surprised when my host slipped through the door.

"I... Uh, I didn't expect to see you again tonight," I stammered.

"It's okay. You're safe," she assuaged my doubt. "I'm not coming in here to try to seduce you or whatever stupid fantasy you have going on in your head right now."

"That's not what I was thinking."

"*Mmm hmm...*" she demurred, sitting on the toilet lid as I rinsed my mouth out. "What's with you and the girl?"

"Teagan?"

"Yeah. The way she's guarding you is cute."

"Guarding me? I don't know what you mean."

"That girl has got you marked as hers and isn't afraid to let anyone know it. And a few of the glances I saw you give her makes me think that you two are a thing—much more than you led me to believe when we were seeing each other. How long have you two been together?"

"You mean, were Teagan and I together when you and I were… Well, when we were doing whatever we were doing?"

"Casual sex," she clarified.

"I thought it was a lot more than that."

"You thought wrong."

"No. Teagan and I were just friends until a couple of days ago."

"Alright," she said, straightening her back and cupping her breasts. "I thought maybe the girls had lost some of their power over the years."

"Haha, funny," I replied, without laughing.

"We had a good time together, Zach, but we both know that it wasn't going anywhere. I couldn't handle your constant bullshit. Take this case for instance. You're a fugitive from the law one day, exonerated the next, but now you have a two hundred and fifty thousand dollar price on your head. That's *way* too much for me to handle."

"I guess you're right."

"Teagan seems like a nice kid. But at the end of the day, she's still a kid. You can't treat her the way you treat everyone in your life. If you do, you'll ruin her."

"I—"

"Zach, it's me. We know each other, *intimately*. I know it's only a matter of time before you fuck up, whether it's with alcohol or with pissing off the wrong ganger. Hell, her apartment's already been destroyed and you've only been dating for a couple of days."

"That wasn't my fault."

"It never is," Avery sighed. "I know you don't mean for things to happen, but they do. Trouble seems to follow you around. Think about that before this girl becomes head over heels for you and you break her heart—or she gets killed because of you."

She didn't wait for me to rebuff her statement. Instead, she stood and kissed me lightly on the cheek. "Good night, Zach. I need you out of my life after tomorrow."

I watched her back in the mirror as she slipped though the crack in the bathroom door.

"What was that about?" I asked my reflection.

I knew what she meant, though. I was bad news. It was only a matter of time before Teagan got hurt—or worse. Why did I let our relationship move past friendship?

*Because I'm a stupid motherfucker. That's why.*

# TWENTY-FOUR: MONDAY

I crept along the wall of the Biologiqué International headquarters building. I didn't see any cameras, but that didn't mean I wasn't being watched. The advances in site security were phenomenal these days; I could be staring directly at a camera and not even know it. Most of the visible cameras were for show anyways; professionals used nanofiber cameras that were about the size of fishing line.

Avery's strange late-night visit in the bathroom last night had really messed with my head. I tried to determine her purpose all day, but I'd come up with a goose egg. The best I could figure out, she wanted to remind me that I was an asshole and that being around me was dangerous. *Thanks, Captain Obvious.*

Even though she'd told us to leave her home, she did us a favor by renting a hotel room for the week under her name. It saved any of us the problem of trying to book a room and getting recognized by someone at the hotel.

She'd also given me four more magazines for my pistol and a box of bullets, bringing my total load to eighty-four rounds in seven magazines, plus one in the chamber and an extra bullet jangling loosely in my pocket. I hoped I wouldn't need them, but my gut told me I'd need every round.

My hand trailed lightly along the wall. I wanted to keep as close to the structure as I could without exposing myself too much in the alley. It was a fool's hope to think I hadn't been spotted yet.

"Good evening, Detective," a hushed voice came from the darkness a few feet in front of me.

I reacted by kicking outward into the darkest part of the shadows and was rewarded with my foot impacting into something slightly softer than the brick wall.

"*Oof!*" the synthesized voice responded.

I pressed forward quickly, wrapping my arms around the attacker's neck, positioning myself behind him for a chokehold.

"*Hey! What the fuck!*" the man screeched in a harsh whisper. "*It's me, Paladin!*"

I realized that my "attacker" wore a type of flexible black armor and a helmet with a visor that covered his face. My grip relaxed, allowing the oxygen to flow, but I didn't completely relinquish the hold so if he didn't prove to be the Paladin, I could reestablish control.

"What are you doing here?" I hissed.

"I knew you were planning to come here, remember?"

"Didn't I tell you yesterday that we were through?"

"Yeah, you did. This isn't about me and you, Detective. This is about shutting down the illegal activity in the cloning facility."

I released him completely. I didn't have to like his methods, but having someone here to assist in the search would be helpful.

"Fine," I relented. "We need to get in there and figure out what's going on *before* we kill anyone. The first priority is to get information about the mayor's involvement and how many people have been replaced by clones in the government."

"You got it. No killing—unless we have to."

I couldn't ask for anything else from him, so I beckoned over my shoulder, leading the way to the back of the building. We traveled for at least four hundred feet before we came to a door. The building was huge. There were four floors above ground; no telling how many they sunk into the swampy ground below.

"Hey, why aren't we going in this door?" Paladin asked as we passed by it.

"Too obvious. We're gonna find a window."

"What if we don't?"

I sighed. Shit like this is why I liked to work alone or with Drake, who thought the same way that I did.

"If we can't find a suitable window, then we'll come back to the door."

He nodded and continued to follow me. I began leading the way once more until I saw what I wanted. Four large dumpsters and a biohazard container sat close together underneath a large window.

"This is where we're going in," I said, bringing the Paladin to a halt.

I reached for the window and my *partner* grabbed my hand. I looked at him questioningly.

"Let me check it first."

"You didn't do that good of a job disabling the last alarm," I reminded him. "What makes you think you'd be any better here?"

"Let me just try," he groaned.

I stepped back and he clamored on top of the trash can. Some type of rod extended automatically from the end of his arm, close to where the blades had emerged when he murdered the guard in Slidell.

Paladin waved the rod slowly over the entire window, paying special attention along the seams where the window would open. When he was finished, he nodded and put the probe away. Then, he dug in the pouch on his belt for a moment until he came out with a small suction cup and a glass cutter.

Within a minute, he'd cut out two small holes in the glass, about where you'd expect the latches to be. Then he climbed down and leaned close to me.

"I can't fit my arm through the holes because my suit is too bulky. You're gonna have to unlatch the window."

"Sure," I answered, pulling my upper body over the lip of the garbage can and then pressing down until I could get a leg up onto the container. The Paladin's plan was already better than mine; I'd planned to break out the glass and deal with the consequences that the noise made.

I squatted and reached through the first hole, then angled my arm up to search the top of the window for the latch. I patted around for a moment and didn't find anything.

I was starting to get frustrated when I noticed the latch at the *bottom* of the window, along the sill, in the center. I tried to reach it through the same hole my arm was stuck through, but I couldn't. I pulled out and hopped down.

"The latch is at the bottom in the center," I told Paladin.

He chuckled and climbed back up, cut the hole and hopped back down. When he hit the ground, I saw his ankle twist and he flailed backward, threatening to fall into the side of the metal biohazard garbage bin.

I grabbed his suit's breastplate in time to avoid what would certainly have been a loud crash if the bin overturned.

"Thanks," he breathed out heavily.

"Be careful. You could have alerted everyone in the facility."

For the hundredth time, I wished for the police drone backup. It could have scanned the building and told me exactly how many people were inside, where they were and whether they had any type of blaster—they couldn't detect standard, mechanical firearms, but blasters lit up like a Roman candle.

"Sorry," he replied.

I didn't answer and went back up onto the garbage can. The window swung open from a hinge at the top. I peeked over the ledge, the floor was a good six feet below, but there didn't seem to be anything underneath that would trip me up if I went through the window here.

I went through feet first and then turned over to my stomach, sliding down slowly. When I hit the floor, I pulled out my pistol, turning rapidly to scan the room.

Above me, the sounds of Paladin squeezing his way past between the glass of the window and the metal on the windowsill echoed across the room we'd broken into. I moved out of his way and he fell heavily onto the spot I'd vacated.

We were in a storage room. Boxes of medical equipment covered metal shelves along the walls, reminding me of the room with supplies at the warehouse where I'd found Sadie. Beyond the standard stuff, there were spare parts and containers that I had no clue what they were—likely medical supplies used in the production of clones.

"I can disable the security system at the access panel over there," Paladin said, pointing at a large plastic lockbox near four circuit breaker boxes.

"And then we'll need to clear any guards down here," I replied, hefting the police baton that Avery gave me before I left. It was her attempt to stop the tide of scattered bodies in my wake. There were two problems with the weapon though. First, I had to get within arms' distance to use it and second, I didn't like the idea of leaving guys behind me who weren't dead, but I had thirty heavy-duty zip ties to secure anyone we found. If we were going to make this a legitimate case against the mayor, we needed live witnesses who could testify in court.

Paladin went to work bypassing the security system, taking special care to avoid the same pitfall he'd hit at the theater when the hardwired alarm went off after a delay. It took him a few minutes until he said we were good to go.

"The main bank of offices is on the fourth floor."

"What makes you think that?" I asked, raising an eyebrow questioningly.

"I've been here before." He didn't elaborate, so I did.

"You've got to come clean with me. Why have you been here before? Who the hell are you?"

He stared at me for a moment as if he was thinking. Then, one of his hands drifted slowly over to the opposite arm. He typed a quick code and I heard a *click* from his helmet.

"Son of a bitch!" I muttered when he pushed the face shield up. I'd halfway been expecting that rookie cop Hannity to be behind the mask. Thankfully it wasn't the kid. Staring back at me was the clone who came to my apartment last fall and then gave me Paxton's memory chip later at the ceremony with the governor.

"Ladeaux's been playing me this entire time," I growled.

"I don't work for Ladeaux anymore," Kaine stated.

"Bullshit. That's how you've known where to find me. You knew about the theater because Tommy Fucking Voodoo fed it to you."

"I used to work for him as a tech supervisor in this facility before the mayor took over," the Paladin admitted. "After that, I began looking into the unauthorized cloning practices. I came back here to see if I could get any answers and got captured by some of the mayor's goons. When they found out I was a clone, they chopped me up and left me to die."

"You look fine to me."

"Emotional scars run deeper than physical ones. They cut off both my arms and my right leg at the knee. Then they slit my throat and left me to bleed out in an alley. I was probably the mayor's first foray into the torture business. A few weeks after my ordeal was when we first heard about the torture tourism ring."

"So…you didn't die and you don't seem to be missing any body parts."

"Ladeaux's people found me and he had a surgeon work with a prosthetist to patch me up."

"A prosthetist? You mean someone who makes prosthetic arms and legs?" I thought of the girl I'd stopped from making the biggest mistake of her life back on The Lane a few nights ago.

"The same—except I've got the athletic enhancements that some professional athletes get."

"Fuck," I muttered. "That must have been expensive."

"It cost me an arm and a leg." Kaine delivered the line perfectly.

Even though we were moments away from leaving the storeroom to continue the investigation, I had to ask a question. "So, how'd you end up hunting down the denizens of Easytown? Did Ladeaux send you out to eliminate his competition?"

"No. Mr. Ladeaux didn't know about it at first. I had enough of a supply of the serum to keep me alive for a few months. The doctor who'd operated on me was murdered by a tweaker who came into the hospital trying to get a fix."

"I think I remember that case," I stated. "It wasn't one of my cases, though. Didn't it happen at Saint Catherine Memorial in Little Woods?"

"Yeah. I was given a second chance at life and I promised myself that I would make the most of it and try to honor the doctor's memory. Since the doctor's murderer was already locked up, I decided to try to clean up the worst places in

New Orleans. That's how I ended up in Easytown. Ladeaux gets me the serum as long as I don't interfere with any of his people."

"*Hmpf*," I grunted. "I guess it makes sense. I don't have to like it, but now I understand your motivation for revenge a little more. Once we've finished here tonight and I return to the police force, I've still got to come after you. You know that, right?"

A look of surprise passed over his face before he hid it behind a stoic mask. "Why would you need to arrest me? I'm cleaning up the streets of New Orleans."

"It's the same thing I said the first time I met you, Kaine. You're *murdering* people in the streets. It doesn't matter if they're the bad guys or not; murder is murder."

I paused, waiting to see if he would reply. He chose not to say anything else, so I said, "For now, we can put that aside. We've got to stop whatever the mayor is doing out here. What else do you know about this place?"

He shrugged. "Basic stuff that you could have gotten off the web if you bothered to do any prep work. The second floor is clone education and storage, the third floor is where they grow the clones—that's where I got caught."

"I haven't exactly had access to the web or my phone, jackass," I countered, not allowing his little jab to go unremarked upon. "What's on the first floor? Do you know how many guards there are?"

"The first floor is mainly offices, client meeting rooms and supply storage. There's a security desk in the lobby, and just a few doors down the hallway is a security room with computer monitors and vid screens. That's where I used to work, so we'll have to take control of the security room before we can have a full run of the place."

We'd talked long enough. "Are you ready?" I asked.

"I've been waiting months for an opportunity to come back here," Kaine said as he secured his face shield and helmet back into place. "I'm ready."

I looked at my watch out of habit. It was time to put an end to this mess.

# TWENTY-FIVE: TUESDAY

We crept down the hallway toward the security room where the Paladin used to work. The building seemed quiet, like it should have been after normal business hours. Everything seemed exactly like it should have—which concerned me.

The mayor knew I was coming for him. He'd tried to frame me and failed. Then he tried putting a price on my head. So far, that had been a failure as well. Logically, it made sense that I'd go after him. *Unless he thinks I'm going to try to take him out at his house*, I thought.

I wished that I still had all of my usual resources at hand, but I still couldn't risk going in to the department. A drone over his house could have told me if he had more guards than normal. Communications with Andi would have allowed me to scan the email servers for any information. If the Jeep's nav system were enabled, I could have even sent it over there and gauged the reaction. As it was, I was blind, bumbling along like some detective in my grandfather's time.

Given my psychological profile, showing up to the mayor's house and trying to kill him made more sense than me sneaking around the cloning facility did. I was known as a hothead who dealt with issues head on. However, this case had never truly been about Mayor Cantrell—sure, he was a major part—but this case was about the clones. First, it was about getting to the bottom of the triple homicide that nobody wanted to touch, then stopping the torture tourism insanity and helping Sadie figure out who she was.

So, in reality, I *was* living up to my psych profile by going to the heart of the cloning problem. I couldn't help it if the mayor thought he was more important than I did.

The Paladin stopped in front of a closed door and gestured that he was going to go in.

I shook my head violently and pointed at him, then the floor. He shrugged and reached for the handle. *Maybe we should have worked out our communications signals beforehand.*

I grabbed his arm and pulled myself close to his helmet. "No killing!" I whispered.

He nodded and twisted the handle. The servos in his suit snapped the metal like brittle glass with a loud *ping.*

"*Fuck,*" he mumbled and shouldered the door open, quickly slipping inside. I pulled the Sig Sauer from its holster—so much for being quiet.

I scanned the hallway in the direction of the guard desk while the Paladin was inside the security room. Through the door, I heard a muffled cry of alarm, then a few soft thuds as they struggled inside. I didn't know how large the room was, or if there was a giant red alarm button like the bad guys always had in action vids, but one thing was certain. The Paladin sucked at being quiet. Probably why he got caught the first time around.

The noises stopped and I prepared for the alarm to sound or for backup to come running down the hall.

Thankfully, neither happened and the Paladin's mask appeared in the door. "Give me one of those zip ties."

I dug one out of my duster's pocket and handed it to him, getting a peek inside the security office as I did so.

There was nothing special about it, just a few empty desks with personal computer screens and a wall of monitors, row upon row of them rotating between the views of cameras within the facility. I decided to check out the monitors while Paladin tied up the guard, so I slipped inside and closed the door.

I watched each one closely for several seconds, beginning with the bottom row labeled appropriately as "first floor." I cross-referenced the view on the monitors with the large floorplan map on the wall to the right of the screens. From what I could tell, the only other person on this floor was the guard at the front desk.

The second row, which corresponded with the building's second floor, showed several rooms with glass walls, reminding me of a racquetball court. People slept on beds in the rooms or read books by the light streaming in from the main hallway.

"You said the second floor was clone storage?" I asked.

Paladin looked up from where he'd used the zip tie to secure the guard's hands behind his back around a metal railing. "Yeah. They go there after they've had their memory implant and are waiting to be used."

I grunted at his choice of the word "used," although I didn't know what else to call it. They stayed in a cell until the person they'd been cloned after needed them for medical reasons—or they were used as a replacement in Mayor Cantrell's scheme.

I noticed movement on one of the monitors and saw a pair of guards patrolling together. They walked alongside each other, both equipped with pulse rifles. *Shit.* I'd figured there would be some type of roving patrol, but had hoped that it would only be a single guard. It would be harder to get the drop on two people.

Nothing else seemed to be happening on the second floor, so I moved up to the third row of monitors. That's when things got weird.

"What the fuck are those people doing?" I asked, pointing at a monitor.

"Pre-memory implant. They're basically fully grown infants."

The first five monitors showed similar rooms from a high angle, looking down. The rooms were completely bare of any furniture or fixtures and appeared to have padded walls. Each held two or three naked adults and all but one of the rooms showed activity. The clones stumbled around into walls, slapped at one another when they got close and some appeared to be screaming. Shit and piss was everywhere.

"Well, this is a lovely place," I mumbled.

"The clones don't remember it—I don't," he shrugged. "It's probably a lot cheaper to make sure the clone's body is healthy before they implant the memories and move them to the second floor."

"I guess that makes sense…" I trailed off. I didn't know what the process was for implanting memories into the clones, but since they were genetically impossible to differentiate between a human and scans didn't show a memory chip stuck on their brain, there had to be some other way that they did it. How did they get the memories from the original, stored on a computer, into the flesh and blood brain of the clone? Science was scary sometimes.

And it certainly didn't sound cheap.

I did my best to ignore the monitors showing the pre-memory implant clones as I scanned the rest of the floor. Large tanks of fluid held bodies in various stages of growth on the other monitors. Maybe an open vat of fluid was a more appropriate term than a tank since they weren't covered. Brightly colored tubes ran along the floor and disappeared into the fluid in each vat. I counted four technicians. Two men and a woman played cards while a third male was on his phone.

"What about these technicians?" I asked.

He squinted at the screen and then shrugged. "I don't know those people. They replaced everyone after I stopped working here. The mayor's goons grabbed me when I tried to free the clones at the other end of the hallway, so I didn't make it that far."

"Fair enough. It looks like they're technicians to monitor the clones that are growing. I don't see any guards on that floor, do you?"

The Paladin watched the screens for a moment before replying. "Not on the third floor—the top floor is ready for a party, though."

My eyes drifted up to the fourth row where two men sat near the stairs and another two sat outside the elevator, effectively covering both entrances to the corporate headquarters. I squinted to see if they had weapons and then

I saw who the guards were, their heavy jawline prominent in the monitor.

Of course it would be those guys.

"Goddammit!" I hissed.

"Yeah, there's no easy way onto that floor."

"I ran into those guys before—well, copies of those guys. They're clones, some type of martial arts masters."

"You sure we can't just shoot them?"

"Yeah, I'm sure. We'll need to subdue them so they can be prosecuted under the law."

"Prosecuted? You mean punished," the Paladin retorted. "I understand that you're a cop, but clones don't get the option of disobeying the people who own the juice. Without that injection, they're dead, so they'll do whatever they're told to do. I'm not against killing them to get them off the street, but at the end of the day, they may be cloned from a good guy."

"Or they could be cloned from a maniac. I understand what you're saying, but I don't agree with you. They could choose to come forward to the authorities and not do illegal shit."

"Really?" he asked, crossing his armored arms awkwardly over his chest. "We have zero protection under the law and these guys know that. Given where they're at, they also know that the mayor would have them silenced the moment they were in police custody. Plus, there's the little problem of the serum. Without it, we die."

I thought back to the two clones that I'd managed to arrest outside Chris Young's studio. They were summarily executed after they were out of my sight, before I could interrogate them. They had zero chance at life under the current laws regarding clones.

"You may be right. Prosecuted or persecuted, it doesn't really make a difference under the current system—but that's why we're here. We're going to put an end to the corruption."

"I'll believe it when I see it," the Paladin stated. "You need to see anything else?"

I gave the monitors a quick onceover and shook my head, then took off my duster and fedora.

"No," I replied, setting my jacket and hat on one of the desks. "Stay here and keep an eye on those two guards on the second floor. I'll be right back."

⚜ ○ ⚜ ○ ⚜

I didn't wait for the Paladin to acknowledge me before slipping out the door with the baton in my hand. I padded quietly down the hall until I came to the lobby. The guard desk was about thirty feet away in the center of the large, two-story lobby.

I hadn't been expecting that.

A quick peek around the corner showed that the second floor had a balcony overlooking the lobby. I assumed that the hallways I'd seen with the clones in their rooms were on either side of the open space, not that it was open to below.

The layout was a problem. If the guard made any noise when I hit him, the roving patrol would probably hear. Even if he was quiet and they didn't hear him, they'd surely notice his absence the next time they walked by the open space. I ducked back into the hallway and went back to the security room.

"No dice," I stated once I made it back. "We're going to have to split up."

"We were just split up," he pointed out.

"I mean I'm going to have to go upstairs and take out the guards on the second floor while you knock out and tie up the one in the lobby. You could have told me about the balcony that overlooked the guard desk."

"I didn't think it was relevant."

"Well, it is."

I studied the floorplan once again and then pointed at the monitors on the wall. "When those guards get to the other end of the hallway, I'll take the stairs to the second floor and find a place to jump them. You take out the guard in the lobby, then bring him back here and tie him up. Any questions?"

"Why don't I go to the second floor against the two guards? I'm the one with armor."

"Your armor isn't going to do any good against a pulse rifle. It'll punch a hole through it like Sha'andre Diggs charging through the D-line."

"Huh? Who's that?"

"Sha'andre Diggs?" I asked in disbelief. "The number one running back in the country; plays for the Saints? First guy ever to rush for thirty-five hundred yards in a season?"

"I don't watch football."

"Of course you don't," I remarked. "Even with that guy, they didn't make the playoffs this year.

"The pulse rifles will kill you," I continued, dropping the subject of football. "I'll take the two on the second floor, *then* you take out the guard at the desk."

"Fine." He held out his hand for another zip tie, which I handed over. "Do you want me to meet you on the second floor after I tie the guard up or do you want to come back down here after you take out your two?"

I didn't consider it long before I answered, "Make sure the front doors are locked and then come up to the second floor. I'll probably need all the help I can get."

He pointed at the monitors. "The patrol passed the balcony."

I followed his extended finger. The guards had indeed passed the open space that I'd decided would be my trigger point to go up the stairs.

"I'm going up," I said.

"Good luck, Detective."

"Thanks," I replied. "Same to you."

# TWENTY-SIX: TUESDAY

My heart pounded as I went up the stairs. I felt something that I'd never really felt before while I was on a case. Was it nervousness? Fear? Neither of those seemed right. Finally, I settled on apprehension. I had a good thing going for me with Teagan and I *wanted* to return to her, to see her lovely face again. I'd never had those feelings about anyone before, so I hadn't really cared about getting hurt—or worse—on the job. Now I needed to stay safe and it made me question my decisions.

That was not a good thing.

I made it to the top of the stairs and stood on the landing for a moment before shoving my feelings deep down inside, where they belonged. The door to the hallway opened quietly, which was a relief since I'd imagined it creaking and the guards shooting me the moment I stepped out onto the second floor.

Immediately in front of me was a glass-fronted room with an older, thin, blonde clone inside. The room boasted a single bed, couch and a desk, where she sat. Her eyebrows shot up in surprise when she saw me come out of the stairwell.

The clone was Senator McMahon—*United States* Senator McMahon. They were expanding their network.

I waived slightly and put my finger to my lips, hoping she would be quiet. She watched me questioningly as I fumbled for my wallet. Once I retrieved it, I showed her my badge and mouthed the words, "*I'm a cop.*"

She nodded her chin subtly and went back to reading on the tablet in front of her. If they'd given her the senator's memory implant, then she should be astute enough to realize that me being here meant things were going to get interesting, but she needed to keep up the appearance of being a simple clone in her education room.

I peered down the length of the hallway and saw the two guards. They were almost to the other end and would be turning around any moment. *Dammit.*

I'd taken too long coming up the stairs, thinking about my feelings. I was supposed to intercept them on the far side of the balcony. The entire length of the hallway held education rooms, most with soft lighting spilling out into the hall. There wasn't anywhere to hide, so I ducked back inside the stairwell and closed the door.

My only hope was that Kaine was still in the security room and hadn't made his move toward the lobby yet, otherwise, we were done for. I considered going back down the stairs, but discarded the idea. I was here; we needed to do this now.

The building wasn't exceptionally large, so the two guards were back on this end of the hallway in a few minutes. I heard them talking long before they arrived and it sounded like they stood immediately outside the door. One of them laughed softly at some unheard joke.

"Hey! What was that?" somebody shouted. The Paladin must have hit his target.

I jerked the door open with the club raised above my head. Two men stood in front of me, both in the process of turning toward the balcony. The club crashed down onto the temple of the taller guard, dropping him like a sack of potatoes as I backhanded the second with the stubby end of the baton in the nose.

Blood erupted everywhere, but he was able to swing the pulse rifle toward me. I gripped the end of his rifle and pushed it toward the side. The air sizzled with electricity and a small shockwave of pressure pushed me back slightly as he discharged the weapon. The sound of shattering glass behind me was the only noise while my hand gripped the rifle to keep from falling. The heat from the barrel seared into it, burning my flesh and causing me to cry out in pain as I released the barrel.

I swung the baton up, under his chin, hitting the nerve that ran just beneath the skin along the jaw and he fell backward. I advanced, not allowing him the opportunity to recover and delivered a vicious blow to the side of his head.

A quick glance showed that the pulse rifle had hit the glass of the cloned senator's room. Then I dragged the two unconscious guards together and zip-tied them to one another in a way that I hoped would make it impossible for them to move.

I grabbed one of the pulse rifles and looked into the senator's room. She sat where she'd been when I saw her a few minutes ago, but she was slumped over the desk, her upper body hidden by the monitor. I slid across the hallway for a better angle.

"Shit." The pulse rifle had taken her head. There was nothing left of it, except a fine mist of blood along the back wall around the burn mark in the brick.

I jogged the length of the hall to the balcony. Beside me, clones beat against the glass of their rooms, demanding to know what was happening and to be released. They reminded me of animals at the zoo, which may have been the idea since they were on display for potential customers to see the product.

The barrel of the rifle clanged loudly as I slammed it against the balcony railing and aimed into the lobby toward the circular guard desk. No one was there.

I cast about the room, changing my angle along the railing to get a better view. Then an armored head popped up from the middle of the desk. Paladin waved and dragged the guard's body toward the security room.

I relaxed and pulled the rifle back. As long as they didn't hear the shattering glass, there was little to suggest the technicians or the quadruplets upstairs had heard the commotion. The pulse rifles were almost as quiet as a silenced rifle; you could still hear them, but nothing like the unsuppressed version.

The burn on my hand flared. I'd been able to ignore it up until now, worried about the guards possibly alerting a strike force to come and wipe us out. I winced as I forced my hand open to see the wound. It was an angry, puckered mess, swollen and red around the edges. That wasn't what concerned me. A two-inch wide strip of white skin ran from the outside of my palm to my thumb. That was a third-degree burn.

*Not good.*

"Fuck," I winced. I wasn't sure that a medical droid on the corner in Easytown could fix that; I might need to go to an actual hospital—which was out of the question as long as the mayor's people were still looking for me.

The dull *thuds* of hands beating against glass reminded me of my mission. I had to try to compartmentalize the pain from the pulse rifle's burn and see this thing through. There were still two floors to go, and my biggest concern was on the fourth floor.

The door that I'd come through at the opposite end of the hallway banged open and I whirled, dropping into a crouch with the rifle. The Paladin's black armor appeared and I eased up.

"Hey!" he whispered loudly. "I checked the monitors in the security room. The people on the third floor didn't seem to have heard anything."

"Good," I replied. "Is the front door locked?"

"Yeah. I made sure it was secured before I came up here."

I flexed my burned hand. I couldn't open or close it completely, but I'd have to get past it. "Are you ready to go?"

"I was *born* ready." he deadpanned.

*Clone joke, I get it*, I thought as I chuckled softly.

"Then let's go up to the third floor."

"What about all of these people?" Paladin asked, gesturing at the clones behind the glass walls.

"We can't do anything about them," I replied. "We should leave them and go up to the top floor. When we get the evidence that we need from the offices upstairs, we can free them."

"Are you sure?" the Paladin asked. "What if we fail? Then they're left trapped in their rooms. That's the same mistake I made last time."

I nodded in acknowledgement. "I understand. As it is, though, they could screw things up if they get in the way or trip an alarm somehow. If we succeed, we're cutting off their possibility of infiltrating our society. We're making things much harder for them, and some of them may not like that."

"Fine" he relented. "Let's get this over with. I'm warning you, the third floor is enough to make you sick. You'll have to check your emotions at the door."

"Emotions? What are those?" I asked. *Two could make stupid little jokes.*

The third floor was worse than what I expected.

I'd seen the video monitors with the clones who inhabited the floor—the ones who hadn't gotten their memory implants yet and had the mental capacity of an infant. I hadn't been prepared for the reality of what I saw, though.

We stepped off the stairs into a nightmare of sights, sounds and smells. For some reason, the building's architects decided to use metal bars to separate the clone holding cells from one another and from the hallway, only the back walls were padded. Outside of each cell, a hose sat, ready to use in order to suppress the clones' activities as well as clean the enclosure.

The clones hooted and hollered the moment we emerged and I had to dodge a flying turd when they saw me. All of them were nude, screaming and gesticulating wildly. I even saw two clones having sex through the bars from one cell to another while a clone in the female's cell smeared feces into his hair and grinned like a maniac. This was so much more evil than I'd thought it would be—rivaling the torture tourism on a more base level of depravity.

"Are you sure these clones are without their memory implants?" I asked. "It looks like they're insane."

He watched them for a moment before commenting. "Physically, they're fully-functioning adults—like those two over there," he gestured to the ones having sex. "So they know what feels good, and that they feel better when they eat and defecate. But, mentally they don't know *why* it feels good or that their body *needs* to eat and drink.

"Even so, they're learning right now," he continued. "So, some of the other clones may observe the two copulating and decide they want to try it themselves. Left to their own devices, they'd probably figure things out eventually and learn to hunt for food."

"So, Ladeaux's company created cavemen?"

"Sort of," Palacin agreed. "Once they get the memory implant, it overwrites everything they've learned here."

"Too bad. That guy's got a great technique," I mumbled. "Alright, let's go."

The clones continued to call after us with hoots and clicks as we walked past the remaining cages that lined both sides of the hallway.

A technician appeared around a corner. "What's got them so—"

"Hold it right there," I hissed, raising the pulse rifle up to his midsection. "Come here."

The clones in the last cage went crazy seeing him. Two of them threw themselves into the bars, bashing their faces into the metal as they reached through to grab him while a third ran to the far corner and hid her face.

"You're certainly popular," I remarked when he was two feet from me, just out of reach of the end of the barrel.

"I—"

"Shut up. Cuff him," I directed the Paladin.

The technician complied, putting his hands behind his back while Kaine put a zip tie on his wrists.

"Besides the three playing cards, is there anyone else on this level?" I asked as I shoved him roughly from behind toward the incubation pods.

"N-n-no," he stuttered.

His fear was palpable. *Good, I'm glad he's scared.* The way the clones reacted to seeing him, I was positive that he'd abused them.

"Tell your friends to get away from the equipment," I ordered, pressing the muzzle into the guy's spine when we rounded the corner.

"Hey, uh, guys?" he said with a tremor in his voice. "You need to get away from the computers and come over here."

They took one look at me and started scrambling for the elevator. Playing cards and poker chips flew in all directions from the little card table they'd sat around. I kicked the technician's knee out to make him collapse and fired a shot from the pulse rifle into the computers behind them. Several computers burst into a shower of glass and plastic.

The card players stopped, raising their hands above their heads. They knew there was no surviving a shot from the rifle.

I kept it trained on their backs as the Paladin zip-tied them together like he'd done the two men from the roving patrol on the second floor. He jumped back from something that I couldn't see from my vantage point.

Then the entire wall of monitors, computers, and medical equipment came crashing down on top of the subdued technicians.

The noise was horrendous. There was no way that the guys upstairs didn't hear it.

*Well,* that *will shut the production down for a while,* I mused.

I dragged the remaining technician to an incubation pod and tried to tie him to it, but my burned hand refused to cooperate, so I bashed him in the back of the head. His body went limp and he fell onto his face beside the pod.

"You're gonna need to tie him down for me, I can't do it," I yelled. "And then get ready; we're about to have company!"

# TWENTY-SEVEN: TUESDAY

We waited for a full five minutes with no response from the clones above. Either they were deaf, or, more likely, they were waiting for us to come to them.

"Goddammit," I cursed. "What do you think?"

"I think they've got an ambush set up for us upstairs," Kaine replied.

He was right.

"Do you still wanna go up there now that they know we're coming?" I asked.

"To be honest with you, I don't think it matters. Those guys up there would have been ready all night anyways."

"Do you want to go together up the stairs or should we split up?" If I was asking him to put his life on the line, I needed to get his opinion instead of simply telling him what we were going to do like I'd been doing so far.

"I think it'd be better if we split up," he said, surprising me.

I hadn't expected him to say that we should split up.

He must have seen the surprise on my face. "As long as they don't use pulse rifles or blasters, my armor can take a lot of punishment that will keep me safe. Thomas Ladeaux paid for it after all. It's the best military-grade composite armor available right now."

"Keep talking," I said rolling my hand.

"I can go up the elevator, distract them, and you can come up the stairs. Hit 'em from behind." He paused for a second before adding, "But you're gonna need to kill them.

None of that only knocking them out bullshit you're doing tonight."

"Agreed," I replied. "I fought against these guys before— well, copies of them. They're good."

I hoped that they hadn't alerted the mayor's security staff after the noise the collapsing shelf made. I didn't relish the idea of fighting my way *down* like I had to fight my way up.

"You ready?" I asked.

He nodded. "Let's get this over with so we can start looking for evidence to implicate the mayor."

Once again, we split up. Kaine lumbered toward the elevator and I went to the stairwell door. I peeked through the small glass square, making sure no one was inside, and then gave him a thumbs up. He pushed the button to call the elevator.

I heard the cables squealing in the elevator shaft all the way over by where I stood. The building was old and its owners hadn't bothered upgrading the elevators to the standard maglift system in use across most of the city.

There was zero chance the clones weren't on high alert now.

The elevator chimed when the car arrived and the doors slid open. I half-expected him to get shot the moment the doors parted. Miraculously, the car was empty.

He waved nonchalantly in my direction and stepped into the elevator.

My mind went into overdrive. He was awfully calm, was I being double-crossed once again? Was this all some elaborate way for the mayor to set me up so that there were legitimate charges against me? He'd already had at least one cop murdered and an unknown number of clones, what were a couple of security guards and medical technicians?

"Fuck it," I told the door before I shoved it open and ran up the stairs.

I heard the commotion on the fourth floor when I was on the landing. The Paladin must have come out swinging. Even as I ran, I heard something large and heavy crash through glass.

I paused for a breath when I reached the upper door and then pulled it open. A fist came out of nowhere and clocked me in the side of the head.

"*Ugh*," I groaned, my knee giving out on me.

It was a good thing that it happened since a foot swung right where my face would have been if I hadn't collapsed.

The world swam in front of my eyes. In the distance, I could barely make out the Paladin fighting with two of the clones, and a third lay in a heap a few feet from them. A cloud of smoke swirled out of the elevator and light's flickered wildly in all directions.

I struggled to my feet and got kicked in the stomach. The force of the blow knocked me backward and my arms flailed wildly. I grasped at the air, trying desperately to reach the railing. Momentum threatened to take me, but I thought I had it—until the asshole punched me in the face.

And then I fell down the stairs.

I don't know how many times the back of my head hit the concrete steps as I tumbled feet over head. It was enough to make me black out temporarily on the way down.

My body crashed onto the landing's flat surface, jolting me awake. I was dimly aware of someone rushing down the stairs toward me. I lifted the pulse rifle and fired a shot before my fractured mind had time to decide if it was Kaine or one of the clones. It didn't matter.

"*Aiyee!*" someone screamed and crashed down on top of me, knocking the air from my lungs.

I fumbled at the clone's throat until my hands wrapped around his windpipe and I squeezed. I gritted my teeth, willing my fingers to come together. My burned hand was little more than a club that blocked him from squirming away as my good hand strangled him. The edges of my vision began to close in from the effort of trying to strangle him.

He punched me repeatedly in the ribs, each blow weaker than the last as the combination of blood loss from wherever I'd shot him and lack of oxygen overwhelmed him.

He stopped punching after a while. I didn't stop squeezing.

"*Die you fucker!*" I wheezed, still not having caught my breath from when he landed on top of me.

The door clanged against the wall above me and a shadow worked its way down the stairs. I released the man's throat and groped for my rifle; I was in no shape to handle another clone.

"Forrest! Forrest, are you okay?" Kaine's synthesized voice echoed around me.

I turned my face to the side and vomited.

He lifted the body off me and blood poured from the stump where the clone's leg had been. Kaine flung the body away like a rag doll.

I coughed and wiped at my mouth with the back of my hand. "Are the others?"

"Dead," he confirmed.

"You sure about that?"

"Very." He knelt beside me and put a hand under my back to lift me up.

"*Ugh*. I feel like crap," I said as a wave of nausea hit me and I closed my eyes.

"You look like it," he responded.

I half-listened while he told me that three of the clones jumped him the moment he came off the elevator and the fourth stayed at the stairwell door. They'd been martial arts masters, but his armor was impenetrable and they hadn't been able to do anything to him.

"Where do you want to start?" Kaine asked.

"Desk drawers? A safe?"

He helped me to my feet and I limped up the stairs beside him. My back was twisted and there was a fluid-filled bulge of skin on the top of my head where I'd hit it when I fell. I would need to be examined by a doctor soon. Brain injuries were about one of the only things modern medicine didn't have a cure for. If there was swelling in my brain, and the pressure wasn't relieved, I'd end up in a coma—or worse.

I had trouble focusing on the task at hand, but it didn't take us long to find a sealed safe in Kelsey Bloomfield's former office. They hadn't even bothered to clean out the pictures of her with a dog and one of her and another woman at the Grand Canyon when they murdered her clone two days ago.

"I should be able to get it open," Kaine stated.

"I doubt it. Those—"

Smoke rose from the hinges on the safe as he pointed his arm at them. Son of a bitch had a laser in the suit too.

The hinges were no match for the military-grade laser. He stepped back as the door fell to the floor. I shuffled around his bulk to look at what we'd uncovered.

"Jackpot."

# TWENTY-EIGHT: TWO WEEKS LATER

"Are you awake, Zach?"

"I am now," I groaned.

"Good," Andi stated. "There is a new vid message from Christopher Young that came in with the subject line, 'You need to watch this.' I previewed the file for you and I agree with the sender's assessment that you need to watch the vid. There is also a video message from Chief Robert Brubaker received at 9:04 a.m."

"Wait. What time is it?" I asked.

"It is 10:17 a.m. Ms. Thibodaux requested that I not wake you before 10:15 a.m. I complied with her request."

"Good morning, Andi," Teagan mumbled, snuggling her body close to my uninjured side. "I didn't mean exactly at 10:15."

"Good morning to you, also. The message from Mr. Young is important. I determined that I should wake you as soon as possible. Do you want me to make coffee?"

"Yes," we replied in unison.

"It will be ready in four minutes."

I rolled away from Teagan and limped to the bathroom to relieve the pressure in my bladder.

"Urine test complete. Zachary Forrest, in cross-checking the public health records, the blood in your urine has lessened significantly over the past week. This is…"

I smiled as the toilet computer droned on. Even though it was annoying, I was glad to be home instead of in the hospital where I'd been confined until last night. The Paladin dropped me off at the emergency room of University Medical Center the night we raided the clone factory, hitting every curb and trashcan from St. Rose to Tremé-Lafitte as he drove my Jeep. He called Teagan for me and then disappeared. Nobody had seen him since.

The doctors admitted me, forcing me to remain in inpatient care for two weeks. They wanted the skin around the composite alloy plate they'd placed over the hole in my skull to heal before they released me. My body had been so battered from the fall that it took longer to mend than usual. Hopefully, that was true instead of the more depressing option that I was just getting old.

The fourth day I was there, Teagan notified Chief Brubaker that I was in the hospital under an assumed name. He came alone, with an arrest warrant issued by Judge Hennessey. Apparently, Judge Carlson had died in a freak fishing accident the week before and the mayor had appointed Hennessey in his place. I was charged with murder of the two guards in Slidell, aggravated assault and unlawful detention of the factory workers, criminal trespassing, and destruction of property, namely Biologiqué's mainframe computer, four clone guards and an unnamed female clone—which I knew to be the illegally grown clone of Senator McMahon.

I convinced Brubaker to look at the evidence that we'd uncovered at the Biologiqué International Headquarters which implicated Mayor Cantrell before he arrested me and broadcast it over the net that I was in the hospital. If any of the mayor's people knew where I was, I'd be dead by morning.

I had documents showing the early contract between Ladeaux and Cantrell to clone a few prominent local figures—with their permission. Then, there were six pages of emails between Kelsey Bloomfield and Ladeaux outlining that she thought the mayor was trying to edge him out of the business and then another fourteen pages between her and the mayor, threatening to go public about his scheme to replace politicians with clones.

Included amongst the papers was a list of politicians, business owners and even a few local celebrities that had been cloned, some with their permission in the early days when they thought it was a way to preserve their health, others without. According to the document, *all* had been replaced and were dependent upon the mayor's people to give them their injections, which ensured they would do whatever the mayor directed. The list stopped one week before I rescued her from the warehouse in Easytown so there was no telling how many more had been cloned and replaced in the time since.

Kelsey had even managed to get a picture of the mayor having sex with a television news anchor while he slit her throat. She'd put a handwritten note along with the picture stating she bribed one Joseph Kleer—the same thug that stole the clones and was later perforated with a few hundred rounds of 5.56 millimeter—into taking the picture, stating it was the real woman, not a clone.

The most damning evidence, and I assumed what ultimately got her cloned and replaced, was a series of messages to Mayor Cantrell stating that she knew he was involved in the torture and murder of multiple humans that he told investors were clones—which is why the ones I'd rescued had their memories wiped. They were the real people, replaced by clones, and they were sold into the torture tourism business for the entertainment of a twisted segment of our population.

Brubaker took the documents without serving the warrant and told me I had a week before he'd be back. Three days later, uniformed cops showed up and stood guard outside my hospital room door. Judge Hennessey had granted a petition for the removal of Mayor Cantrell signed by a majority of the city council and withdrew the warrant against me until an independent investigation was complete. The mayor disappeared ahead of the warrant, so someone on the court staff had tipped him off.

Then, surprisingly, Andi called me. Police officers who showed up to remove the crime scene tape from my apartment had plugged her back in and she was pissed at the mess. During the "investigation" they'd torn my place apart, looking for any evidence that would have told them where I'd gone when I slipped their net. I had her document everything for an insurance claim and then hire a cleaning company to do what they could. I also required new furniture since they'd "searched" through my couch cushions and mattress with a knife.

Assholes.

Once my apartment was restored to a semi-normal state, Teagan moved out of the hotel in Slidell and into my place temporarily while they repaired her apartment. It was the least I could do since I'd dragged her into this mess.

Sadie visited me in the hospital as well and I told her about Kelsey's involvement in the scheme. She took the news hard, questioning how the person she'd been could have done such things. Kelsey knew about the illegal cloning and tried to get a piece of the action, first by attempting to blackmail Tommy Voodoo, then the mayor. It didn't work out for her. Instead, she got her memory wiped and now Sadie would have a lifetime of therapy for it—or a lengthy prison sentence.

I felt bad for her. The woman I'd rescued and gotten to know was *not* the woman who did those things. But, it a jury probably wouldn't differentiate between Kelsey Bloomfield and Sadie. The public would demand justice for the crimes the other woman had helped to facilitate.

Now I was home, doing mundane things like ignoring my toilet computer and trying to avoid hitting my head on anything accidentally.

When I came out of the bathroom, Andi started immediately. "You really should view the video that Mr. Young sent right away, Zach."

"Hold on, Andi. I want to get a cup of coffee first. Can I do that, please?"

"Of course, boss. I apologize for my exuberant behavior."

"Eh," I grunted. "Let's remove exuberant from your vocabulary. Nobody uses that word."

"Understood. Removing the word 'exuberant' from my speech patterns."

"I like the word," Teagan murmured from underneath the covers. She slid them down so just her face showed. "It's a sophisticated word that should be brought back. It sounds so much more educated than excited or cheerful."

I smiled at Teagan, her hazel eyes seemed more green than brown this morning. "I stand corrected, Andi. You may continue the use of the word."

"Understood. Reinstating the word 'exuberant' to my speech patterns."

"So, you *can* teach an old dog new tricks, huh?" Teagan teased.

"Maybe for the right person, that old dog is willing to learn a few tricks."

"Okay," she responded, flipping the covers open completely to reveal her nude body. "You can come back over here."

"I really must insist that you watch the video," Andi pressed. "You will both be pleased."

I took one long wistful glance at Teagan and sighed. "Fine. I'm sorry, Teagan. I want nothing more than to spend all day in bed with you."

"I get it," she answered. "I've got class in a couple of hours anyways—and I've missed *way* too much lately," she added. "How long is the vid?"

"Four minutes, thirty-two seconds."

Teagan slipped on one of my t-shirts that she'd adopted while I was gone and we went into the kitchen for coffee.

"*Ugh*," I groaned, staring at the large mound of old case files on the table. "I'd forgotten about those."

The cleaning crew hadn't been able to recreate my elaborate filing system of stacking case files in certain places across the entire surface of the dining room table. It would take me hours, maybe even days to fix it.

"Maybe you should get a filing cabinet," Teagan suggested.

"No way. I knew exactly where everything was the old way."

"But how often did you have anyone else eating over here?"

She had a point. Her stay was temporary, but hopefully she'd be coming over more often. Without the table, the options were standing in the kitchen, which I often did, or eating on the couch. Neither of which were exactly civilized.

"I'm not asking you to change your whole way of life, Zach. Please don't think that."

"Huh? Oh, sorry." I guess I'd taken too long to respond to her. "I was just thinking about where a cabinet would go."

"How about right there in the corner next to your gun safe?"

I glanced at the safe. There *was* enough space for an upright filing cabinet that wasn't being used.

"Sounds good. Andi, can you order a filing cabinet that will fit beside the safe?"

"Metal or composite? Three or five drawer? Lockable or not? Do you require an additional alarm system?"

"Uh… Composite, five, yes and no?"

"We're in luck, boss. There's one in stock, in town. It will be here by 3 p.m."

"Whoa," Teagan exclaimed. "That was crazy."

"*That's* why I have her," I replied. "Let's see this vid you're so *exuberant* to show me, Andi."

She didn't reply. Instead, Chris Young's message displayed on the wall:

```
Zach, you need to watch this. I wouldn't
  have believed it if I hadn't been on
  site when my cameraman recorded it.
  This is the raw footage from our live
  feed yesterday and I haven't had the
  opportunity to edit or prepare the
  voiceover yet, which we'll broadcast
  on the megavid screens throughout town
  this afternoon. But, since you have so
  much invested in this case I decided
  to let you get the first look.
Ignore the rocket comment. I was
  obviously dazed and we'll edit that
  out. Your troubles are over!
```

Cheers,
Chris

After a couple of seconds passed to allow me to read what he'd typed, the vid began playing. It showed several marked state police cars and what I assumed were unmarked cars parked in a vee formation blocking the entrance to the parking lot outside what looked like a large hotel. I didn't recognize the place.

In the video, Chris said, "Are we live? Are we— Hello, this is Chris Young. I'm coming to you live from the prestigious Windmere Resort & Spa in Gramercy, about fifty miles west of New Orleans. As you can see, the Louisiana State Police, the Gramercy SWAT team and members of the FBI have been called to this location because of a potential hostage situation.

"We have word that the New Orleans mayor, Mayor Derek Cantrell, is involved. You may remember that Mayor Cantrell was recently removed from office after he was implicated in the so-called torture tourism ring, kidnapping and murder, and the illegal manufacture of human clones. He's been missing since being relieved of his office.

"Our sources say that Mayor Cantrell is inside the Windmere Resort & Spa and may be a hostage." He put his finger to his ear and nodded. "No, I'm being told that the mayor may be the one who took the hostages, not the other way around."

The video cut between scenes and it was obviously later in the day, the sun beating down onto the police officers on the perimeter.

"So, if you can see behind me, the building is laid out almost like an uppercase H-design when viewed from above. As you can imagine, a building this large is exceptionally hard for police officers to raid and secure since there is so much space to hide and so many potential exits. Additionally, we don't know where the hostages are being held at this time. If I had to guess—"

The camera shook and then fell to the ground as a massive explosion took out the top two floors of the far right wing of the front building. One moment everything was seemingly peaceful, the next, it had gone to shit.

Large chunks of burning drywall and roof shingles rained down around the prone cameraman. "Get up, Danny!" Chris said.

"Gail, are you getting this? There was some type of explosion at the Windmere Resort & Spa. We'd been following the developing story of Mayor Derek Cantrell, the recently removed mayor of New Orleans, when the building exploded."

He pointed to the missing floors. "As you can see, it was a massive explosion. It looks like it destroyed the top two floors of the resort. We don't know yet whether the explosion came from inside the resort or if the police fired some type of rocket at the building. It's too early to tell."

The camera focused on officers opening a clamshell trailer. Once the roof and sides were out of the way, a drone similar to what the NOPD used lifted skyward. It circled the building multiple times and I knew it was scanning. I didn't know what type of equipment it was equipped with, so it could have been scanning for people or more explosives.

Chris remained silent for the first pass and then continued talking. "As you can see, Gail, the police have released a drone. We're being told it's an EOD drone—that's Explosive Ordnance Disposal—that is searching for more explosives."

The camera zoomed out to show police officers running forward. "The drone must have cleared the building," Chris stated, "because officers are now moving in."

Chris and his cameraman advanced several feet until they were stopped by a uniformed officer. "We're being told that we can't go any closer, Gail. This is as close as the state police are going to allow us to go. There's—hey! Look over there, the SWAT team appears to have two people in custody.

"Can you? Yeah, zoom in on that." The camera zoomed in and I recognized the mayor. He was in handcuffs between two cops. Behind him, a giant bear of a man was also in handcuffs. Neither looked like they'd gone down without a fight.

"That's Mayor Cantrell! He was probably trying to use the explosion as a distraction to escape on the opposite end of the building.

"Can you see this, Gail? It appears that New Orleans Mayor Derek Cantrell is in custody after a dramatic chain of events. We don't have positive identification yet, but from what we can tell, it certainly looks like him. Of course, if you remember my exclusive report on illegal cloning last week, the FBI will still need to conduct DNA testing to determine if he's a clone. If he is a clone, then the real Derek Cantrell may still be on the run."

The video ended and I glanced at Teagan, who stared openmouthed at the blank wall where the video had played.

"Um, *that* did not play live yesterday," she managed to say.

"They're keeping it under wraps," I answered. "Smart. That way, they make sure they've got the real Cantrell and not a clone."

"Are you ready to watch Chief Brubaker's message?" Andi asked. "It correlates directly with what you are discussing."

"Yeah. Go ahead and play it back."

"Forrest, this is Brubaker," the chief's gruff voice echoed over my apartment's speakers as his craggy face filled the wall. "Your AI tells me that you're still sleeping. Good. Get some rest now because we have a giant backlog of cases that Cruz couldn't handle on his own. Seems there's some new type of killer robot wars happening between rival gangs and civilians are getting caught in the crossfire.

"I'm sure you've heard about the standoff in Gramercy by now. DNA evidence confirms that the real Derek Cantrell is behind bars. The DA's office had a field day with the evidence you provided and subpoenaed Biologiqué International's network servers and every computer still functioning. It seems there was a massive amount of damage to the local network the other night by unknown vandals.

"One more thing. There's been a string of deaths among prominent people in the city. Seems they're all dying of some type of inoperable kidney failure. They go in to the hospital and ten, twelve hours later they're dead. Some of them were on Bloomfield's list of known clones, most of them aren't. Seems like without the juice from Cantrell, they shrivel up and die. The department has taken a few of them into custody and provided the injections that will keep them alive.

"They're singing like birds as long as we give them their daily shot of life. We recovered four cases of the stuff in Cantrell's home, but we'll have to lean on your pal, Ladeaux, to get the manufacturing process turned back on for that serum—it's going quick."

He paused to spit out a bit of chewed tobacco, which echoed around my living room and caused Teagan to blanch.

"Oh yeah, before I forget," Brubaker's message continued. "You're a lucky son of a bitch. Thomas Ladeaux has decided not to press charges against you for breaking and entering his building, destroying his property, restraining security personnel and setting his cloning business back by several months and an untold amount of money. The DA is also dropping the two murder charges against you since the video only shows the Paladin in Slidell, not you. Saint Michael must be watching after your sorry ass."

He cleared his throat and continued, "In all seriousness, I'm glad you're alright and that none of those bullshit charges against you panned out. I'll see you Monday at the precinct."

The message ended and Andi said, "You have four more days until Monday, Zach. I recommend you get as much rest as possible. Studies show that rest and decreased activity are key factors in the healing process."

I took a long sip from my coffee and then set the mug back on the coffee table. "I'm sick of lying in bed, Andi. I need to *do* something."

Teagan grabbed my hand and interlocked her fingers in mine. "You *could* take me out to dinner tonight. We still haven't had our official first date yet."

"We had that picnic," I stated.

"Oh, no you don't, mister. You're gonna take me someplace nice. I'm sure that New Orleans *Hero Cop* Zachary Forrest can get us reservations somewhere last minute while I'm in class."

I groaned at her use of Chris Young's term. "I'm not gonna live that one down, am I?"

She threw her leg over mine and then straddled me. "Maybe in time—but you're gonna have to work it off."

I met with Sadie a couple of days after I learned of the mayor's arrest. The police department had allowed her to return to her home in Lakeshore, a posh neighborhood that only the very rich could afford. They'd completed their search and hadn't found anything at the house.

"How are you holding up?" I asked. She'd been devastated when I'd originally told her that she was implicated in the torture tourism case.

"As well as can be expected, I guess. I've been put through a battery of medical and psychological tests, but they can't find any trace of my memories from my time at Biologiqué International. Since my mind was wiped by those sick bastards, the district attorney has decided not to seek criminal charges against me, although there may be a civil case in the future by families of the victims."

"No jail time," I stated. "That's huge. Congratulations!"

"Thanks."

She frowned and fretted with a string on her pant leg. "It's just… What kind of a person would *do* that stuff? Condone the torture and murder of anyone, let alone potentially hundreds of people. Am *I* a monster?"

I shook my head. "No, you're not. In fact, you're not even Kelsey Bloomfield anymore. You're Sadie, the strong, independent woman who's been through a fuck-ton of shit. You just happen to have the same name as that other person."

I paused to arrange my thoughts and put my experience dealing with murderers, rapists and thieves every day for more than a decade into words that would mean something to her. "A monster doesn't ask whether they are a monster. They accept it, they revel in it. Being evil defines them. That's not you. You, the person who you've been made into *today*, is not like that. You have a completely blank canvas to paint your masterpiece on. You can be anybody that you want to be."

The nod of her chin was barely noticeable. "I don't want to be like that. I want to help people, not hurt them. I just don't understand how I—how Kelsey could have gone down that road. I remember her childhood. It was totally fine, there wasn't anything bad that happened to her that would have made her turn out the way she did."

"Sometimes people start out gradually, a faked report here, a lie about a project there, and then before you know it, they've slid completely down that slope to become so mired in their lies and misdealings that they'll grasp at whatever comes along. Maybe that's what happened to her. Maybe she turned a blind eye to one illegal cloning or needed money for something and eventually it became commonplace. Then, when she tried to blackmail the mayor, she ceased to exist, and then you were born."

I didn't really know what else to say. Even though I'd been on Jasmine Jones' couch on more occasions than I could count, counseling wasn't my thing.

"The slippery slope argument, huh?" she asked.

"It's real. I see it every day."

"Can I recover from the things that she's done?"

"That's up to you," I replied. "You could sit here and dwell on all the negative things that the media will surely throw your way, or you can accept that Kelsey Bloomfield was murdered by the mayor's thugs and her body was left in the street to be discovered and broadcast across the city.

"If you can do that, accept it and move on, then you'll be able to begin anew. *You* hold the keys to your future now, not some dead clone."

"I want to be a good person," she whispered.

"Then make it happen. Campaign for clone rights, donate your time at a food shelter, whatever you want to do. The future is wide open for you."

She smiled and a few tears dribbled down her cheek. "I guess, in a way, being cloned was the best thing that ever happened to me, huh?"

"Without it, you wouldn't be who you are right now. You've been given a new life. Go live it."

"Okay. I will," she agreed, standing up quickly and then leaning over, hugging me.

My arms drifted up awkwardly and I hugged her back the best that I could. She'd be alright. With that kind of determination, she'd be just fine.

*Now, what about those killer cyborgs in Easytown?*

# THE END

# Want more from Brian Parker?
# Find all of his books on Amazon.com:

www.amazon.com/Brian-Parker/e/B00DFD98YI

## About the Author

A veteran of the wars in Iraq and Afghanistan, Brian Parker was born and raised as an Army brat. He's currently an Active Duty Army soldier who enjoys spending time with his family in Texas, hiking, obstacle course racing, writing and Texas Longhorns football. He's an unashamed Star Wars fan, but prefers to disregard the entire Episode I and II debacle.

Brian is both a traditionally- and self-published author with an ever-growing collection of works across multiple genres, including sci-fi, post-apocalyptic, horror, paranormal thriller, military fiction, self-publishing how-to and even a children's picture book--Zombie in the Basement, which he wrote to help children overcome the perceived stigma of being different from others.

He is also the founder of Muddy Boots Press, an independent publishing company that focuses on quality genre fiction over mass-produced books.

### FOLLOW BRIAN ON SOCIAL MEDIA!
Facebook: www.facebook.com/BrianParkerAuthor
Instagram: @BrianParker_Author
Twitter: www.twitter.com/BParker_Author
Web: www.BrianParkerAuthor.com

# Discover more works by Brian Parker!

## Easytown Novels
*The Immorality Clause*
*Tears of a Clone*

## The Path of Ashes
*A Path of Ashes*
*Fireside*
*Dark Embers*

## Washington, Dead City
*GNASH*
*REND*
*SEVER*

## Stand Alone Works
*Enduring Armageddon*
*Origins of the Outbreak*
*The Collective Protocol*
*Battle Damage Assessment*
*Zombie in the Basement*
*Self-Publishing the Hard Way*

## Anthology Contributions
*Bite-Sized Offerings: Tales and Legends of the Zombie Apocalypse*
*Only the Light We Make: Tales From the World of Adrian's Undead Diary*

Printed in Great Britain
by Amazon